Suddenly Summer

By

Lyn Miller LaCoursiere

In association with
Nightwriters Books

Cover design and format by Genny Kieley

ISBN # 978-09842151-3-3

Suddenly Summer

Suddenly Summer takes the reader on another hair-raising journey when Lindy Lewis saves the life of the Mayor of Monterrey, Mexico. "I know all about your deceptive life," he threatens when she rejects his advances. In desperation to get away, she flees back to the US. She is soon kidnapped by Mario D'Agustino's henchmen and left in a forest to die as payback for testifying against him in court for the FBI. Antagonist Reed Conners, always doubtful of her clairvoyance, is finally convinced that she may be on to something when she has a vision of the place a psycho has taken his best friend's wife. And later identifies the two men found drowned in his home town lake.

Quotes from readers

Tragedy leads to career for LHS graduate!
---TRF Times

Hey mom, you're on it!
---Jeff L. MN's #1 Greatest One Man Band.

LINDY LEWIS will keep you guessing.
 ---Jud, writer, stand up comedian and musician.

You will fall in love with LINDY.
---Ross Tarry, author of third best seller, Eye of the Serpent.

Lindy rocks!
--Sue, author of the Blossom adventures.

The eclectic escapades of LINDY LEWIS surprise the reader again and again.
—John S, author of two best-sellers and more.

We all wish, sometimes, we could be LINDY LEWIS!
---Laura V, author of Blue Bells of Scotland.

Her writing gets better and better!
---Lola, Rolling Green Gazette

Whatever tight spot Lindy is in, a new look and identity is imminent.
 ---Genny K, author of Green Stamps to Hot Pants & Northeast's three best sellers.

Books by Lyn Miller

LaCoursiere

Nightmares and Dreams

Tomorrow's Rain

Sunsets

Suddenly Summer

A note from the Author

My novels tell the story of Lindy Lewis, a woman who has had her perfect world abruptly taken when her husband becomes ill and dies. Of the things that happened that compel her to burn the beautiful home they had lovingly renovated, to claim the huge insurance policy on it. Believing all that gorgeous money would bring back her happiness.

Actually, some of Lindy's dilemmas are similar to events in my life, although I didn't burn the house my husband and I did remodel. Some of her actions could be mine too, but then, as a writer I do embellish!

When I picture Lindy Lewis, I see a woman that looks like the actress Meg Ryan, with a personality like Goldie Hawn. She is intelligent, and thinks of herself as worldly, but at times, can be naïve. Acting and dressing with class is very important to her.

She has lived in Dallas, Texas where she was mugged and robbed. While there, she proclaims she had to work her body to the bone to make a living. She had a romance with a drug lord and watched him kill an innocent man. She discovered her clairvoyance in Rhode Island and later spent time in jail in the Midwest. All the while, her old college boyfriend, Reed Conners, an investigator for insurance fraud, is always just around the corner with his lawyerly help and his bed.

I've always said you have to make your own music in life, so writing about Lindy and her travels is an early morning routine for me that makes me smile. And taking my coffee and sitting down at my computer keeps me motivated and focused.

I love all of you who follow Lindy's adventures! Happy reading!

Acknowledgements

Once again I need to thank my
writing buddies,
Ross, Judy, Jud, Steph, Sue,
Jack, Laura, Genny and Janet,
THE NIGHTWRITERS OF MAPLE GROVE
for their demanding vigilance.
Also my niece Marylou
for editing this book, and again,
Mary for her constant
technical expertise.

This book is for
my mom
Signe Sjulestad Miller

-1-

Lindy's first instinct had been to run like hell when she opened her door and found Reed Conners there. She had given up all hope of any help from him, but now here he was! In a sagging t-shirt, baggy socks and tear-stained eyes she gaped at him as he stood, his western boots firmly planted on the portico of the rambling adobe house in a prestigious neighborhood of Monterrey, Mexico, where she lived. They stared at each other.

"Reed," she stammered, "how did you--?" He stalked past her into the foyer and bellowed, "Lindy, we have to talk!"

She stood there uncertainly then stammered, "Reed I'm sorry. But I called."

He stood rigid and unrelenting. "Why the hell did you hang up?" Drakkar, his familiar cologne drifted over as he stood just a few feet from her.

A tear fell on her cheek. "Reed," she wailed, "I thought you probably wouldn't want to talk to me after I left you in South Carolina." She wiped her eyes on her hand and went on, "But don't you see, I had to leave Charleston when I heard the jury had found Mario innocent at the trial!"

Reed's fair complexion darkened in his aggravation. His arms locked at his side as he growled, "Goddamn Lindy, how many times have you taken off and left me hanging?"

"But," she whispered, "You didn't see the threat in Mario's eyes when I sat in that witness chair and pointed him out as the killer!" She shivered as she remembered the moment.

"Lindy," he yelled, "didn't you think I could protect you?"

Tears sprang into her eyes at his concern for her. Had she heard just a little spark of caring in his voice? Maybe he would forgive her for leaving. She was so lonely. She stepped close and wailed tearfully, "Please Reed, I'm so sorry!"

But he avoided her eyes, then after a few minutes he muttered, "Lindy, stop!" Then said something under his breath that sounded like, "goddamn it," after staring off into space. When he finally reached out and pulled her to him she snuggled into his arms.

When she lifted her lips to his and then sighed at the taste of his kiss and the familiar feeling of his body, she was safe at last. And soon they were both caught up again in their same age-old tryst, and hours later lay spent in her king-sized bed after a delicious love fest.

Feeling totally relaxed now in his arms, she said "Reed, you remember the visions I have sometimes don't you?"

She watched anxiously as he sat up and untangled himself from the twisted covers and punched a pillow into place behind his back. "Yeah, why what's going on?"

Her voice faltered. "I keep having nightmares and seeing someone chasing me, and trying to kill me. I can't sleep, I haven't slept for days," she managed to say and sat up unconcerned that her breasts were bare. "Reed, I keep having this same nightmare about these men after me!" She closed her eyes and lowered her chin to her bent knees and rocked back and forth.

He ran a hand through his ruffled hair. "For God's sake, Lindy," he said, "what the hell are you talking about? What men?" He reached over the side of the bed to the floor and fumbled in his shirt pocket for a cigarette.

Lindy dropped her knees and was silent for a minute. Then she whispered, "I think I'm losing my mind!" She wiped at her eyes and turned to him.

"Reed, something like this happened once before when I was in Dallas!"

"You saw men chasing you?" He lit a cigarette and reached for an ashtray.

"No, then I lost my memory, but now I can't forget!" She sniffed and moved in closer to him. "Reed, I'm really scared!"

She shivered and he put his cigarette down in the ashtray and reached out to her, and then said, "Lindy, no one is chasing you. It's just a dream!" He pulled her close.

"I knew you would come," she whispered. "Can you stay?"

She waited for his answer as he slid down in the bed and settled the covers over them in her bed and said, "Well, I need to stay long enough to let you know the other reason why I came to Mexico!" She heaved a happy sigh as he put one arm behind his head and she lay in the other.

She tried to keep her eyes open and listen as he began to talk, and then snuggled in closer to him, completely content.

***

Reed went on, "I can tell you now, you're a free woman, Lindy," he said. "My company has their million dollars back and those fraud charges against you have been dropped!" He waited for her to jump up and happily exclaim with some expletive, then thinking she's dumbfounded by the good news when she didn't, he went on. Her warm breath rustled the hairs on his chest.

"Lindy," he went on to say, "I worked out a deal with the FBI that when you testified for them at the D'Agustino trial, they would spring for the million and pay back my company. And listen to this; they had to pay regardless of the outcome!"

He talked on and on in the darkened bedroom. "See, I didn't tell you before because I didn't want it to influence your testimony when you got on the stand at the murder trial.

"You understand don't you, Lindy?" He asked her, but she still didn't throw her arms around him with excited gratitude.

"Goddamn," he blustered disappointed, then went on. "Now I've got something else I need to talk to you about."

When he still didn't get any reaction out of her and sensing something must be wrong, he leaned down and saw she was sound asleep and gently snoring.

"Well, the least you could do--," he mumbled, then exhaustion caught up with him and he too, fell asleep.

Their tranquility was suddenly interrupted the next morning by the shrill ring of a telephone. She opened her eyes and saw Reed fumble amongst the pile of clothes they'd tossed on the floor the night before for his cell.

The familiar voice of Murphy, his friend from the Minneapolis Police Department boomed through the telephone and into the room as he said, "Conners, where the hell are you?" His harried voice cracked.

"Huh?" Reed mumbled as she sat up, wide awake.

"Conners," Murphy asked again, "Why the hell don't you answer your phone?"

Reed sat up at the tone of the detective's stressed voice. "Murph, what's up?" he asked wide awake now, too.

"What is it? "Lindy whispered through kiss-swollen lips as she listened.

"Buddy, I need help. Anne's disappeared!" Murphy's voice rasped.

Reed swung his legs out of the bed. "What do you mean she's disappeared?"

"She's been gone since yesterday noon," Murphy's voice broke.

"Goddamn," Reed exclaimed, "I'm out of town and it'll take most of the day for me to get there. But I'm leaving now!" He tossed the cell-phone on the bed and threw the covers aside.

'What is it?" Lindy asked again frightened after being awakened suddenly by their loud exclamations. She'd been so warm and safe in his arms.

"Anne, Murphy's wife has disappeared," Reed said as he rushed into the bathroom. "I've got to get out to the airport and catch a morning flight out of here!"

- 2-

"Annie's been gone since yesterday noon. And I've got to find a morning flight out of here!" Reed repeated.

"Now? You're leaving now?" Lindy asked flabbergasted.

"Lindy, you know she's my best friend's wife," he said over his shoulder as he rushed into the bathroom. She heard the splash of water from the shower and minutes later stood in the doorway and watched him drive away.

It was just before dawn and the Monterrey neighborhood was still asleep. She swallowed back tears as the familiar pang of loneliness shot through her chest again. It had felt so good to be held as they had lain together during the night. She hadn't thought ahead as to what was going to come of their meeting and had just reveled in the moment.

She pulled the robe around herself tighter and used a corner of the sleeve to wipe her eyes. Lord, she hadn't even had a chance to finish telling him about all the things that were happening to her. They'd made love and she had started to tell him about her nightmares, but they both must have fallen asleep!

What am I going to do now? She wailed to her empty house. Last night had been the first time she'd slept in almost a week. Sure, his friend Murphy was in trouble back in Minneapolis, but she needed him too!

She huddled in a corner of the couch, and then eyed the edges of the window blinds as something seemed to move outside in the shadows.

Was someone out there? She sucked in her breath and remembered running for her life, desperate to get away from those faceless men who chased her in those nightmares. But she was awake now, she reminded herself. She wiped her eyes again, still hurt at Reed's abrupt departure.

What had he meant when he said he had something important to tell her? Why hadn't he just told her whatever it was and not made such a big production out of it! Now she was mad. And suddenly her anger made her feel stronger! *Get it* together, she told herself sternly in the silence of her house.

She jumped up and opened the drapes and shades and the gloom in the living room brightened. As the sun started its ascent over the horizon it began to soften the shadows around the white couches and the red easy chairs in the room. As she sat huddled again on the couch and watched dawn creep into her house, her tangled thoughts began to sort themselves out.

To hell with Reed Conners, she said out loud to the walls, I don't need him! She was still for a minute and waited to see how that felt. She didn't feel any remorse at her decision, and went on boldly, be damned if I will ever call him again!

And, these god awful nightmares? She sat up and with a determined look said, well, that's why there are drugstores! She'd get some pills and knock herself out at night and those dreadful dreams wouldn't have a chance to creep into her sleep! There! She marched over and yanked another window blind open.

The sunlight lit up the rooms and blazoned over the shelves of colorful teapots by the fireplace. The collection had come with the furnishings in the house and she never tired of looking at them. There was porcelain, pottery, china and a variety of metals and styles that someone had lovingly gathered and left. Al Guiness, the banker she had bought the house from said that he had gotten the place in a foreclosure after the owner had disappeared.

Things were starting to sort themselves out now for her as she gazed at the teapots. A little giggle escaped her lips as she thought suddenly, what would Reed have said if he knew his precious million bucks was right here, and that he had been standing right next to all those dollars!

Then a pensive look came over her face. I suppose he thinks I've spent it all, but wouldn't he be surprised if he knew I got it all back and more when I invested it in stocks in that Rhode Island Bank. Her head began to clear as she thought about all that lovely money just across the room, all those crisp bills in neat rolls nestled safely in the teapots on the shelves.

She wiggled her toes as she sat with her feet propped on the coffee table, and then saw she needed a pedicure. And a manicure! Lordy, it had been weeks since she'd been to the Spa. She rushed into the bathroom and showered and when she saw the wet bath towel Reed had left hanging on the hook on the door she tossed it into a corner. Before leaving her house, she reached for a fat china teapot and counted out a handful of bills, then added several more just in case she saw something she really needed.

Hours later, her purse almost empty after all the lovely extravagances she'd undergone, she emerged a platinum blonde with a smart spring in her step. The stylish yellow linen dress flattered her slim shape and matched her high-heeled sandals.

Well, now feeling like a million, she thought with a smile, she looked too good to go home. She hailed a taxi and warily watched as it backed up to her at break neck speed.

"Señorita, where to?" The driver asked as he jumped out and opened the door of the cab for her, all the while appreciating her looks with roving eyes.

By now, it was late afternoon in Monterrey, the streets jammed as the tourists and natives moved around. Horns blared and whistles pierced the air as vehicles of every era flew around traffic circles. When she groped for a seatbelt she saw there wasn't one and slid off the seat onto the floor as they careened around a corner.

Turning to glance into the back seat at her, the driver asked again, "Señorita, where do you want to go?" As he brought his attention back to the front, he swerved just in time to avoid a truck that had broken down loaded with squawking chickens.

Lindy righted herself and braced her hands up against the front seat to keep from falling again as the taxi driver yelled something in Spanish and waved his fist at the truck-driver. Then glanced back at Lindy again and laughed.

By now, she was frantic in the hands of this lunatic and shrieked, "Let me out of here!" She threw a bill over the seat at the man and jumped out of the taxi as it screeched to a stop.

She was in downtown Monterrey where the streets were alive with people jostling for space amongst the shops. After calming down after the hair-raising ride she'd just had, she walked and gazed at the sights. Then saw a huge building on a corner with a flashing sign that said, The Grand Ritz Hotel. Well, now she felt better. The Grand hotel was the company she'd worked for years ago. She'd heard that they had joined forces with the Ritz chain and developed a major line of up-scale hotels worldwide. She quickened her step and crossed at the light.

The building was terra-cotta colored with a roof of round tiles. Bright green awnings adorned windows and balconies reaching up four floors. Palm trees and tropical shrubs sat in fat pots around a manicured lawn that glowed in the mist from the air coolers. As she neared, the scene vibrated with whistles and honking as valets opened car doors for arriving and departing guests.

"Good evening Señorita," a uniformed doorman said and saluted smartly as she approached, then rushed to open one of the big glass entrance doors for her.

As she walked into the elegance of the Grand Ritz, heads turned as she entered the bar and perched on a stool.

"Buenos dias! Señorita, what would you like to drink this afternoon?" a tuxedo clad bartender asked.

Lindy ordered a margarita and reached in her purse for her cigarettes and the elegant silver holder she'd snitched and just found in a jacket pocket the other day. A reminder of her days as Lili Lane and part of the costume she'd worn for her job at the Ashton mansion in Newport.

"Señorita, allow me," the bartender said after placing the drink before her. She touched her cigarette to the flame, and then sat back. She didn't need anyone anymore, certainly not Reed Conners! She was safe and secure again.

-3-

Reed hurried out of Lindy's house to the rental car, sick at heart at the helplessness he heard in Murphy's voice when he'd called and told him that Annie had suddenly disappeared. That she had not been seen since the day before, around noon. Being with the police force for twenty some years in Minneapolis, Murphy had put hundreds of sleazy characters away who could be out for revenge. It was a law enforcer's worst nightmare that their work might reflect back on their family.

The early morning traffic in Monterrey was a mix of shiny cars, rusty buckets that resembled cars, limousines and taxicabs, all fighting for space on the road as Reed sped to the airport.

"How soon can I get a flight out to Minneapolis," he asked impatiently after standing in line for what seemed like hours to get to the ticket counter. "First class," he added and slapped his credit card on the counter.

"Buenos dias!" the agent purred, and then dazzled him with a smile as she turned her attention to him.

Taken aback by the woman's charm, he swallowed his frustration at the seemingly snail's pace the whole country operated at. He cleared his throat and said in a more civilized tone. "It's an emergency; I need to leave right away!" He impatiently ran a hand through his hair.

But goddamn, he hadn't accomplished the one thing he'd come to Mexico to do! He exhaled. His resolution had gone to hell when he had stood at Lindy's door and she had turned those woeful eyes on him, and within minutes, they had ended up in bed. Disgusted with himself, he kicked his carry-on bag. And mumbled again, she still didn't know she was a free woman since falling asleep like that. Hell, she would be so angry that he had kept it from her! However, he could not have just blurted it out, he had to explain.

"Señor," the agent broke into his thoughts, "I can get you on a 10 o'clock flight and you will be in Minneapolis in the early afternoon. Will that be satisfactory?" She smiled at him.

"Is that the earliest I can get there?" Reed asked.

"Sĩ," she murmured.

"I'll take it," he said, then left a call with Murphy's secretary of his time of arrival. As he waited for her to make the arrangements, being someone who appreciated the appeal of a beautiful woman, admired her lustrous black hair, slim shape and classy uniform. That was one thing that he had noticed about the young female generation in Mexico, they dressed and moved with style.

The small Monterrey airport was filled with travelers arriving amid boisterous greetings, and tears and waving handkerchiefs as loved ones departed. He picked up his bag and looked around. He needed coffee. Then seeing a cafe, ordered the largest and minutes later was at his gate with several hours to spare. At least here in Mexico, the country did not dictate where you could smoke, he grumbled and lit a cigarette.

After the apprehension of getting a flight out of Mexico and back to Minneapolis, his thoughts went back to Murphy and his wife Annie. Theirs was a genuine love-story. He remembered Annie talking about their early days, smiling proudly as she recounted their struggles paying bills and finishing their education. They had known each other since grade school and had grown up in the "projects"; a government subsidized part of Minneapolis. They had been together through high school, soul mates in college and married after they had both landed their first jobs with the city. Annie had been a "stay at home mom" when the girls came along, but had been back at work as a social worker for a few years now. He had stood up with them at their wedding and was Godfather to all three daughters.

He stared off into the distance as he remembered the many times he'd been a guest at their home in Minneapolis for special occasions, and smiled again at Annie's efforts to line him up with a "nice girl" as she put it. He had met Murphy years ago, when early in their careers he had sought him out for help in hunting down a stalker that had been plaguing Lindy. Murphy had been a cop working the streets then and they had hit it off, and had been close friends since.

Goddamn, here he was thousands of miles away and could not do a thing! Why had he decided to go on this wild-goose chase right now?

It was almost twenty-four hours since Annie had disappeared, and time was important. Past cases had proven that after a certain amount of time, the chances of a victim being found alive decreased at an alarming rate.

Reed took another drag on the cigarette. Murphy idolized that woman! What would the man do without her? And those kids!

Impatience ate at Reed's nerves and he jumped up and began to pace. Back and forth, he walked as his mind raced. He stopped short as a group of young women walked by swinging their hips and clicking their high-heels smartly on the tiled floors. He did a double take and stared at the redhead on the left, his heart doing a flip as she smiled at him.

For a minute, he had thought it was Lindy, then realizing he was wrong, felt let down as the women disappeared into the crowds. He inhaled hard on his cigarette, blew out a smoke ring.

Damn, he had to call her, and took his cell out of a pocket. He had time now to explain to her as he waited at the airport. He stared at the coffee in the Styrofoam cup, raised it to his lips and drank deeply.

Well, maybe, not yet. She more than likely had gone back to bed. It had been early when the telephone had awakened them that morning. He chewed on his lower lip as he looked off into the distance. Against his will, his thoughts roared out of control and zeroed in on his feelings. He remembered how perfectly she'd fit in his arms and then how all his resolutions had vanished. Again!

Well goddamn it, he muttered to himself, face it old man, you have always had a thing for that woman. All she has to do is turn those blue eyes on you and you lay down!He took another drink of his coffee as he wrestled with his thoughts. Dismay burned through his agitated reflections that he had let her do it to him again.

How many times does it take? He thought again, pissed at himself for being so lame. As he sat down, engrossed in his grueling thoughts, time flew by and an announcement caught his attention calling his flight.

He listened, and then checked his ticket. Well I'll be damned; he said to no one in particular and hurried to get in line. Without another thought, he put his cell phone back in his pocket and hurried onto the plane.

After settling into his seat, he leaned back and closed his eyes but Lindy's face suddenly flashed before his eyes. Now he saw the tears she had been trying to hide when he had run out the door without taking five minutes to explain things to her. He felt guilty, but what the hell could he have done? He had to get to the airport fast!

He felt a presence at his side and opened his eyes as a flight attendant stood before him.

"Buenos días! Señor, may I bring you something to drink?" she asked.

Reed swallowed over his skidding nerves. "Yes, thank you," he said, "I'll have a double shot of Hennessy and water on the side."

When she brought the brandy, he drank greedily and felt the heat loosen the tightness in his belly. But after a second drink, as the liquor mixed with the coffee his stomach rebelled and the rest of the trip was agonizing.

Goddamn, he growled and wiped his clammy brow and tried to remember when he eaten last. When the flight attendant brought around crackers and cheese, he devoured the snack and asked for more.

Finally, arriving in Minneapolis he was one of the first out the door. When he got past the secure area, to his surprise Murphy stood waiting for him.

"Buddy," Reed said and clapped him on the shoulder, "Sorry, I was out of town. Is there anything new since we talked this morning?"

Murphy's voice shook. "Not a goddamn thing!" he said as they started walking fast through the airport. Today, Murphy's usual attire of perfectly fitted suits and pristine shirts and silk ties was missing as he wore faded jeans and a sweat-shirt. His black hair seemed mixed with more gray than Reed had noticed before. His green eyes were blood-shot. "I've got an unmarked parked over here," he said then pointing to a close lot.

"Tell me what you want me to do Murph," Reed said following him and not mentioning he had his Corvette parked in the ramp.

Murphy exhaled, "I'll catch you up on the way in, but we started going over my files this morning. But Christ, there's so many!"

They raced out of the airport and Murphy was silent as he maneuvered the car out to the freeway, and then continued, "She went to work yesterday at 8:30 and spent the morning in her office seeing her clients. Her appointment book was full. She's the best social worker that welfare department has!"

Reed agreed and reached for his cigarettes. Then remembered Murphy hated the smoke and put his craving aside.

"When was she last seen again?" He settled back into the car seat.

Murphy banged a fist on the steering wheel. "Her secretary said she left at 12:30 to go across the street to get a quick sandwich, but she never got there!" He wiped a hand over his jean clad thigh as he drove.

Over the years, Reed and Murphy had hunted deer together, fished the deep waters of northern Minnesota, even gotten falling down drunk together but, Reed had never seen his friend so troubled.

"Was she working on something new?" he asked.

"As far as we know, there was nothing different going on." Murphy slowed with the traffic. "It was her job to sift through the needy and the seedy. Jesus," he growled then as they were forced to come to a complete stop in back of four lanes of backed up traffic. Without a word, as Murphy put the window down Reed handed him the emergency flasher which he clamped on the roof of the car.

"Hang on," Murphy growled and Reed grabbed for the dash and braced himself, then gained new respect for his buddy as he maneuvered the car through ditches, over culverts with the siren screaming and lights flashing. As they left the traffic behind, Murphy slowed the car. "Assholes don't know how to drive," he muttered and threw the red light in the back seat. Reed felt sweat run down his forehead and reached for his cigarettes.

"Murph," he asked instead and looked at his friend, "do you have any ideas?"

"Jesus, not yet," Murphy replied brokenly. "We've got people going door to door downtown this morning in a two mile radius. Plus, we have crews going through the neighborhood around the house. They'll all report in now at two o'clock!" He exhaled and shook his head. "Conners, I just can't believe this, but goddamn I'll kill anyone who hurts a hair on her head!"

Reed reached over and put a hand on his shoulder. "Hang in there buddy, we'll find her!"

Murphy stared ahead at the road.

"Have you said anything to the girls?" Reed asked then.

"No, I just told them their mother had to go out of town, and they were happy to get out of school and spend time with the folks." Reed saw the pained look on Murphy's face as he continued, "We have had an APB out since midnight, with a description and a picture. Christ, she just disappeared into thin air!"

"Where is this café she was going to?" Reed shifted in his seat.

"Conners, it's just across the street and down at the corner of 6th and Hennepin. Peter's Grill, you know the place. She told her secretary she was going to grab a quick lunch and spend the rest of the afternoon in her office catching up on her paper work." Murphy cleared his throat. "When she wasn't back in an hour, the secretary thought it seemed unlike her and began to watch the clock. After two hours went by, the secretary called the security department. They called me at five!"

Murphy's voice was grave with fatigue. "When she wasn't home at dinner time I knew something was terribly wrong. She never missed!" Then he added, "I spent all night trying to remember every threat, every asshole had made to me over the years!"

Within minutes they hit the Minneapolis city limits and in another ten they were in the underground parking lot at the police station. They raced to the elevators and then to Murphy's department, and were just in time for the meeting. The room was jammed with officers.

"Murphy," the Chief said seeing them rush in the door, "take a seat." He nodded at Reed. "Good to see you, Conners."

"Have you found anything?" Murphy asked.

One by one the detectives recounted the results of the search. One neighbor thought he had seen a strange car in their area. An employee of an antique store downtown thought he had seen a woman matching Annie's description walking by on the street accompanied by a man. She hadn't seemed to be in a distressed situation. Nothing concrete!

The chief looked around at the men, and then nodded at Murphy, "We will find her! Go on home, Murphy, get some sleep, we'll call you the minute..."

Murphy stood up, "Can't do it, Chief. Come on Reed, let's take a walk, someone has got to have seen something!"

"I'm with you, buddy," Reed said and joined his friend.

-4-

Lindy sipped her tequila as she sat at the bar in the Grand Ritz hotel. She felt great after spending all those hours at the spa. She refused to think about Reed anymore and had made up her mind she wouldn't tolerate any more nightmares sneaking into her sleep and scaring the daylights out of her. On her way home, she was going to find a drugstore and buy a supply of those sleeping pills.

She raised the cigarette in its silver holder to her lips and inhaled, then blew out a cloud of smoke as she glanced around the room. The bar and dining room was located off to the side of the lobby of the Grand Ritz Hotel. The lighting was low in the large open area and Spanish music played softly. She didn't notice as a new customer took a seat a few stools over, didn't feel the curious look he gave her, as he glanced over a second time.

A group of women also entered the lounge and settled at a table nearby. When someone called out "Lola," the name didn't register, but when she looked up and saw a woman approaching her at the bar, she recognized Rita. Whom she'd met when she'd first come to Monterrey and began using the name Lola Lang.

"Lola, my dear, I've been so worried about you," Rita whispered. "Where did you go?" Gold and diamonds sparkled on her fingers, wrists, and neck.

Lindy swallowed her sudden alarm. "I was out of town for a few days."

"Well, I gathered that. Why didn't you tell me, my dear? I even came over to your house!" Lindy remembered someone ringing the hell out of her doorbell!

"Well, for God's sake, wherever you went, it agreed with you. Lola, you look marvelous!" Rita boldly scrutinized her new look and she swallowed her alarm.

"Join us," Rita said, "I'm here with friends."

When Lindy hesitated, Rita picked up her drink and stood aside and looked at her expectantly. Lindy slid off her stool and followed.

"Ladies," Rita said then, "I want you to meet a friend of mine. This is Lola Lang." All heads turned to Lindy. Then Rita added with a wink as she made room at their table, "Lola is a new resident of our city, and she has the gift!"

Now the group, mostly of Spanish descent studied her.

"She's clairvoyant," Rita whispered proudly and added, "She can do readings!"

The women began talking all at once.

Rita, better known as Margaret Ames was an American who had resided in Monterrey for decades. As a woman of sixty years plus, she was an active member of the prominent social set. She was an artist and her watercolors hung in galleries around the world. The story was her millionaire husband had died mysteriously at an early age after amassing a fortune in lumber and railroads, and shortly after his death, Margaret Ames had gathered up her inherited fortune, left the US, and moved across the border into Mexico. She was a diminutive woman, but commanded respect with her aggressiveness.

She was childless, and suntanned with beautifully styled silver hair. Lindy had been to her home several times and had been awe-struck at her vast estate.

Lindy had also saved her life several months ago when they had been having lunch together in a local restaurant. That same day after an earthquake had destroyed part of the business district in the city miles away, she had had a sudden vision of another quake about to happen, collapsing the roof and bringing the huge chandelier over their table down on them. She had reacted intuitively and pulled Rita to safety with just seconds to spare. Rita had guessed and recognized her extrasensory ability and encouraged her to take advantage of those powers, and had already introduced her around to her country club friends.

"Lola, my dear," Rita had said, "The Spanish people are very spiritual and strongly believe psychic predictions play an important part in their lives!"

And Lindy had followed the advice and had made money, huge amounts. She forced a smile at her new acquaintances now and said, "Yes. I do readings in my home." She reached into her purse for the business cards Rita had said she needed and caught up in the moment said, "Call me anytime!"

But it had been several weeks since, and those visions had suddenly turned into horrible nightmares and her new and safe life had come crashing down around her.

Since her own mother had died when she was a youngster, Lindy felt a connection towards Rita, and felt guilty that she had not told her, her real name. But that would have prompted too many questions!

Well--, Lindy murmured as she left the group and climbed into a taxi, I'll tell her later.

"Can you find a drugstore?" she asked the driver as they careened through the streets of downtown Monterrey and she hung on to the seat for dear life again. Irritated, she yelled at the Spanish man, "Why do you all drive so fast?"

In broken English he replied, "Pesos, Señorita pesos!"

Lindy found the pills in the store she needed to sleep and heaved a sigh of relief after getting home in one piece. Inside, she stepped out of her shoes and unzipped her dress on the way to her bedroom. She put on a robe and decided to make a cup of tea.

Things looked so promising she even hummed a little tune as she padded barefoot into the kitchen and filled the teakettle, and turned on a burner on the stove. As she waited for the water to boil she stared dreamily out the window over the sink. And then froze as a voice whispered, "Hello, Lola!"

She stood paralyzed, then whirled around and came face to face with Rio, the Mayor of Monterrey lounging in a chair at her table. A man she had met months ago and had saved his life after seeing a vision. He had wined and dined her in thanks one night, but later she had awakened in his bed. After being drugged and raped.

"What are you doing here?" she managed to gasp and tugged the robe tighter around herself.

Rio smiled. "I hardly recognized you as a blonde at the Ritz!" The man was dressed handsomely. His oiled features resembled a Latin movie star.

"You broke into my house," Lindy huffed to cover her shakes. "Leave right now!"

"Ahh-Lindy Lewis, I don't think you mean that," he said with a sly look on his face.

My God, he knew her name! She sucked in her breath and managed to whisper, "I do mean it. I'll call the police!"

Rio smiled, "Well, you can call them; they're all friends."

Then Lindy remembered that was the exact reason she hadn't gone to them before to report what he had done to her. She had heard things! A chill went down her back as he added, "By the way, I like your new look Lindy. I have a passion for blondes!"

She cringed. "What do you want?" she asked bravely.

"Answers, Señora Lewis," Rio said with a cunning look on his face. "Have you come to my country to hide?"

Lindy looked him squarely in the eye. "Whatever makes you think that?"

Rio laughed. "That's usually the reason why foreigners move here and change their name!"

Lindy shrugged her shoulders and looked innocently at him as he continued, "I make it my business to find out who takes up residence in my town! What's your reason?" He barked at her.

"I just love the food!" Lindy exclaimed boldly.

Rio stood up. "Señora, I have given you a chance to exonerate yourself, but you choose to lie!" He started to the door, then stopped and turned back to face her and with a cagy look in his eyes said, "I know all about you, Lindy Lewis. I'll be in touch!"

-5-

Reed followed Murphy out of the Police department and into the street. Murphy's steps were fast, his shoulders hunched down in his shirt.

"I want to retrace her steps," he said and turned down the busy street. "Her building is just over two blocks."

"Good idea," Reed said.

Murphy blew out a shaky breath. "Christ, someone had to have seen her. How can someone just disappear into thin air?"

"We'll find her," Reed reassured him. But they both knew people disappeared without a trace every day.

The traffic in downtown Minneapolis was at its peak; buses roared down the streets belching fumes as pedestrians raced for a seat. Car horns blasted and tires screeched as the rush hour exodus began. Reed and Murphy's footsteps slapped against the concrete as they made their way to Annie's office building.

Social Service stood on a busy corner in the midst of the downtown warehouse district. Peter's Grill, an old, but established restaurant was across the street and down on the next corner.

"Okay, we've gone over this numerous times already, but we'll start here again," Murphy said as they stood by the building. He looked up and down the streets with an anxious look on his face.

"Would she have crossed here?" Reed asked as he looked back and forth, seemingly measuring steps.

"I don't know," Murphy mumbled as they started walking. The block between her building and the diner housed various businesses and also a parking lot.

"It's that lot that scares me!" Murphy nodded towards it as they neared, where a fenced off area held what looked like about a couple of dozen cars.

"Come on, let's check it out," Reed said and they walked over to a small shed wedged amongst the cars. A black man stuck his head out the door as they approached.

"I'm full up," he yelled.

"We just want to ask you some questions," Reed said as Murphy took out his Police ID and asked, "Did you see this woman anytime yesterday?" Murphy held out Annie's picture.

The parking attendant, a man in his twenties blew out a breath as he studied the picture, maybe relieved that it wasn't about him.

"Probably, sometime around twelve thirty yesterday," Murphy added and studied the man as he replied, "Nah, never seen her."

"Are you sure?" Reed asked.

"Yah, it's busy around here at that time!" The attendant shrugged his shoulders and hurried away, then disappeared into his shed.

The next block held a dry cleaners, a boutique, a beauty shop and at the end of the street, a bar. After stopping at each and getting nowhere, they turned into the bar. A downtown landmark called Russell's, which had stood on the same corner for decades and was owned by an Irish family. It was a hangout for the police department, where officers gathered for drinks after shifts and where Murphy was well known and respected. As they opened the door and stepped in they were blasted with cigarette smoke and loud conversations, but as they came into the room it quieted down. Friends and acquaintances nodded at them.

Dick Russell appeared out of the crowd and came over and put a hand on Murphy's shoulder. "Tell me what I can do." He motioned to the bartender.

Murphy sank down on a stool and shook his head. "Jesus Dick, she's just gone. I can't believe this!"

"Easy now, buddy," Dick Russell exclaimed to his friend. He nodded towards Reed.

Reed said, "Everyone knows Annie, but why don't we pass around some photos, just in case!"

"Good idea," Dick Russell said as Murphy took several out of his pocket.

By now the bar was quiet. "Pass these along," Reed said nodding especially to several groups of customers that had just come in. "This is Murphy's wife Annie, she disappeared yesterday around twelve thirty on her way from the Social Service building to Peter's Grill. She never got there and she hasn't been seen since!" All faces were turned to his as he spoke.

The bartender set two shots of whiskey on the bar. Murphy gulped one and Reed lit a cigarette before taking his. Then one by one, a steady stream of officers came up and clapped Murphy on the back, many just coming off duty after volunteering to do an extra shift combing the area searching.

Murphy put his elbow on the bar and placed his forehead down on his hand. His face was gray and his eyes bloodshot from loss of sleep.

"Got any coffee?" he asked?

"Sure, and I've started the big pot," Dick said. "I passed the word we've got free food here for everybody who's working overtime. I'm going to stay open after hours as long as we need to until we find her."

"Thanks Dick," Murphy nodded. Minutes later a waitress came over with a tray of buns piled high with ham, steaming French fries and pickles. "Here, Murphy, eat something before you fall over in your tracks," she said and set it down on the bar before them.

Reed was famished and helped himself, but Murphy just looked at the food, and then stood up. "I can't, I don't have time," he said and appeared to stumble.

Reed reached over and steadied him. "Murph, sit down, you need to eat something!" Murphy blinked several times.

"Here, have a sandwich," Reed said then. He checked his watch. "It's almost time for the next briefing with the chief." He looked at his friend. "Could be someone has found something!"

Just then Reed's cell-phone rang and recognizing Ed's number from the insurance company he worked for, he stood up and walked outside to take the call.

"Conners," Ed said. "We just got word that Ann Murphy is missing. She just disappeared?"

"Yesterday," Reed answered Ed's abrupt question. "I'm with Murph now and we're on our way back to the department for another briefing."

"Christ, a good family. What'll happen next?" Ed swore in the background. "It's not a good time, but you know we've got a million dollars covering her."

"Well, we can only hope we don't have to get into that!'"

"Yeah, how's Murphy holding up?"

Reed took a breath. "He's okay for now. But he's starting to lose it."

"I'm coming over to the department when I lock up here. Tell him I called. My wife is wondering if she can help with the girls."

"I'll tell him. They're at the farm with his folks for now."

Reed and Murphy left Russell's bar amidst exclamations of good will from his associates and hurried back to the police station for the early evening briefing.

Ann Murphy had been missing for thirty hours, from just past noon the day before until six o'clock that evening. Warehouses, rooftops, vacant houses and buildings had been searched in the area. Business owners and their employees had been questioned. Normally, a person wouldn't be considered missing until forty-eight hours had passed, but in this instance, she was the wife of one of their own and that pushed it up to top priority.

"Alright, we're all here," the chief said standing in front of the detectives in the conference room, "let's see what we've got so far."

One by one the detectives took their turn reporting in, but again in the end they all had come up empty, each of them looking at Murphy apologetically as they ended their reports.

"Here's what we're going to do," the chief said after a moment and held up his hand for silence as everyone started talking. "I'm extending the search to include a helicopter search of all the Hennepin county parks and I'm bringing out the canine units. We've got four hours until dark, and then we'll use the searchlights. We'll work through the night!"

Everyone was aware the focus had also changed from finding Ann Murphy alive, to include searching for a body. Reed glanced over at Murphy and saw his face had turned a greenish color. He was breathing hard.

"Conners," the chief said then, "I want you to get Murphy home and see that he gets some sleep. I'll call if we find anything!"

Reed followed Murphy out of the conference room and was on his heels as he yanked opened a restroom door and disappeared into a stall, where the man began to retch.

Minutes later, he came out and put his head under the cold faucet and let the water wash over his face. He mumbled "Jesus!"

"Can you make it?" Reed asked.

"Yeah," Murphy said and ran a hand over his hair. "Let's go, I need to check the house. Maybe she's there!"

Reed didn't say anything as they hurried out of the police department, through the halls and then outside. They got back in the blue unmarked car in the parking lot and within ten minutes they were in the north suburb and Murphy's driveway. Reed followed him as he opened the back door and went inside.

"Ann, Annie," he called out as he hurried from room to room, opening closet doors and then running upstairs calling out her name in a hoarse voice. Reed stood just inside the door, uncertain as to what to do.

Seconds later, Murphy came back into the kitchen. "I just thought maybe--." For the first time his voice broke.

"Come on let's take a break, Murph, thirty minutes." Reed nodded towards the couch in the family room. "I'll take the recliner." And, finally Murphy gave in and his snoring echoed in the room.

Reed stretched out. Goddamn, he was tired! Every bone in his body ached and his head was ready to explode. The whole day had been like something out of a horror story.

Just hours ago he'd been thousands of miles away, warm and cozy in Lindy's bed, when Murphy's frantic phone call had abruptly awakened him out of a sound sleep.

"Goddamn," he mumbled now as he glanced over at Murphy's inert form as he lay out cold on the plaid couch. He went into the kitchen and called a taxi, then wrote a note.

"Call me on my cell when you get up!" He propped it on the coffee table by the couch, next to Murphy.

The Corvette was still standing safely in the airport lot where Reed had left it. Christ, it felt more like a week since he'd left it there. He hurried back downtown. All along an idea had been niggling in the back of his mind. He parked the car and began walking the streets in the downtown area in search of another woman. Brita was her name and she lived on the street. One cold winter, when Reed had come into Minneapolis from Willeston, he found her nearly frozen to death in a doorway downtown and had taken her to a hospital. After days in a coma, she'd survived. Over the years, he would track her down, give her money, and try to talk her into coming in off the street, but she always refused saying she had a family out there. He had done some checking and found she was in her sixties, had a Master's degree in physics, and had come from a prominent family in Wisconsin. Reed was aware of the tight network of the street people and knew Brita would have heard if anyone had seen or heard anything suspicious going on!

It was dark now as Reed headed up Hennepin Avenue, and then walked down a seedy alley. As he got further into the warehouse district, he stopped a lone woman pushing a rusty shopping cart, loaded and overflowing with bulging plastic bags. He held up a ten dollar bill.

"Have you seen Brita?" he asked. The bag lady's eyes grew weary and she hurried by. "She's a friend of mine," Reed said then. The woman stopped and stood hesitant for a moment. Then the sight of money apparently got the better of her as she hurried back and grabbed it and pointed off in the direction of the downtown Greyhound bus depot, then took off running and pushing her cart of worldly goods.

Reed yelled thanks to her fleeting back and hurried to the depot and within minutes found Brita sitting placidly amongst the travelers, her cart of treasures close.

"Hello, beautiful," he said and sat down in an empty seat beside her.

"What?" the woman said and jerked away, then turned and looked him over good. "Motherfucker, if it isn't my boyfriend!" she gasped and smiled her toothless grin.

Reed had to smile at her greeting. "Good to see you, Brits, how are you?"

"I got here early tonight for my shower before the bums showed up."

"Good thinking," Reed nodded his head in agreement.

"I've got a new outfit," she said then and smoothed the skirt. She stood up and twirled the flared skirt.

"You look just like a movie star," Reed said as she sat down again.

Brita's hair was silver gray, and wet and curly from her shower. Her frame, small and wizened and her face lined. The dress was purple and red flowered and many sizes too large, but she had tightened it up around her waist with a piece of pink ribbon. On her feet she wore a pair of shiny gold sandals; black socks came up over her knees.

"I need your help Brita," Reed began and held out a picture of Ann Murphy for her to see. "This is my friend's wife, and she disappeared yesterday at around noon. She's got three daughters. I'm wondering if you have heard anything on the street that might help us find her."

Brita held the picture close to her face and squinted to see better, then sucked in her breath and whispered, "Motherfucker!" Apparently one of her most favorite words.

-6-

Lindy watched Rio, the mayor of Monterrey, walk out her front door after finding him sitting at her table when she'd gone into her kitchen to make a cup of tea. It had been weeks since he'd invited her over to his house for dinner, when she had awakened later out of a drugged sleep to find herself in his bed. Now the man had broken into her house!

She shivered as a chill spread down her back. He had called her Lindy Lewis! And, had implied she must be in hiding since she'd crossed the border, changed her name and was now living in his country. What else did he know?

The tea kettle on the stove in the kitchen suddenly shrieked its temperature alert, and she fumbled in the cupboard for a cup and saucer and made the tea. Then walked on unsteady legs to the table and sat on the edge of the chair.

It was going on midnight and pitch black outside the window in her kitchen. She glanced up at her reflection in the glass.

Lord, was Rio still out there? Was he watching her?

She reached over and yanked the shade down and forced herself to sit and drink the tea, then finally made her way to her bedroom. As she tossed her robe on a chair, she reached for the pills she'd gotten at the drug store. The directions read adults; take two before retiring. And just for good measure, she took four and then slipped between the sheets of her king-sized bed.

The white adobe house with the red tiled roof in Monterrey was silent as the wee hours of the night ticked away on the small clock as she slept, finally oblivious to the world around her. But suddenly, a picture flashed through her sub-conscious and she awakened abruptly. She sat up and looked around bewildered, and brushed a hand over her newly blonde hair as she sat in her bed. She couldn't erase the feeling that the incident had had an ominous ring to it!

Seeing it was almost noon, she threw the blankets off and stepped into the shower. As the water sluiced over her body she peeked through the curtain, just to reassure herself she was alone in the bathroom.

Needing to get away from her sinister thoughts, thirty minutes later she called for a taxi and went to check out an interesting looking restaurant she'd seen advertised.

Zelda's, the sign said over the door. Well, it was going on early afternoon and she was starved and besides she was at loose ends. And after Reed's sudden departure and Rio's threat, her nerves were shot. She was going to have a strong drink. She settled on a stool then froze as the bartender exclaimed, "Oh my God, Lindy, it's you!"

Lindy sucked in her breath. And after all these years, a friend from the past stood behind the bar.

"Monica," she said astonished, "What are you doing here?"

Monica laughed, shaking her mane of black curly hair. "Lindy, I've lived here for years. What the hell are you doing in this country?" She came out from behind the bar. Lindy stood up and they hugged.

For a minute Lindy was beyond words, torn between happiness of running into an old friend, then anxious about yet another person knowing her identity.

She found her tongue and managed to say, "I live here now, too!"

"You do?" Monica said and went back behind the bar. She raised her eyebrows. "Lindy, the last time we talked, you were hunkered down in that mausoleum of a house with your old man, in the middle of one of those god-awful Minnesota blizzards!"

Lindy smiled. "Things have changed!"

"I'd say. Girlfriend, I'm fixing you a strong drink, so talk." After sliding an amber filled glass over the bar to Lindy, she added, "I better have one, too!" After which, she put her elbows on the bar and eyed Lindy expectantly.

Needing time to collect her thoughts Lindy asked, "You tell me first, when did you move from Texas to Mexico?"

Monica tossed her hair back over her shoulders. "I came here on a vacation and never left."

"Really," Lindy murmured and remembered her friend had always been restless and independent. "What happened to Lee?"

Monica lit a cigarette with a slim gold lighter. Her nails were perfect ovals with blood red polish and glistened as she held the long black reed to her lips. She shook her head. "Oh, we were over years ago."

Lindy took a sip of the drink Monica had mixed, and then choked as it burned its way down her throat.

"Okay, your turn," Monica said again.

'Well," Lindy said evasively, "the same with me. I came down and decided to stay too. I bought a house not too far from here."

"You did!" Monica glanced around the bar. "Lindy, give me five minutes to catch up here and I'll be back." She left to take care of some new customers.

Lindy thought back to the time when they had worked together and became good friends. Over two decades ago now, she remembered.

In her job for the Grand Hotel chain, she had traveled to Dallas to help set up the dining rooms in their new complex. She'd been there for months as the mammoth building took shape. Monica had been hired to train the mass of wait people the finer points of dining and together they'd worked to give the restaurant a "five-star" quality. They'd been young and unattached and had shared many bottles of champagne as they had worked and partied in the town. Later as their lives sent them in different directions they'd kept in touch, but then over time their letters and telephone calls dwindled to just every couple of years. Now here they were both living in the same city in a new country. Outside of her friend, Mitzi, who lived in Hilton Head, South Carolina, and Solly, who she assumed still lived in Savannah, Georgia with her boyfriend, she hadn't had the good fortune of having a close friend for a long time. And, she was lonely. Of course she had met Rita, the rich American artist who was introducing her to the country club set. But would they have welcomed her if she hadn't had the gift?

She opened her purse, found her cigarettes and put one in the long holder. As she exhaled a cloud of smoke toward the ceiling, she fluffed her blonde hair and smiled as her friend Monica said, "Okay, Lindy Lewis, it's your turn, out with it!"

-7-

"What is it?" Reed asked Brita. They were sitting in the Greyhound bus depot in downtown Minneapolis. Just then an announcement boomed over the sound system listing the towns the next bus would be going through. Nauseous fumes crept into the crowded room and mixed with the odor of dust, sweat, cheap cologne and burnt popcorn.

Brita's elfin features were contorted in a mass of wrinkles as she concentrated on Annie's picture, then her bright blue eyes anxiously darted to the main entrance of the depot.

"Have you seen this woman, Brita? Or heard anything?" Reed prompted.

Brita's breath whistled as it swirled around in her toothless mouth. "No, ----no," she whispered and pushed the photo back into his hand.

"Please Brita; this is my friend's wife. They've got three little girls!" He asked, "Have you heard anything on the street?"

"I can't--," Brita whispered again and put a hand over her mouth. She turned her face away and he saw her blink away tears.

He put a hand on her shoulder. "Brita, what is it? Tell me if you know anything!"

"I can't!" She shuttered, then whispered, "He'll get me!"

Reed's heart started to pump faster. "Who, Brita tell me, who will get you?"

Brita stood up and nervously began tucking her plastic bags deeper in the old shopping cart that stood by her side. "Someone will see me," she gasped, then whispered again, "He's called Wolff! He's bad!"

"Wolff, where is he?" Reed stole a quick glance over the mass of people milling around amongst the suitcases and boxes, waiting to get on the buses.

Brita closed her lips into a thin tight line. Her wizened face paled. Her eyes darted furtively over the crowd, and then she whispered, "He's over on First Street!"

Reed's face hurt from holding back his impatience.

Brita averted his eyes as she busied herself rearranging her worldly goods, and then muttered. "I've heard things!"

"What things Brita, what have you heard?" He forced himself to control his voice. He began again, "Please Brita, I need your help!"

Brita looked around anxiously, and whispered under her breath, "Please. I've got to go before someone sees me talking to you!"

He put a twenty dollar bill in her hand and watched as she slipped out a side door of the depot pushing her rusty cart. Her gold shoes gleamed in the streetlight and the purple and red dress she was so proud of, dragged on the ground. He'd seen the fear in Brita's eyes as she had told him as much as she had. Now he had a name!

Reed drove over to First Street. Even though it was getting close to midnight, the street was teeming with people and the bars hummed with activity. All the action brought out the street people who lived off the money they were able to collect. Prostitutes walked the concrete, their eyes piercing the crowds for a knowing wink or a come-on of some kind. Pan-handlers stood with their hand out for a dollar.

Reed searched for a parking lot, parked the Corvette and walked the streets, his eyes wary as he searched the faces of the masses of people.

He approached a man standing on one corner playing a guitar with a hat down on the sidewalk in front of him. He put a ten dollar bill in the hat and stood off to the side. After the song was finished he stepped up.

"Good show, man," he said, and then saw the man was a young boy around sixteen years old. His hair was long and dirty, his clothes ragged. He shook his hair off his face and gave Reed a second look.

"Have you seen Wolff tonight?" Reed asked

The boy hastily picked up the hat and stuffed the dollars in his pocket.

"Hey buddy, I'm not interested in you. I'm just looking for Wolff," Reed repeated.

"Get the fuck away from me," the boy said in a rasping voice and took off down the street clutching his guitar.

Reed watched him run. When he asked a woman loitering on another corner if she'd seen Wolff, she yelled, "Get lost!" As he continued searching the streets, apparently word had spread quickly throughout the network of street-people, as silence preceded him now as he approached and tried to question them, averting their eyes as he tried to make contact. Finally after several hours, he gave up and went back to his car. When he got back to Murphy's he tiptoed into the house.

"I'm up," Murphy said in a hoarse voice.

He followed the voice into the kitchen. "You were out cold when I left, figured you'd be good for a few hours."

Murphy ran a hand though his wet tousled hair. "Jesus, I can't! I've got to find Annie. It's been too long already!"

Reed looked his friend over and saw his pallor, the dark circles around his eyes.

"Where were you?" Murphy asked as he gulped coffee. He leaned against the cupboard dressed in faded jeans again and a black t-shirt. Then turned and poured a cup of coffee for Reed.

"I had a hunch!"

"What?" Murphy asked.

He took a drink of his coffee. "Murph, I think I found something!"

Murphy jerked to attention. "You found something?"

Reed reached for a cigarette then slid his hand into his pants pocket instead. "Have you heard of a homeless person by the name of Wolff?"

Murphy's eyes burned. "Wolff?"

"Yeah," Reed said. "Apparently, he's got some kind of hold over the streets. All the residents are scared of him!"

"Christ, I've heard of him!" Murphy put his cup in the sink and started out the door leading into the garage on a run. "You think he took her?" his voice rasped.

Reed sucked in a breath as he followed, "Christ man, I got a feeling about him!"

Murphy smacked a hand against the door jamb. "Jesus Christ, I'll find the fucker even if I have to pick up every last bum out there. Someone will talk, by God!"

-8-

"For God's sake, it's been years since we talked," Lindy said to Monica, her best friend from the past she'd just run into, "I wouldn't know where to begin!" She was sitting at a bar in Monterrey, Mexico where Monica worked as a bartender.

"Well, first of all, you used to be a brunette, when did you become a blonde?" Monica asked.

Lindy laughed and fluffed her tresses. "Just lately, I like to change now and then."

Monica stepped back and sized her up. "I like it," she said. "In a few minutes this place will be jammed with the lunch crowd, so talk fast and tell me everything! Are you here in Mexico with your husband?"

She sucked in her breath.

"Well, where is he?' Monica looked around expectantly.

Lindy saddened as she said, "he died."

Monica's face sobered. "Oh my God, I'm so sorry," she said and reached over and took Lindy's hand and asked, "What happened?"

A sudden lump caught in Lindy's throat as she said, "He got cancer, and just a few months later he was gone."

"Oh Lord, I'm sorry," Monica repeated again, and then said in a hushed voice, "I can't believe he's gone. It seems like yesterday when I stopped at your house while I was there for that class reunion." Monica shook her head. "Lord, that's ten years ago!"

"We'd only been in our new home for a couple of years then," Lindy said and sniffed as her nose stuffed up.

Monica went on, "You guys were so happy! He was so proud of that house."

"He was," Lindy said and for a moment felt like she was going to cry. She forced herself to brighten up and sipped at her drink.

"What am I drinking?" She asked then to change the subject.

Monica tossed her mane of hair. "You're in Mexico, its tequila!"

"I should have known." Lindy put a smile on her face and started to feel better.

But Monica continued, "So, I got to tell you when I first saw that run down relic of a house, I thought you were both nuts to buy something like that." She blew a trail of smoke through her red lips.

Lindy smiled. "It was pretty bad, wasn't it?"

"Good Lord, when you sent me the picture and I saw the place later, I couldn't believe the changes you two had made, how long did it take?"

"You know, just over three years. The first year we spent rebuilding the outside; we had to repair all the windows, replace the porches that ran along the three sides, shingle the roof." Lindy waved the glass of tequila in the air and joked, "I could hire out as a carpenter if I had to!"

"Jeez, I couldn't believe it was the same house!"

Lindy shook her head. "When we started on the inside, it was a full year of eating dust; many times I was sorry we'd ever gotten involved. I sanded all that woodwork myself you know."

"Good Lord," Monica said and grimaced, and then turned as a new customer slid onto a stool. She greeted the man, "How are you doing, Al?"

Out of curiosity, Lindy looked over, but hastily turned her head away, but not before he said, "Hello, Lola!"

Lindy nodded at Al Guiness, the banker.

"Mind if I join you?" he said and before she had a chance to think up a reply, he had moved over. He said in his clipped accent, "I've been trying to reach you!"

"Really," Lindy replied innocently.

"Yes, well, I've been concerned about your assets, so I've worked up a portfolio that will bring you unbelievable returns! When can we meet?"

She smiled sweetly at him. Today the man was dressed in gray; Suit, tie, shirt, even his shoes were gray.

When Lindy had researched the banking world for a way to get her money out of the US, she remembered overhearing Mario D'Agustino and his brother talking about Al Guinness, an unscrupulous banker across the border, who for a price was sympathetic to wealthy Americans who wanted to relocate their riches. He was British and his demeanor, conservative. She had successfully gotten her cash out of the country and into Mexico disguised and posing as a pregnant woman returning to her home country. She'd put it in a safety deposit box in his bank, temporarily, promising to invest in his suggested ventures as soon as she got settled. But, she had started having nightmares again, dreadful ones that scared the daylights out of her; visions of upcoming events that sometimes actually happened. She'd had an image of an earthquake, where she saw the bank that held her fortune clearly pictured, demolished. Not wasting a minute, she'd rushed right over and gathered her fortune. And sure enough, inside of hours a quake had taken place and turned that area into a pile of rubble.

Because she'd gotten her money out of his bank before he'd had a chance to collect his due, she knew Al Guiness had become obsessed with finding her.

She almost giggled as she thought, wouldn't he have a conniption fit if he knew I have all that money safely tucked away in my teapot collection at home!

Lindy glanced over at Monica, who stood a short distance over polishing the bar and listening unabashed. When their eyes met, Monica looked astonished.

Just then Al's cell-phone rang and he abruptly hurried out of the bar without a backward glance.

Monica stared at Lindy dumbfounded and then asked, "What the hell is going on?"

Lindy downed the tequila. After the distress of running into Al Guiness, she needed another drink. Raising her empty glass she gasped, "Lord, I need more!" Then suddenly, the place began to hum as waitresses bombarded Monica for service and lone customers lined the bar.

After an hour of intense lunch action, the crowded restaurant and bar emptied quickly as the throng of customers made a mad exodus back to their desks and cubicles. Monica came out from behind the bar and took a stool next to Lindy.

"Okay, Lindy or should I call you Lola, what's with the alias?" she asked and slid her shoes off and let them drop to the floor under the stool. She stretched her long legs and adjusted the short shorts she was wearing. She was in her middle forties too, and looked like a streamlined thirty five, with long black curly hair, naturally stand-up boobs and a golden suntan.

Lindy lit another cigarette and took her time inhaling through the elegant holder. Lord, she was happy to have found her good friend. When they had run around together twenty some years ago, they'd been young with taut skin, no wrinkles and thought they were immortal. They'd dressed in denims and silks, and drank only champagne. Even though it had been years since they'd seen each other, they both fell into the straightforward closeness they'd always shared as they sat in Zelda's, far away from their roots.

By now, Lindy was feeling no pain. Even though it was early afternoon, she was in high spirits. The nightmares were forgotten, along with Reed's quick exit, Rio's threat and now running smack into Al Guiness, the banker.

She looked at Monica. Should she tell her friend everything? The only other time she'd told anyone about the last year was when she'd seen Mitzi in South Carolina. Of course, she'd shocked the heck out of her, but Mitzi had gotten over it and they'd had a lot of fun, until they'd met the D'Agustino brothers.

Lindy shivered remembering the murder she'd witnessed and the trial she'd been forced to testify at.

Well, Monica was her best friend. They'd had plenty of adventures together years ago, sometimes pretty close to breaking the law. She took another swallow of the tequila.

"Lindy, for Christ's sake, what is going on?" Monica asked impatiently, and then went on, "Al is a pretty shady character, and he called you Lola, why?"

"Well, I put some money in his bank," Lindy began.

Monica shook her head. "Lindy, you can kiss it goodbye. He's a thief! I heard his downtown place got hit by the earthquake we just had, but he's still got branches all over the town!"

Lindy sat back in satisfaction. "But Monica, I got it out just in time before the place crumbled! He is pissed though!"

"Well, I guess I'm surprised he let you." Monica looked at her. "Just how much money are we talking about?"

"A little over a million," Lindy answered stone-faced.

Monica's eyes widened. "A million dollars?" She gasped and stared at Lindy who calmly smoked her cigarette.

"Well, did you win a lottery or something?" Monica asked.

Not able to contain a tequila induced grin, Lindy said. "No, I collected it after I burned that house I had slaved over!"

"For Christ's sake, are you nuts?" Monica raised her glass and drank, then said, "Now I know why you've changed your name! Jesus Lindy!"

Lindy just placed another cigarette in the long silver holder and smiled.

-9-

It was nearing midnight as Reed followed Murphy in his own car to the Police Department downtown. As he drove through the streets, his eyes swept over the crowd of people as they left the Target Center searching for the man who might be Wolff, though as yet, they didn't have a description. The air vibrated with thunder and the black sky above the city lights sparked with lightning, spiraling with each brilliant crescendo.

They hurried into the department and on into homicide. "Anything come in?" Murphy asked as they stopped at the Chief's desk.

The Chief turned from his phone. "Murphy, why didn't you stay home and get some sleep?"

Murphy just shook his head.

Ann Murphy had been missing for thirty-six hours now. They all knew that every hour that went by the likelihood of finding her alive diminished rapidly. The air in the department hummed with tension as the men checked in. Each nodded at Murphy soberly as they gathered for another briefing.

The Chief strode over to the detectives, "What do you have?" he asked.

The lines on Murphy's face deepened as each one related his efforts to no avail again. When the officer with the Canine Department reported searching the park reserves and wetland areas, Reed put a reassuring hand on Murphy's shoulder.

Murphy asked, "Have any of you heard of someone on the street who goes by the name of Wolff?" He ran a hand over the stubble on his face, "Reed heard a rumble tonight!"

One detective spoke up, "I've heard of that name. It's someone new from out of town and goes by that name!"

"Do you have a description?" Reed asked from where he stood off to the side. When no one did, he added, "He'll stay away now for sure when he hears we're looking for him!"

The Chief held up a hand to quiet the group who had all started talking at once.

"We've a new picture of Ann Murphy. It was taken by the security camera yesterday morning as she came into the department for work. I want this placed on every door of every business place in the area. Every corner pole or post! Tonight, it'll be on every television in the country!"

Reed's hand tightened on Murphy's shoulders as the Chief passed the photos around.

Ann's full length frame was pictured as she had stood before a security camera waiting to be admitted to the Social Service division. Reed was reminded of her resemblance to the actress, Jane Seymour, with her long red hair and sparkling hazel eyes. The description included her height at 5'8"and weight at 142 pounds. She was wearing a red and purple floral print dress and low heeled black shoes. Her purse was a large black shoulder bag and she wore a gold necklace with matching hoop earrings.

The minute Reed saw the photo, his heart began to pound. He studied it as something tugged at his thoughts. But what the hell was it? Then the Chief interrupted by saying, "be careful out there men!"

"Come on, I'm going on foot," Murphy said to Reed and they headed out of the homicide department.

The night was hot and steamy as was common in late August in Minneapolis as they walked the streets leading to the downtown area. The state fair would start soon, then a long weekend and the opening of a new school year. Reed's mind was still in turmoil as he followed Murphy. This time of the year always put him in a depression as nature's growing season began to decline, and his spirits didn't lighten up again until winter's chill settled him in front of his fireplace with his collection of Western novels.

He brushed sandy hair off his forehead, forced the gloominess aside. "Buddy, what do you want to do?" he asked Murphy.

Murphy's pale features hardened. "I'm going to find this freak Wolff and choke the truth out of him," he hissed. "I'll kill the bastard if--." He clamped his mouth shut and their footsteps echoed on the concrete as they walked.

Reed turned to his friend. "Murph, we don't even know what the man looks like yet!"

"Yeah, I know," Murphy said not slowing his steps, "but I'll find out!"

They searched faces in the crowds and walked through dark alleys. The same street people averted them as they prowled the streets and tried to show Ann's picture.

Suddenly, Murphy took off in a run down the street and headed into a parking lot chasing someone. Reed followed and when he caught up, Murphy had a black man on the ground, his gun in the guy's face, and the heel of his boot on his throat.

The man lay on the ground gasping for air, fear in his eyes.

"Hello, Duke," Murphy yelled down at him, "I don't give a fuck about you this time asshole, when I take my foot off, start talking!"

Reed took out his gun and moved in.

"Where's Wolff?" Murphy growled, and then held out Ann's picture. "See this," he jabbed at it with a finger, "That's my wife! Word's out Wolff's got her!" Murphy's voice cracked, "Where is he?"

Duke's eyes bulged.

"Where is Wolff?" Murphy repeated, dangerously close to putting his foot down harder on his throat and smashing his windpipe. The foul smell of Duke's unwashed body and dirty clothes filled the air. "Think hard, asshole," he growled.

Duke struggled for air. The white of his eyes glistened in the dim street light.

"Okay, fucker, if you so much as move an inch. You're a dead man!" Murphy said

"Talk!" Reed hissed as he pointed his gun at the man's head too.

Duke whispered hoarsely, "He got a crib in that big old place, that ol' Grain Belt place!"

"What does he look like?" Murphy barked.

"Big, big man, gray hair!"

"Is he white?" Reed asked.

"Yeah!" Duke moaned as he lay on the dirt in the parking lot.

"Get the fuck away from me," Murphy said then and within seconds Duke jumped up and disappeared into the murky alley.

"Let's go," Reed said and they hurried back to the department parking lot for Murphy's unmarked and out into the bustling street traffic. Within minutes they were in Northeast Minneapolis and parked by the old Grain Belt Brewery building. The windows had been boarded up for years in the German castle-like structure. There had been talk of a renovation to turn the place into upscale apartments, but as yet it stood forlorn and bare.

"Jesus," Murphy said brokenly and adjusted his shoulder holster as they stood by the car, "This place is huge, how the hell can we find her in there?"

As Reed looked up at the towers that crowned the six stories of brick, the same turmoil he'd felt earlier, returned. And suddenly he knew what had been bugging him.

It was that dress! That red and purple dress that Ann Murphy had been wearing in that picture the chief had shown was the same dress Brita was wearing when he talked to her at the bus station! And Brita's wardrobe came out of garbage cans!

His gut hurt, he could not tell his best friend that! But goddamn, he'd get the bastard even if it took his last breath.

-10-

"Well Monica, I did change my name so you've got to call me Lola now!" Lindy said as she sat calmly drinking tequila in Zelda's bar in Monterrey where Monica worked as a bartender.

"Okay--," Monica said as she looked at her old friend curiously, "I remember you used to do some crazy things, Lindy, but this? Did you really burn your house for the million dollars of insurance?"

Lindy nodded and calmly smoked her cigarette, then blew out a plume of smoke.

"Why?" was all Monica managed to say, "You loved that place?"

Lindy was silent as a picture of her home came back to mind. Almost tearfully she whispered, "Honestly, I had to!"

Monica stared at her friend and rolled her eyes.

Lindy went on soberly, "After my husband died and I lived there alone weird things began to happen in that house! The lights would go on and off in the middle of the night!" Then added, "Sometimes a cold draft would blow through the house even though everything was closed, and pictures would fall off the walls." Her eyes grew large as she said, "And then, after that I'd always smell my husband's cologne in there."

"Really?" Monica murmured and still stared, transfixed at Lindy's saga.

"Monica, this went on for months. And," she whispered, "One night I woke up and a ghost was standing by my bed watching me sleep!"

"A ghost?" Monica put a hand over her mouth and almost laughed. "Who was it?"

"My husband!" Lindy whispered and stared hard at her friend, just daring her to laugh. Monica tried to conceal her amusement.

"Lordy, then you won't believe this, just days later I found the place was infested with ants!"

"Ants?" Monica choked this time and then cleared her throat.

"Yes, huge black carpenter ants!" Lindy held out her thumb and forefinger measuring inches. "In the attic, right over my head and that did it!" She shivered and shook her head.

"But, you could have had all those things fixed and the house fumigated for those ants. Are you sure, Lindy, maybe you just dreamed seeing your husband's ghost."

"Maybe--," Lindy murmured doubtfully, but then remembered that edgy feeling she'd felt living alone in that enormous house. She watched as Monica took a bottle off a shelf and poured a shot of whiskey into her coffee cup.

"Good God, Lindy, this is nuts!" She said and swirled the cup to mix the drink. "Do you mean you actually got away with burning your house and collected a million dollar insurance settlement?"

"Well," Lindy smoked her cigarette, "Yes, and no!"

"What do you mean?" Monica's brow wrinkled in confusion.

"I got the money and then they wanted to take it back!" Lindy looked warily at her.

Monica shook her head and raised her liquor laced cup of coffee. "Were you arrested?"

"No--not really," Lindy answered evasively. "You remember Reed Conners, don't you?"

"Sure, I remember how you liked to string him along. What's he got to do with it all?"

Lindy swallowed hard. "It just happens he works as an investigator for the same insurance company I was insured with, and later when some evidence turned up against me, he got the case!"

"Did he arrest you, then?" Monica lit a cigarette.

"Well, it's a long complicated story." Lindy made rings on the bar with the wet bottom of her cocktail glass.

"God, Lindy, I can't believe this! Tell me honestly, are you wanted by the law in the US?"

"Well, yes," Lindy admitted finally, "that's why I left!"

Monica just shook her head as she went to wait on a group of tourists that had just come into the bar.

"Guess what," Lindy said some time later as Monica stood across the bar from her again. "I've sort of started a business here in Mexico."

"A business?" Monica asked. "What for when you've got all that money?"

Lindy laughed at her friend's curiosity. "It just sort of happened, they say I'm psychic!"

"Psychic, for Pete's sake," Monica choked, "You sure they don't mean psycho?" Then both women began to laugh and finally their merriment dissolved into tears of delight at finding each other again, and they slipped back into the same camaraderie they'd shared years earlier.

However, that night as Lindy slept an image began to hover, edging closer and closer, threatening to steal her peace and she awoke the next morning feeling unsettled, sensing something troubling might be about to happen.

Could it be all that tequila I drank last night? She questioned. Then as always, when her thoughts were in disorder, she cleaned. Although, she could hire someone to do it for her, she needed the time to try to figure out why she felt this way.

She ripped the sheets off her bed that Reed had slept on. In the kitchen, she furiously polished the table where Rio, the Mayor of Monterrey had sat and threatened her. In the living room, she dusted each and every teapot and cursed Al Guiness, the banker, and vowed to never, ever let him get his hands on her money. But after falling exhausted into bed that night, she had not resolved that disconcerted feeling and her dreams drifted back into the same state of turbulence.

-11-

Reed and Murphy slipped through a hole in the chain link fence that surrounded the Grain Belt Brewery. There were five entrances into the structure and huge metal double doors stood before them, padlocked and corroded with decades of grime.

"For Christ's sake Murph, what's with all these doors?" Reed asked at he took hold of the lock on one. Flakes of rusted iron drifted down to the concrete. He leaned back as he looked up six stories, then around the sides of the building.

Murphy wiped a hand over his sweating brow. The building loomed monstrous and sinister in the eerie illumination of a streetlamp on the far corner. "Each entrance leads into a different department,"

Murphy said and kicked at the door when it did not budge. "I've got a crowbar in my trunk! I'll get in this place!" He mumbled and his voice shook.

"Hold on, let's check the other side," Reed said and they walked to the corner of the building. Here the wall was solid brick with no windows or doors. A small copse of trees with overgrown bushes leaned up against the building. Seeing the possibilities, both men took off on a run. Two tall cottonwood trees, heavy with silvered green leaves quivered in the damp night air, and stood high above tangled overgrown bushes. Weathered litter covered the weedy small spot.

"Here," Murphy yelled as he pushed and shoved bushes aside and sure enough, found a door. Almost completely covered with a vine that had grown up the wall, a back entrance was visible.

The door was metal and it too had a padlock. "I'll be right back," Murphy said and took off. Five minutes later, he was back carrying flashlights and the crowbar, and breathing hard, jammed it in between the door and the hatch. The rusty metal resisted for a few moments, then with a clunk the wood around the connection gave and the apparatus fell to the ground. Murphy pushed at the door and it swung open, banged against the inner wall. As they stood silhouetted in the doorway with their lights shining into the cavernous space, a sudden floury of motion erupted, then an ear-splitting shrieking shook the night as a cloud of screeching bats flew at them, circling around their heads in a frenzied attempt to escape the disruption.

"Jesus," Murphy yelled and fell backwards and put his hands up over his head.

Reed turned away from the oncoming onslaught of rodents as they escaped into the dawn.

After several minutes they flashed their lights into the room again. Piles of boards, chunks of cement and pieces of insulation lay in heaps around the cavernous space.

"Look at that," Reed said and moved his light around. The beam reached high and then became lost and disappeared into nothingness. The floors had fallen, leaving parts still clinging precariously to the sides of the upper walls.

As they stood awestruck at the scene before them, the overpowering smell of guano hit their nostrils, causing their eyes to burn.

"Goddamn," Reed said under his breath. "Murph, bring the crowbar and let's try another one of those doors on the front." He eased the door shut and Murphy picked up the tool he had dropped. This time when Murphy jammed the crowbar into the door frame and connection, the padlock fell off, and Reed put his weight on the door and it swung open with a groan. Light seeped in from a high window and they saw the walls and floor above seemed to be intact. They stepped in cautiously; sidestepping piles of pigeon muck, and saw huge metal containers that had evidently held the fermenting beer.

Trying to lighten the moment Reed said, "I wonder how many six packs they could cook up at a time."

A metal stairway stood off to the side, but when he put his foot on it to test the stability, it swung loosely away from the wall. Then Reed saw the anguish in his friend's eyes and the fatigue on his face.

"Okay Murph, here's what we're going to do, come on," he said and walked outside. After hours of sweat and covered with grime, he gulped the fresh air. When Murphy followed, he continued, "Buddy, you need to go home and catch some shut-eye!"

"Nah," Murphy croaked, but he sank to the ground and dropped his head in his hands.

Reed reached down and put a hand on his shoulder. "Buddy, you haven't slept for forty eight hours! Come on!" He pulled Murphy up and they walked to their cars.

"I just need some coffee--," Murphy said, but his steps were unsteady.

"Murph look, I'm going to follow you home, just to make sure you get there okay, then after you've caught a couple of hours of sleep we'll get some help and come back," Reed said then and watched as Murphy put his precinct's unmarked in drive.

After he had seen Murphy safely into his house, thirty minutes later he was back at the brewery, this time the Corvette hidden in some trees across the street. With a giant cup of coffee clutched in his hand, he growled, "Okay, Wolff, show me who you are asshole." He was ready to watch and wait!

-12-

As she lay on the floor, her chest heaving for each breath, she forced her voice through parched lips and cried out, "Help me, someone please help me!" But no one heard her desperate plea.

Her body was twisted awkwardly and her hands were tied behind her back. As she tried to sit up, her head exploded in pain. Through terror filled eyes she saw she was in a window filled room and then realized they lined the four walls. And as she lay on the grimy floor she had the sensation of being somewhere high up.

She was wearing a flowered dress of purple and red. She never wore purple and red, Lordy, it would not go with her make-up and hair! She brushed at long strands of it sticking to her cheeks, hanging in her eyes. Then Lindy awoke and her heart began to slow its frantic beat as she realized she was safe in her own bed.

What was that dream about? She worried later as she sat in her kitchen drinking coffee. It did not make any sense! But something seemed to tug at her memory. But what?

The next day flew by as she busied herself. She joined Rita, her country club friend for lunch. As Rita declared would happen, word had spread of her visions and predictions and as Rita advised, she began to set up appointments in her home for readings. The first evening she had five appointments.

She bustled around her house that day, trying to decide how to stage her art. She pictured a sort of gypsy look to her new business. Should she fix up the guest bedroom, hang black curtains at the windows? She still had that glass ball Rita had given her for that gala earlier at the club. She could put one of her black bed sheets on a table; drape a gold scarf over the side next to the ball.

She collapsed on the couch in the living room, after her frantic search for the proper setting. And what should she wear? Another scarf tied over her head, long dangling earrings. Did she have a long skirt and some kind of a flimsy blouse?

The clock was ticking away as she studied her options and now it banged out its hour. She had thirty minutes to set a scene to hone her craft. She teased her blonde hair into standing tufts, dug in her closet for a pair of granny glasses she thought might enhance her look, and then hunted through the hangers in her closet for one of those long skirts and skimpy blouses she'd bought on a whim when she first came to Mexico. She added a chain belt, three necklaces around her throat and the biggest hoop earrings she had. She checked her look in a mirror.

Lordy, she looked like she belonged to a carnival! What was she thinking?

She threw the get-up on the closet floor, smoothed her hair into the fluff she normally wore. Then slipped on a pale yellow shift and slid her feet into sandals, just as the doorbell rang. She took a deep breath and hurried through the house.

"Buenos tardes!, Señora Lola," a matronly Mexican woman said as she stood on the doorstep. "I am here to see you."

Lindy smiled despite an attack of panic that began to eat at her nerves. Could she really do this?

"Hello, please come in," she managed to get out finally. "Let's sit in the kitchen," she said then and led the way.

"My name is Rosa," the woman said and adjusted the skirt around her legs as they sat down at the table. "I have come a long way to see you Señora, you see I am going to die and I want to go in peace!"

Lindy put a hand over her mouth to refrain from gasping at the woman's outburst. "I'm sorry, Rosa," she said, "What can I do for you?"

Rosa took a rosary out of a pocket, "Señora, I need to know something important! When I'm gone, will my husband take that slut of a sister of mine into my bed?" Rosa looked to be around fifty years old. Severely dressed in a black dress and shawl, her nylons and sensible shoes matched her outfit.

Lindy took Rosa's hand and studied the lines on her palm. Then felt a jolt as she saw this woman lying dead in a casket, and a man in the arms of a young woman as he stood at a gravesite. It did not necessarily mean anything, Lindy thought, but good grief; she could not tell the woman what she had glimpsed. She was silent for a few moments as she considered her options. She consulted the crystal ball, studied the woman's lifelines on her hand again. People wanted to hear happy things! Then looking into Rosa's anxious eyes Lindy said, "Rosa, you're going to be surprised at the things that are going to happen to you. Pleasant things and they will start soon. I see a trip for you, somewhere, to see good friends!" Then Lindy exclaimed, "Rosa, I see numbers, by any chance do you gamble?"

"Oh no—I wouldn't," Rosa whispered, "I just play bingo at my church."

"I see you are going to be very lucky!" Lindy paused for a few seconds, "Rosa," she said then, "I see your husband will be heart-broken when you're gone, and soon your sister will be going to live in another place."

"Gracias, gracias Señora," Rosa said, as she held her beads. "I will die happy now!" She placed a mound of pesos in Lindy's hand and got up to leave. Then praised and thanked her profusely for her gifted visions as she left.

That night she fell into bed exhausted after seeing all her waiting customers. They had gone away happy even though she'd had to embellish at length when her magic did not seem to surface when she needed it. However, she smiled as she counted the number of bills they had thrust at her and stuffed the money into a teapot.

The southern moon sent its beam over the city as she pulled the covers up and fell into a contented sleep. However, the feeling did not last long and she was back in the same nightmare she had had the night before. Bound and locked in the same square room with windows all around, a castle it seemed, wearing that flowered purple and red dress. She screamed again weakly, "Help me, please someone help me!" Then at the height of her anguish, Lindy awoke, and furtively righted herself to her surroundings. As she sat up in bed, her distress lessoned and a startling realization took form. The woman in the dream was someone she had met years ago. It was Ann Murphy, the wife of Reed's friend! The woman he had said disappeared and the reason he had left Mexico and rushed back to Minneapolis!

She clutched the sheet. Good lord, this was just like those other times. Just weeks ago, when she had seen a vision that an earthquake would soon destroy part of Monterrey, and then again that Rio, the mayor would be shot. So many times, she had seen things about to happen, and they did! She shook her head to clear her thoughts. It was just past two o'clock in the morning. She threw the bed covers off and clutched her robe, now wide-awake.

Should she call Reed and tell him about her dream? She turned on all the lights in her house as she walked to the kitchen and knowing she was up for good, made a pot of coffee.

This definitely was a clue to that woman's whereabouts, but, would Reed believe her?   She poured herself a cup of strong brew and sat at the table. She had to tell him what she had seen, even if he did not take it seriously!

She looked up his cell-phone number and dialed. Beads of perspiration broke out over her upper lip as she heard the connections meet, and then heard his voice.

"What," he growled.

Her stomach lurched at his cold greeting. "Reed," she said, "it's me."

There was a pause before he said anything. "It's the middle of the night, Lindy!"

Lord, she had made a mistake calling him, but she pushed on. "I know where Ann Murphy is, I've seen her, twice!" There, she had told him.

Reed exhaled tiredly, "What do you mean, you've seen her?"

"Reed," she whispered "She's tied up and locked in a room with windows on all four sides. She is wearing a purple and red dress," Lindy added.

"No shit," was all Reed could say as he thought about this. Goddamn, Lindy made him mad as hell at times, but he had to admit, sometimes she was right on the money when she had one of those wacky dreams. "Describe the area," he said.

Lindy thought for a moment, bit her lip. "I think-, Reed, I felt I was in a castle, in a room with a lot of windows and up high." She went to the stove and poured another cup of coffee as the scene righted itself in her memory. "It was a square room with windows on all four sides!"

There was silence on the line. Then his voice echoed over the miles as he growled "goddamn" and the line went dead.

If she had been there, she would have seen him throw the cell phone on the seat of the car, jump out, stand and study the building. Then when he figured out the room, the square room with the windows on all sides, up on the top floor that she had just described, she would have seen his excited reaction when he located the exact spot Ann Murphy was in!

But tears blurred Lindy's eyes as she sat alone in her kitchen. Reed had not believed her, again!

-13-

Reed got out of the Corvette and studied the building before him, and the room Lindy had described she had seen in her dream was right there atop six stories. And, it appeared to have windows on all four sides.

Could Ann Murphy really be there? After the conditions he and Murphy had seen earlier in the place when they'd opened a back door, just how the hell could he get up there to find out!

Sweat ran down his forehead and he wiped it on his shirt sleeve. He opened the trunk of his car and took out the tire iron, a huge flashlight and an extra box of shells for his gun, then strapped a smaller gun and holster to his ankle. Back at the building, swearing under his breath, he jammed the tire iron into a hinge on the first of the doors and pried, and finally the lock fell to the concrete.

Dropping the tire iron, he kicked the door open, then stood still and looked around to see if the noise would bring anyone to investigate. After several minutes went by and no one appeared he flashed his light into the building and found to his amazement this area seemed to be intact. The room was small and opened into another larger one that held the stairway. The place reeked of dust and mildew. Closing the old door behind himself, gun in one hand and gripping the light, he tested the first step on the stairs, and then cautiously put his full weight on it, and it held. He climbed higher and finally stood in a large room on the second floor, vacant except for rusty pipes scattered around. The smell was a mixture of dust and aging wood. Another stairway stood in the middle of the room and again he carefully tested each step before putting his full weight on it. This time half way up it crumbled under his weight and he clung to a rusty railing and jumped to the next step, then ran up the rest of the way.

As he got to another level his mind raced. How the hell would he get out of here if he made it to the sixth floor? And, what would he find if he reached that room on the sixth floor?

Should he call Murphy? And tell him what? That he'd gotten a call from Lindy Lewis, saying that she'd seen his wife in one of her dreams, locked in a room in this place that looked like a castle? Maybe not! This likely was a fluke anyway. Goddamn, even if he wanted to, he realized in his rush he'd left his cell phone in his car!

His breath burned in his throat and his chest hurt like hell as he made his way up the grimy stairways. On the fourth floor, a window was missing and pigeons had found a home. Feathers, nests and droppings covered the floor and the stairs ahead of him. The smell was sickening. He held his breath as he climbed that stairway, taking two steps at a time.

Could Lindy be right and he would find Ann Murphy? Would she be alive? What the hell would he tell Murphy if she was dead! He wiped his face on his shirt sleeve again.

 He started to run, faster leaping up the creaking and rotten wood steps, and hanging on to the railings for dear life, when there was one still attached. On the next floor, his legs were about to give out as he came into a big room. Striped wallpaper clung to the top of the walls and trailed loosely downward. He stood for a minute to catch his breath. Christ, what floor was this? It seemed like he had climbed a dozen so far!

Gripping the flashlight and the gun, he started up another flight of stairs. This time the stairway was metal, but it swung away from the wall as he flew up over the steps. As he got to the top of these steps and on to flat flooring, he realized he was in the square windowed room Lindy had described. He flashed the light around and saw fast food cartons and old papers littered the dirty floor, then a blanket covered mound on a mat off to the side.

His heartbeat slammed in his throat as he started over, and then froze as he realized it could be Wolff on that mattress. He gripped the gun and this time stepped quietly, and grabbed up the blanket ready to put a bullet in the asshole's head.

And he stared down at Ann Murphy's nude body lying on the dirty mat. Her wrists and ankles were bound. Her body was covered in welts, and strands of her long red hair trailed over her face.

"Oh Christ, Annie," Reed whispered as he knelt at her side and covered her again with the old blanket. "What has he done to you?" He put a hand on her neck for a pulse, and felt nothing. He went cold. No--, it couldn't be! This couldn't happen to his best friends!

"Ann, Annie, open your eyes, wake up," he begged and gritted his teeth as he slapped her face. He repeated her name and when she still didn't move, he began CPR.

Oh Christ, what would he tell Murphy! He blew his breath into Ann Murphy's lungs all the while praying, "Please God help us!" It felt like hours went by, his own body almost collapsing as he worked, but finally her eyelids fluttered. He felt a faint pulse and heard a rustle in her chest.

Bending close, he whispered, "Annie, its Reed. Wake up. You're going to be okay!" He brushed her hair off her face. "Listen Annie, you're safe now and I'll get you out of here."

She moaned faintly.

"Goddamn," Reed muttered as he glimpsed the bruises on her small frame. Saw one eye was swollen shut. He adjusted the blanket around her.

"Annie, it's okay, can you hear me? You're going to be okay!" He put the gun in his waistband, and then picked her up.

"Steady now, we'll take our time, but let's get out of this hell-hole." Carrying Ann and holding the flashlight, Reed began their journey down. All the while his mind was spinning. Would they get out of there?

What if they met this Wolff creature on the way out? If only he had his cell phone with him and could call for help, but he was on his own. He held Ann's weakened body close as they went down the first flight of creaking stairs.

"Hang on sweetheart, we've got a few stairs to go, but we'll make it!" He whispered. "We'll be outside in a few minutes."

They progressed slowly down the rickety stairways, Reed's heart in his throat worrying if their combined weight would cause the stairs now to collapse. On one floor, as he stopped to catch his breath, as he put his foot on the first step to go further on down, the stairs groaned and the step fell out. His heart stood still, and horrified, he clutched Ann closer and forced himself to put another foot out and continue.

Goddamn, he whispered. What if--, then thought, what the hell am I going to do anyway? We've got to get out of here. And he started down the stairs again each step a fearful risk, but as each one held, it brought them closer to safety. Slowly, they progressed down the aged broken stairs, and Reed silently prayed now for God's help as he carried his friend's beloved partner to safety.

Minutes later he kicked a door open and they were outside. Still carrying Annie he whispered as he hurried to his car, "We made it, sweetheart!"

He sat her in the seat and adjusted the dirty blanket around her. "We'll have you checked out at the hospital first and then you'll be home for breakfast."

"Home," Ann whispered weakly, "My girls--?"

"The girls are fine. Your old man is almost crazy though!"

The Corvette roared to life then as they escaped the horrors of the brewery, and he reached for his cell-phone and speed-dialed a familiar number.

"Buddy," he said, "I found her. She's okay!"

"Conners," Murphy yelled, "You found her? She's okay?"

"A little banged up, Murph, but she's going make it! We're on the way to North Memorial Hospital right now. We'll see you there in a few minutes!"

-14-

"Hang in there Annie; we'll be at the hospital in five minutes." Reed reached over and patted Ann Murphy's shoulder. "Murph will meet us there."

Ann grasped at the dirty blanket around her body and rested her head against the car seat as they sped through the downtown area.

She whispered weakly. "How long have I been gone?"

"Since the day before yesterday around noon," Reed said and absent-mindedly patted his shirt pocket for his cigarette pack.

"He forced me into the alley with him." Ann fought back a sob and added, "His hand was over my mouth so I couldn't scream!"

"Asshole," Reed growled as he maneuvered the Corvette through the traffic and pulled up at the emergency entrance at the hospital. Murphy threw open the car door on the passenger side.

"Annie," he groaned and reached in and gently helped her out of the car then pulled her into his embrace and for a minute they stood together in each other's arms. Then an attendant appeared with a wheelchair.

"I don't have any clothes. He took my clothes!" Ann wailed.

"Its okay, honey," Murphy said and helped tuck the blanket to cover her. "I'll run home and get something for you." Ann tried to smile.

"I'll park and meet you inside," Reed said as he stood with them.

Murphy nodded. Reed saw the lines in his friend's face were more prominent than ever and deep dark circles edged his eyes.

He got back in the Corvette and inched his way through busy late night traffic. The bars had closed and now hours later the emergency area of the hospital was filled with an assortment of crises.

Reed lit a cigarette and inhaled as he patiently made his way to the parking ramp then up the inclines in search of a parking place for his car. He rolled his head to relieve a stiff neck, shrugged his shoulders to relax his back.

Minutes later, he was back in the hospital and found Murphy in a waiting room, pacing. "Jesus, she's hurt bad!" Murphy said and his voice shook.

"Take it easy, buddy." Reed unzipped his jacket.

Murphy pointed to a closed door. "They got her in there. A couple of people are with her."

"It'll probably take a while, come on let's find a coffee machine," Reed said nodding, and they took off down the hallway, both men subdued in the surroundings.

"Conners, where did you find her? Christ man, I didn't think--," Murphy's voice faded.

"We got lucky Murph; she was in that old Grain Belt mausoleum we looked at earlier."

"How the hell did you know where to look in there?"

"Murph, it's weird, Lindy Lewis called me. She's in Mexico now. You remember those crazy dreams she would have? Well, get this, she saw Ann in there and described the place. She said Ann was in a room at the top of the building that had a lot of windows!"

"Unbelievable!" Murphy said.

Reed looked at his watch. "Did you get any sleep?"

Murphy shook his head and mumbled, "Nah, I went through the old files again." His eyes glittered, "It was this Wolff character who took her, then?"

"Yeah, Murph and we'll get him. He'll pay!" Reed saw the anger in his friend's eyes. "Have you

called your folks and the kids yet?" he asked to
change the subject then picked up the Styrofoam cups
and handed one to Murphy.

"I just got off the phone before you came in.
Jesus, they were both in bad shape, but held up for the
girls."

"Got to be a parent's worst nightmare," Reed
commented as they walked back to the waiting room.

"I know the pig raped her," Murphy said then.

Not knowing exactly what to say to his friend,
Reed whispered, "Buddy, she's alive and you have
each other. Keep that in mind!"

"I'll tear that asshole to pieces with my bare
hands!" Murphy's coffee spilled out off the cup and
over his shirt sleeve as he growled.

"Take it easy, Murph, we'll get him!" Reed put a
hand on his shoulder and pushed him over to a chair.

The Chief of Police came in then. He nodded at
Reed and sat down next to Murphy. "How is she?" he
asked.

"We haven't heard anything yet." Murphy
exhaled and sank deeper into the seat.

"I'm going to wait here with you and see what the
doctors have to say. Okay?"

Murphy nodded.

Reed stood. "I've got some things to do," he said,
"I'll catch up with you." He hurried out of the
hospital and to his car.

Back in the Corvette, he gunned the motor and sped out of the parking ramp. The sun was up now and had turned the whole world into a glorious shade of gold. A cold morning wind rustled the crimson leaves as they rained down over the streets as he cruised through a parkway on the way to downtown Minneapolis. Back at the same place he'd parked in earlier at the Grain Belt brewery, he slid his car seat back a notch and prepared to wait.

"Okay Wolff, you have to show up sometime," he growled, then checked his gun and laid it on the car seat.

As he waited the sun crept higher in the sky and soon the shade in the copse of trees disappeared and began to appear on the opposite side of the car. His throat was parched and his stomach ached from lack of food. He couldn't remember when he'd eaten last, then thought of the pretzels he'd eaten on the plane when he'd flown back from Mexico.

When in the hell was that? Then realized it was yesterday afternoon. And that black coffee he drank at the hospital was racing unbelievable havoc at the moment. As he sat in the Corvette his thoughts played with many different scenarios how he would make this asshole pay for what he had done to his friend's wife.

He inhaled hard on a cigarette and fumed, "He needs to hurt!"

***

The sun had begun to sink over the horizon as Reed watched the street that led by the old Grain Belt building. To the left, it led directly to the downtown area and to the right, to the old neighborhood that consisted of warehouses and run-down vacant buildings. The man called Wolff could be hiding in any one of them!

Reed turned on the radio and listened as a local announcer said, "Enjoy this weather folks, because tomorrow we will have a rude awakening. It's Minnesota!" And he went on to say falling temps and sleet was in the forecast.

It had been hours since Reed had found Ann in the building and Wolff had to show himself soon! He looked up and down the streets. Goddamn, he'd stay for days if he had to!

The skies were starting to darken now and a cold mist began to coat the windshield of the car.

Then he saw him! A man with wild gray shoulder length hair, wearing a long black coat that flapped around his ankles, ambled down the street towards the Grain Belt building. A shaggy beard covered his cheeks and chin and with all the hair, he did resemble a wolf. Approximately six feet tall and around two hundred pounds, Reed figured. As the man neared, Reed quietly opened the car door and stepped out, the gun in his hand. From where he stood, Wolff would have to pass within three feet of him.

He counted Wolff's dragging steps as he neared, then leapt out of his hiding place. Now they were face to face. He jammed the gun at Wolff's head and in a deadly whisper said, "Move and you're a dead man!"

Wolff stopped dead in his tracks, a surprised look on his face, and growled, "Get the fuck away from me!" Then, with lightning speed Wolff swung at him.

Reed's gun went flying as Wolff knocked the wind out of him. He doubled over and time seemed to drift suspended as he fell, then his body made contact with the concrete. He lay motionless and stunned and when he opened his eyes, Wolff was standing over him with a knife directed at his throat.

He stared at the wild looking man and then his instincts took over, and with his own lightening speed, rolled out of the way and over to the gun he had dropped, grabbed it and pulled the trigger. Suddenly, Wolff's head exploded. Blood and brains rained over the sidewalk as the lifeless body slumped to the ground. The only sound after the earth shattering gunshot was a hideous groan from the bloody corpse on the ground.

Stunned, Reed struggled to his feet and stared aghast at the grisly scene before him. He dropped his gun to the ground as an uncontrollable wave of nausea swept up his throat when he saw pieces of the man splattered on his clothes. He tore his leather jacket off and tossed it to the ground and got sick. After minutes of retching hell, he mumbled "fuck" and straightened up. Then got his cell-phone out of his pocket and made the call to the Police department.

"Get me the Chief," he said," it's an emergency!" When the Chief came on the line he growled, "I got the asshole who grabbed Ann Murphy, but he's dead!"

"Conners, Jesus are you okay?" The Chief of Police asked.

"Yeah," Reed said.

"Christ man, where the hell are you?"

"I'm at the Grain Belt brewery." Sweat ran down Reed's face.

"Hang on; I'll be there in five minutes!" The Chief broke the connection.

Reed had been standing with his back to the scene on the sidewalk. Now he turned and looked again, still in shock at how fast it had happened. Christ, he'd killed a man. He had taken a life!

Goddamn, he whispered in a shaky voice amidst tumultuous feelings of horror at what he'd done, then, pissed for being forced into having to do it. For Christ's sake, he had planned that when he found the bastard he'd handcuff him and call it in. Case closed!

Where in the hell is everybody, he mumbled and searched up and down the street. Not a soul was around. He felt for his cigarettes and when he finally got one in his shaking hand, lit up and inhaled, it tasted like road kill. Then suddenly the forlorn neighborhood's silence was broken by a siren as a car careened around the corner and slammed to a stop.

"Conners," the Chief said as he got out of the vehicle and stood for a minute and surveyed the scene.

Reed stood off to the side. "My gun and his knife are there," he said and avoided looking at the body.

"Jesus, he had a dagger!" The Chief said and then came closer and pointed, "You're bleeding!"

Surprised, Reed looked down and saw his hand was covered in blood.

More sirens ripped through the night and within minutes the street was filled with emergency vehicles.

"You can't do anything for him," the Chief said as the paramedics hurried over to Wolff's body, "but take care of Conners here." He nodded at Reed. "Go with them and get patched up, then get down to headquarters!"

-15-

Lindy swiped at her eyes as she sat at the kitchen table and stared into her tea cup. Reed had not believed her when she had called and told him where to find Ann Murphy. He'd just hung up on her!

It had been another hot autumn day in Monterrey, the heat blasting out a temperature of 99 plus degrees and now the next morning it was still hot and humid. This time in the northern US, she remembered the days would be cool enough for a jacket and more than likely the winds would be blowing furiously stripping the trees of the last remaining leaves.

When Reed had gotten that frantic call from Murphy as they lay entwined in the sheets in her bed earlier, telling him that his wife Ann had suddenly disappeared, he had rushed back to help his friend.

And, that very night Lindy had had a dream that Ann Murphy was being held prisoner somewhere in a castle-like building. Even had visions during the day and had finally called Reed. But after listening to what she'd seen, he'd just slammed the phone in her ear, so that was that! She sighed and thought sadly, I did what I could and now I'm through with that man. With that resolution firmly in place she stuck her tongue out at his memory and finished her tea.

The week spun by as she immersed herself in her new business and on the week-end took time out to have lunch with Rita, her country club friend. They were sitting in an upscale eatery, sipping their cocktails when Rita asked, "Lola, my dear, what do you see ahead for me?"

Lindy looked at her almost guiltily. Truth be told, she had had a sudden glimmer of something involving Rita, but it had just been a fleeting reflection that had flashed through her mind and instantly vanished, leaving her confused.

Not wanting to alarm her friend, Lindy shook her head and said, "Rita, I'm sorry I don't know anything, but I'm sure you have only good things to come."

"My dear," Rita persisted, "You would tell me if you saw something wouldn't you?"

"Of course," Lindy lied and took another sip of her wine.

Actually she was exhausted from all the frightening episodes treading through her head; frightening pictures, fleeting conversations and nightmarish shadows. Most of them fading before she recognized who they involved. But, Rio's threat that he'd find out what she was hiding was still fresh in her mind.

Were all of these premonitions meant for her?

She took a deep breath to steady herself, determined to enjoy the afternoon when Rita asked, "Lola, tell me something about yourself, when did you realize you had the gift?"

Lindy swallowed a mouthful of salad and forced a smile, "You know when I was in grade school, a lot of times I knew the answers to my tests even before I saw the questions."

"Really, how marvelous Lola!"

"I guess. When I got older though I figured I must have a photographic memory. It helped me all through college." She chuckled as she remembered how some of her professors would question her abilities to always score the highest marks in her classes even though she didn't seem to take time to study. Then it had all disappeared, for decades, until lately.

Rita laid her fork down on the table and straightened her diamond rings, then turned her head to admire the gleam of the stones in the sunshine. "Do you have any siblings?" She persisted.

Lindy looked off into the distance and for an instant a frown crossed her brow.

"Oh yes," she answered, "I come from a large family."

"You are so lucky, Lola, I hope you are close."

"Pretty much," Lindy volunteered.

"Do you keep in touch?" Rita went on.

Lindy forked up another mouthful of salad before she answered, just a little irritated at Rita's inquisitiveness. Well, she had sent Christmas cards. But then the more she thought about it, it may have been the year before. Could it be going on two years since she had contact with her relatives? But to satisfy Rita's endless curiosity she replied, "I talk to them all the time!" Wanting to steer the conversation away from herself, she said, "Rita, my life is so boring, how about you? When did you start to paint?"

"My dear, decades ago. Now my work is scattered around the world."

Rita was the picture of a well preserved, well dressed matron again today, as she sat amongst the elite patrons of the restaurant. Lindy had just come from the beauty shop after getting her hair scooped up on her head in an up-do, wearing one of her new chic silk dresses. This one was a mellow orange and pink flowered original she had just gotten in that boutique that had opened in her neighborhood. She looked good today and fit in nicely with the privileged.

Later that week, the telephone awakened her from a sound sleep. Thinking it was a customer she cleared her throat and answered in what she thought was her professional voice.

Monica, her old friend was on the line and said in her customary clipped voice, "What took you so long?"

"Hey Monica, it's about time!" Lindy sat up in her bed, fully awake now and asked, "Did you get my message?"

Monica clunked down something that sounded like a cup on a tiled top. "Yeah," she said, "sorry, I didn't get back to you, I've had to double shift this week so I'm feeling like hell!"

"Monica, how do you do it?"

"I've got nothing but time," she answered and laughed.

"Monica, I want to go to a bull fight. You've gone haven't you?"

"Well, sure many times. Haven't you?"

"No," Lindy said and ran a hand through her tussled blonde hair.

"Well, it's the country's leading entertainment! I'm off this week-end. Do you want to go?"

"Sure," Lindy said.

"Let's go Sunday. Tell me how to get to your house and I'll pick you up at five!" The phone went dead.

Lindy smiled, recalling Monica didn't waste too much time on small talk. She hung up and stretched lazily in her king-sized bed.

Promptly at five o'clock, Monica sped up to her house driving a silver low-slung foreign model car that hummed expensively.

"I love this," Lindy said and hopped in and within minutes they had left the glamour of her neighborhood and were speeding through the dusty squalor of the inner city. Monica expertly maneuvered the car through traffic circles at breakneck speed and they finally arrived at the gates to the park.

"Lord," Lindy gasped and got out of the car. "Does everyone here drive like they are nuts?"

Treading their way through an eager crowd, the women found the ticket booth and then their seats which overlooked a body of water. Heavenly cool breezes ruffled their hair.

Monica said then, "Bullfighting is considered an artistic spectacle. It features skilled matadors from Mexico and Spain, and the action does not start till just before sunset."

The opening ceremonies started soon after with rousing Latin music and boisterous clapping as announcements were made of the events. Then the scene erupted as the renowned matadors were introduced and walked out and bowed to their admiring audience. As the blazing Mexican sun began to descend in the west, the scene changed abruptly and amidst the breath taking silence, a bull walked into the arena. The huge magnificent beast stood with its head lowered and blew great gusts of air through his nostrils and pawed at the ground, raising a cloud of dust.

"Lordy," Lindy shivered. "I didn't realize it would be so big!"

Monica lit a cigarette and waved to some friends across the aisle. "This is just one of them. There will be more."

"Wow," Lindy whispered aghast as she watched.

"Lindy, this is literally a dance with death," Monica said as she smoked. "In the end the bull will die."

"Really!" Lindy looked around at the rapt faces of the audience, not sure if she liked what she'd gotten herself into. Six men were taunting the animal now and driving him into frenzy by jabbing spears into his shoulders.

"They're getting him ready for the Matador," Monica said.

"Oh Lord," Lindy whispered again, "This is awful!"

"Here, you better have some of this," Monica said and took a bottle out of her big purse and handed it to Lindy. "This is just getting good. Watch now!"

Lindy gulped a swallow from the bottle then choked. Her face ablaze as she tried to catch her breath. "What is this?" She finally managed to sputter.

"Girlfriend," Monica laughed, "when you're in Mexico at a bull fight, you drink tequila! Watch, here comes the Matador!"

Lindy sat transfixed as a celebrated Matador took center stage and began the taunting dance with the frenzied animal. Each time he waved the blazing red cape and sidestepped the charging ferocious bull, the audience shouted "Ole."

It took several more gulps of Monica's tequila, before Lindy got over the anguish of the animal's inevitable demise and got in the spirit of the bull fight. And soon she was clapping her hands and shouting "Ole" with the best of them.

"Look at you," Monica shouted through the pandemonium, "When this is over, we'll go to Rosie's. You'll love it!"

The last event of the day erupted with a frenzied display of skill and bravado as a favorite Matador took center stage. By now, Lindy was having a good time although her voice was hoarse, and her blonde hair drooped from the humidity in the hot night.

This time the crowd was extremely pleased with the skill of the Matador and after he had sunk his sword into the bull's body and killed the beast, he held up an ear amidst thunderous applause. Then the audience continued their clamor as the Matador was carried around the arena on the shoulders of his devoted followers. It was totally dark now and finally the event was over.

As the women left their seats and joined the throngs of people leaving the arena a man pushed in close to Lindy. She sucked in her breath at his audacity, then gaped at him as he grabbed her arm in a vice-like grip and whispered in a guttural voice, "Scream lady and you're dead!"

-16-

Reed sucked in a shaking breath as he leaned against a squad car. The Minneapolis Police had followed the Chief's car and were swarming around the scene at the Grain Belt Brewery building. He held his left hand and felt his wet warm blood ooze out of a slash the madman had tried to aim at his throat. Still in shock at what had happened in that instant, Reed tried to steady his breathing. But he'd killed a man!

The night air had cooled and the sky began to turn a soft pink as morning began to make its way into a new day. This was the time of day at his home up north when he would rise early and take his boat out on the lake and fish. Most of the time, the awesome colors of dawn held his attention and he didn't get into serious fishing until the sun was up.

Right now, I'd give my right nut to be out on the water, he grumbled under his breath as the Chief walked over to him.

"We're lucky to have that character off the street Conners, most of the people out here are pretty low key. They just want to be left alone."

"Good riddance then. I heard he's been terrorizing the homeless for weeks now."

Reed recalled Brita's fear. "What he did to Annie, she wouldn't have lasted much longer."

"You got there just in time. Christ, it could have been anyone's family!" By then the Coroner had arrived to claim the body and the paramedics hustled Reed into the ambulance for the ride to the same hospital he'd brought Ann Murphy to just hours ago.

Goddamn, his hand was hurting and he gratefully followed a nurse to an enclosed area and lay down on the skinny sheet covered bed. The first thing they did was give him a shot that calmed him down. Minutes later, another shot that immediately began to numb his hand and take away some of the pain. He turned his head away as a doctor cleaned the wound.

"You were lucky; Mr. Conners, another inch and it would have sliced into your wrist and caused all kinds of trouble."

"Yeah?" Reed mumbled, suddenly feeling weak and clammy. Sweat broke out on his face and he felt it trickle down the side of his face now as he watched the doctor began to stitch him up. Soon the only sound in the room was an odd clicking noise as the needle went in and out of his flesh. After another half hour of attention and instructions, he was let go with his injured hand in a sling. He found a uniformed man waiting for him outside the emergency.

"Mr. Conners," he said as he stood, "The chief is waiting for you down at headquarters. I've got a squad car right outside."

"Thanks," Reed said and sized him up; a fresh-faced kid, he thought in a surly mood. His head was in a fog as they went through downtown and didn't really clear until he had drank a cup of some sludge they called coffee in the Police Department.

"Conners, how are you doing?" the Chief greeted him and shoved a mountain of papers off to the side on his desk. "This shouldn't take more than an hour, think you can make it?"

Reed just shook his head in agreement. Actually, he had the headache from hell, and after tossing his lunch his stomach was on fire. He'd thrown cold water on his face and rinsed his mouth out at the hospital, but he still felt wretched.

"I'll live," he mumbled and found a seat by the side of the Chief's desk. The door opened and a uniformed woman walked in carrying a laptop and sat down.

The Chief nodded at her and said, "Start at the beginning, Conners, what time did you get to the Grain Belt building and go on from there."

Reed inhaled a breath to steady his nerves and began. As he relived the moment of terror when Wolff had the knife aimed at his throat and he leveled the gun at him, the horror of the explosion blowing the man to pieces right before his eyes sickened him again.

"I shot in self defense. I'd dropped my gun when I fell and luckily got a hold of it again just in time!" Reed repeated the scene and his statement were recorded in court records.

The same fresh faced officer gave him a ride to pick up his Corvette at the Grain Belt Brewery and he finally got back the hotel room, he'd rented earlier. By now it was mid morning and Minneapolis was in full swing of a glorious fall day. Reed threw off his clothes, downed a couple of the pain pills he'd gotten and went to bed, hoping the horror filled pictures would quit racing through his mind. The important thing is, he kept reassuring himself, was Annie Murphy was alive and home with her husband and kids.

Reed slept through the day, got up and took some more pills and slept through the night. Waking at dawn the next day, he showered and dressed. First of all he needed food, lots of food and then he would catch up with Murphy. After that, maybe he'd look up

Mona. It had been months since they'd gotten together and several weeks since they talked. For some reason he was feeling kind of lonely. He shook his head at that revelation. What the hell was this all about, he had never felt alone or needed anyone before?

After eating a hefty breakfast of eggs, bacon and hash browns and washing it down with numerous cups of strong coffee, Reed tossed the sling and felt more like his old self. As he drove out of downtown and into the suburbs, the hum of his Corvette soothed his battered nerves as he came into the familiar neighborhood where the Murphy's lived.

Their house was a tan bricked two-storied contemporary, well kept with a beautifully maintained lawn and shrubberies. Peach colored shutters adorned the windows and terra cotta stone filled pots accessorized the walk. As Reed parked and rang the doorbell, he could see the patient love and dedicated care his friends put into their home. The door suddenly burst open and he found himself clutched in the arms of Ann Murphy.

"Oh my dear," she whispered tearfully. "How can I ever thank you for finding me in that horrible place?" She held Reed in a brotherly hug. Her long red hair was tied up in a pony-tail and she was clad in jeans and tee-shirt. Her feet were bare. Reed returned the hug and soon Murphy and the three girls rushed in and joined in the hug.

"How are you all?" Reed asked then as everyone stood back and smiled happily.

Murphy put his arm around Ann's waist and said, "I owe you Buddy, I've got my family back."

"We got lucky, Murph." Reed had always thought of them as his family and they always included him in their holidays. Several times during the summer, they would come up to his house and enjoy the lake.

"Come on in, Reed, I just made a pot of coffee," Ann said and hooked her arm through Reed's. And they all trooped into the kitchen and sat down at a big round oak table. The morning sun gleamed against the stainless steel appliances; the lovely wood floors and the cozy matching chair seats and curtains, and the fragrant aroma of fresh brewed coffee flooded the room.

"Girls," Ann said to the kids, "we're going to have some grown-up talk now and I want you to go to your play-room. I'll call you before Reed goes so you can give him hugs." The three little girls obediently trooped out of the kitchen, dragging their dolls and blankets as Ann got cups and poured coffee.

Reed and Murphy sat at the table. The hollow circles under Murphy's eyes had left his face this morning, and the tenderness between he and Ann was evident.

"Reed," Ann began, "I want to talk to your friend Lindy Lewis. Murphy said she called you after seeing me in a vision or dream in that horrible place."

"Annie, she did. There was something about that building that drew me back to it Murph, and I was standing right in front of it when she called." Reed raised his cup and drank. This coffee was the real thing and tasted wonderful.

Murphy huffed out a breath. "Jesus, I'm sorry Buddy. I should have been there. I couldn't sleep anyway after you forced me to go home. I just went over those files again."

"It is okay, Murph, it turned out okay." Reed reached over and clapped him on the shoulder.

"Where can I reach Lindy?" Ann asked. "Does she live here in Minneapolis?"

"She lives in Mexico," Reed said and reached in his pocket for the scrap of paper with the telephone number he'd written down earlier.

Later that day, he had a sudden thought, this was not the first time Lindy Lewis had been instrumental in helping him. Twice before, she'd had important information that had enabled him to solve a case.

Goddamn, the woman might have something; he had to admit to himself. But, he still didn't think it was all that trustworthy, just a lucky guess! But now, after the stress of the kidnapping and then the elation finding the victim alive, he had time to dwell on the situation he had left undone when he'd rushed out of her house, just several days ago. He'd just gotten in the door at her house in Monterrey and, goddamn, they'd ended up in bed.

Much later, as they lay spent in each other's arms, he'd told her she was a free woman and his company had its money back. Had she heard what he said before she'd fallen sound asleep? He had left in such a hurry in the morning after getting that frantic phone call from Murphy; he hadn't given her a chance to talk. Guiltily, he took a breath and opened his cell phone.

-17-

"I don't need to tell you what this can do if you try something stupid," the man whispered and Lindy felt the hard metal tip of a gun stab her in the ribs.

Stunned, her legs automatically moved with the throng of people as they surged toward the gates after the bullfight. She walked, her eyes looking straight ahead not daring to do anything that might upset her assailant. She stuck her lower lip out and blew at her blond hair that hung in her eyes, and then stole a glimpse of the man. They were shoulder to shoulder, so close she could see the small red blood veins in his eyes and smell his stale breath. His face was mean and ugly.

"What do you want?" she finally managed to whisper in a strangled breath.

"Shut up, lady," he mumbled and increased the pressure on her arm. As the crush of the crowd forced them along, he began to edge her toward a door almost hidden behind a pile of trash cans.

What had happened to Monica? She had been right there at her side a minute ago! Good Lord, they were almost to that door. And, what the hell was on the other side?

Then out of nowhere, in a split second, Monica jumped in front of the man, aimed a karate chop at his neck and he fell to the ground. Shocked, Lindy stopped and looked wide-eyed, but without missing a beat, Monica grabbed her arm and they continued moving ahead with the crowd, who stepped over and around the fallen man and hurried on.

"Asshole!" Monica exclaimed as they finally got to her car.

By now, Lindy had calmed down, but her thoughts raced. "Thank God you got rid of him," was all she could say at the moment.

"A thief after your purse," Monica huffed. "You're damn lucky you had a good hold on it. They will try it on tourists every time," she added again.

But Lindy wasn't so sure. The memory of the man's threat still burned in her thoughts.

Within minutes Monica had expertly wrestled her sporty car out of the throngs of departing vehicles and the two women were speeding back into the city.

"Rosie's is just up ahead in that run down building you see on your left, everyone goes there after the fights," Monica said and abruptly turned off the freeway. Latin music poured out of the place as they drove up and down a jam packed parking lot looking for a place to leave the car. Three blocks away, they got lucky and trooped over uneven gravel streets back to the bar.

The building was a long low structure of grey cement blocks with a rusty tin roof and a blazing red neon sign on the roof that said Rosie's. Dust in the air from the heavy traffic on the unpaved streets caused the place to have a sort of mysterious look about it. "It looks pretty scary," Lindy said uneasily, "are you sure we should go in there?"

Monica laughed and put her arm over Lindy's shoulder. "It's okay, it's a local hot spot and the owners are friends of mine. I'll introduce you to Rosie and you'll really like her. Watch this." Instead of walking right in the place Monica knocked on the door. It was instantly thrown open and a giant sized Latin man stepped out and immediately lifted Monica off the ground and swung her around in a hug.

Music deafened Lindy's ears as she stood with her mouth open, wondering if anyone could hear her if she screamed for help. Then the man put Monica down.

"Buenos noches! Señoritas," he said in a booming voice. He stood at least six feet plus in height and must have weighed three hundred pounds.

Monica straightened her tube top and pulled down her shorts. "Hey Joe Moe, I want you to meet my friend Lindy, but you can call her Lola. She's a new resident in our town."

Lindy smiled at the man, relieved that he was friendly. And, as her eyes swept over the packed bar she didn't miss the hungry looks on some of the male faces that were turned toward them.

But, was her attacker hiding in amongst them, too?

She followed Monica as they made their way to the bar where right away two male customers stood up and gave up their stools.

Lindy perched on the high chair, adjusting her legs to show off her high-heeled wedgies. Latin music pierced through room with smoke so heavy her eyes watered.

"We'll have tequila," Monica told the bartender and lit a cigarette that sent more smoke spiraling upwards to join the cloud above their heads. Almost immediately, the two women were surrounded by men, all of them of Latin descent.

Lindy took a sip of the tequila and it burned a path down her throat. Her heart skipped a beat as she glanced around and saw they were the only Americans in the place!

Monica was happily engrossed in greeting friends, and then said, "Hey everyone, I want you to meet my friend Lola Lindy, she's living here now." She winked at Lindy who had gulped her drink to cover her nervousness.

The men murmured, "Bueno" and smiled at her. Their white teeth gleamed against their dark skin and hair. One of them took her hand and kissed her palm while another jostled his way over and pulled her to her feet, then out to the packed dance floor as disco music had begun blasting off the cement walls.

"Señorita," he laughed and crushed her body to his and forcefully held her close to the tension in his groin as they circled the floor. When he wouldn't release her after the number was over, Lindy calmly kneed him in the jeans and walked back to her seat at the bar where Monica was engrossed in visiting with friends. She lit a cigarette and joined in the group.

The evening ended with an invitation from Rosie, or Rosita as she was called, to continue the party. Rosie was a native of the country and with the name Joe Johnson; her husband looked to be of good old, Norwegian stock.

Dog-tired from the long evening at the bull fights, they declined Rosie's invitation and left the bar and went outside into the hot humid night. The air was heavier yet with dust from the unpaved streets and the

departing traffic as they tottered on their high-heels
back to Monica's car.

"Well, Lola Lindy," Monica had taken to calling
her, "What do you think of the nightlife here?" She
asked.

By this time, Lindy was pleasantly drunk and had
loved the attention the Latin men had heaped on her.
Wow, she hadn't felt so beautiful for a long time.
Well, maybe that time she'd been in Dallas, when she
had found her money and treated herself to a long
stay at a spa.

"I loved it," she bubbled having forgotten about
the episode earlier that evening when the man had
stuck a gun in her ribs. "I really had a good time, let's
get together again in a day or two and go back there."

"Sure, call me," Monica said and wheeled the car
into her driveway.

She unlocked the door and waved to her friend
who spun away and back into the night. As Lindy
went into the kitchen and rummaged in the
refrigerator for a snack, she saw the message light
blinking on her telephone. When she picked it up and
listened to it a man's voice whispered in her ear,
"You were lucky this time!"

She dropped the receiver and it clattered down on
the cupboard. She sank into a chair and clasped her
arms around herself. Sobered, she remembered the
man with the gun.

Who was doing this and why? And instantly her thoughts flew towards Rio, the Mayor of Monterrey. He knew her real name, and now was this his underhanded way of trying to scare her into divulging her past?

Had that man who had stuck the gun in her ribs as she was leaving the bull fight been one of his flunkies, or just another pick-pocket honing his craft?

As Lindy sat in her dark kitchen in the middle of the night, worrying over the new state of affairs, the telephone lying next to her on the countertop suddenly shrilled.

-18-

Reed sat in the kitchen with Murphy and Ann looking on expectantly, as his cell-phone made the connection across the border into Mexico to Lindy's number. They both waited to talk to her.

But after several minutes and no answer he hung up. "She's more than likely out gallivanting," he muttered under his breath. He also remembered she never did hurry to catch a ringing phone.

"I'll leave her number with you." He said and finished his coffee then stood up.

"What are you going to do now?" Murphy asked.

Reed ran a hand through his hair. He had planned to stay around town for a few days and spend some time with Mona, but goddamn, suddenly he just needed to get away. When he'd talked to her, she had finished the chemo treatments, and was feeling pretty good and her sister had gone home. Now he said, "I'm taking off."

"Where to," Ann asked?

"Up north, home," he said. "I've got to get some fishing in before the snow flies again."

"We're going to miss you. How about we all pile in the car and drive up for a few days soon," Murphy exclaimed.

Reed smiled at his friends. "You bet any time! Just give me a call." With that he hugged Ann and clapped Murphy on the back as they grinned at each other. At the door the three little girls rushed into his arms and plastered his face with kisses. Their red pony-tails danced in the air as they ran, so like their mother's.

Finally Reed was on the road, going home. The Corvette hummed perfectly, and jazz played on the radio. He lit a cigarette and sat back to relax. Finally!

But he couldn't relax. Goddamn, he couldn't calm down, he couldn't forget. He had killed a man! That horrible split second when he'd shot Wolff, the vagrant who had kidnapped Ann, was firmly implanted in his mind. Minute details of the bullet exploding into the man's head, and the gory aftermath was still vividly replaying over and over and wouldn't let go.

He punched the steering wheel. What the hell else could I have done? The son of a bitch damn near killed Annie. And he would have if I hadn't found her in time.

He opened the car window and sucked in the fresh air, then changed the radio to some country. Then muttered, maybe tonight he could get some sleep in his own bed, away from the nauseous memories of what he'd been forced to do.

It had been weeks since he had been home and then it had been for just a short few days when Ed, from the insurance company had called and needed him, pronto, on a case. The Fisher case. And, after working that case he'd accompanied Lindy Lewis to South Carolina for the D'Agustino trial. When she had panicked at the verdict and run to Mexico, he'd followed her, and that's when he'd gotten Murphy's desperate telephone call about Ann's disappearance. And he'd rushed back to Minneapolis to help search for her.

Now as he drove home and had time to see the countryside, he realized the whole goddamn summer had passed. As he got further north, the maple trees were turning a gorgeous shade of red and gold. Sumac along the highway was orange and its flower a rich burgundy. As he got close to Brainerd, a resort town, he caught the faint odor of burning leaves through the lowered car window as he slowed down to thirty miles an hour as he went through the town. It was a late afternoon on a Friday and traffic was bumper to bumper as locals and tourists rushed to their retreats. There was a festive air about it all.

On the road again with another hour before he got to his place, Reed picked up his cell-phone and tried Lindy's number in Monterrey again. By now, goddamn, she should be home and not still out painting the town red. With one hand on the steering wheel he held the phone to his ear with the other and listened to it ring. After ten rings, he grudgingly gave up and mumbled, where the hell is that women?

Now as the Corvette sped over the miles, the small towns flew by. The picturesque town of Nisswa proudly showed off its colorful array of summer homes along its shores, then Backus and Ridge, their main streets gaily peppered with hanging pots of trailing flowers on their streetlights to delight the tourists who sped through their main streets. Then Reed saw the corner ahead that led to his home by his lake.

As he left the highway and started down his private road through the woods he began to feel the tranquility of it all calm his nerves. The glorious colors had started to erupt around him filling the woods with shades of autumn. Flaming maples stood next to majestic pines. Here too, a breeze carried the faint aroma of smoke in the air as he traveled the last quarter of a mile down to his island. Actually it was a peninsula of three acres which he had inherited from his parents. After retiring his law practice and selling his ranch located on the outskirts of Brainerd several years ago, he'd moved to the lake permanently. The gleaming white bark on the birch trees that edged the water had prompted his parents to name it Birch Island. Now as he drove into the yard, the beauty of the place overwhelmed him again as always. Actually, he hadn't had time to really enjoy the place since it had been rebuilt after the ice storm had demolished it months ago, but now he was going to make time.

He sat for a minute in the Corvette and took a good look at the place. He'd made arrangements with the builder to have the painters stain the siding a warm mellow shade of brown, with white trim bordering the windows and especially the three big picture windows that looked out at the water. It looked good! Then he saw that Abby, his neighbor, had been over and filled the decorative whiskey barrels with bright red and white flowers. Damn the place looked really great! He pulled up in front of the garage and stopped, grabbed his luggage and opened the door into his house.

The place looked just as he had left it weeks ago. The same sunflower arrangement stood on the oak table in the dining area and the wood floors gleamed in the late afternoon sunlight. He dropped his suitcases in the bedroom and came out in the living room and sat down in a leather recliner, put his feet up, lit a cigarette and gazed out at the water.

Goddamn, this is contentment he said to the book filled walls. He wasn't going to leave for a long time! After relaxing with several brandies that night he opened the windows and for the first time in days slept soundly as the pine scented breezes whispered through his bedroom. The next morning after awakening rested and starved, Reed showered and went into the town to the local restaurant.

Its logs silvered now, the Woodsmen café had stood on the same spot for generations, nestled in amongst the business district which held a hardware store, a bakery, a well drilling company and of course a liquor store and bar. Down at the end of the block, the church and a real-estate office stood.

"Morning Flo, I'll have the works." Reed grinned at the waitress in the restaurant and swung a leg over a stool at the counter. Flo had been working there when he was a kid, and he added now, "What's your secret, Sweetheart, you just get better looking!"

"Really," she beamed loving the compliment as she put a steaming cup of coffee down in front of him. Flo knew everyone. Her hair was dyed a bright red and her uniform and apron a crisp white. She always had a colorful fluffy hanky stuffed in a pocket over her left breast and she always chewed gum. No one knew her age for sure, but the locals all assumed she was in the same age bracket as Jerome, who had been around too, when Reed was a kid.

Now Jerome sat at the end of the counter, on the same stool he'd occupied in the mornings for years, dressed in his usual plaid flannel shirt with a classy tie, bib overalls and as always wearing a feed cap over his bald head. His clothes were threadbare and he always left a trail of Old Spice in his wake.

"How you doing?" Reed greeted him.

"Oh, I've been better," Jerome said and scooped up a forkful of eggs. He'd spend hours each morning in the restaurant, then go a couple of doors down the block and spend the afternoon and evening in the bar. "Good to see you again, neighbor," he added.

Stan, the cook and owner of the Woodsmen café came out of the kitchen carrying a cup of coffee and joined the row of men at the counter, his apron splattered with spills.

"You back for awhile now, Reed?" He asked and pulled a pack of Camels out of his shirt pocket.

"Sure plan on it." Reed fired up a cigarette and sent the smoke upwards to join the cloud above their heads. The "no smoking what so ever" law in food establishments had not yet reached this small town and they still just shooed the non-smokers to the back of the room.

"You gonna be around for the Fall Festival this year?" Stan asked.

"Well, I should be," Reed answered, "why do you ask?"

Stan laughed, "The wife is on the planning committee this year and we're having a parade. She mentioned having you drive the Corvette in it!"

"My car?" Reed looked up as Flo set a plate down in front of him.

"Well," Stan drawled, "the ladies around here think you're pretty hot."

Reed looked around at the grinning faces of his friends. "Well goddamn, then I better not let them down! Do I get a pretty one to ride with me?"

"We'll probably have to draw a name out of a hat," one of the guys joked.

Stan dragged hard on his Camel. "The wife says Jerome and Flo are going to be king and queen of the festival this year and ride in the parade."

"They're the oldest around here," another man added.

"So Reed, the wife figures you could pull a trailer behind the Corvette. They've decorated up one for them to ride in."

"Oh sure," Reed said as he ate his eggs, and thought; now finally this is the life. Peaceful town, good friends and harmony.

-19-

The persistent shrill ring of the telephone echoed in the night as Lindy sat in her kitchen after getting home from Rosie's bar. Just minutes ago when she'd answered it a man had whispered in her ear, "Lady, you were lucky this time!" And it had sounded just like the man who had tried to drag her off earlier at the arena.

Her eyes darted to the windows in the room and thank God, the blinds were pulled tight. She hurried over and checked the locks in the back door. Then on shaking legs ran to the front of the house and to her horror saw her keys dangling in the outside keyhole when she opened it to slam it tight. Lordy, in her tequila induced recklessness she realized she'd left the keys handy for anyone to just walk right in.

She was scared now, really spooked. Then the telephone rang again. Running into the bedroom she grabbed the cord and yanked it out of the wall, sank down on the edge of the bed and wrapped her arms around her chest to try to stop the shakes.

Her mind raced. Who was doing this? Had Rio sent out his goons to scare the daylights out of her? Or was this some crazy revenge Al Guiness had come up with because she'd taken her money out of his bank. Or had she made other enemies in Monterrey?

She took a deep breath as people and events flew through her mind. Her friend Rita had nothing to gain, and the women she'd met at the country club and done readings for hadn't seemed threatened by her. So, who else could it be but Rio or Al Guiness? And they had succeeded in doing exactly what they had set out to do. To terrorize her! Now she wouldn't sleep the rest of the night worrying about what else they might have in store for her.

Well, she was not going to take it, she'd show them! She paced through the house using anger to boast her bravado. And determined, she showered until the water ran ice cold. Then minutes later dressed in sweats, made a pot of coffee and downed cups of the strong caffeine. Now her mind was clear and she was ready for the bastards if they tried anything.

The night was endless but finally the darkness started to fade and the sun began to show its face. But during the long daunting hours she realized she had to get her money out of the house. That whoever was doing this could break in, rob her and be gone in minutes! She looked around warily. She'd have to bank it again and take the chance that if something drastic happened in the future, like another earthquake, her intuitiveness would alert her.

Well, she had picked up a few things associating with those crooks, the D'Agustino brothers, and one was that you kept your friends close, but your enemies closer. They had done business with Mexican banker Al Guiness with their millions. So, she would have to again too, but she didn't trust the man!

She stood at the cupboard in the kitchen, a coffee cup in her hand as she thought it out. She'd invest in some safe ventures at his bank and then over time would cash out in their currency. She'd take her time and watch the man. Eventually she would slide all her cash through. But for now she would put the rest of her million away in other banks around the city for safe keeping. She sat down with the Monterrey telephone book and made a list of the places she'd do business with.

Her first trip was to Al's bank. Since his main place of business downtown was still a pile of rubble after the earthquake weeks ago, she found he was temporally doing business out of a suburban location. She dressed in a new fashionable dress, fluffed her blonde hair and called for a taxi, her classy Coach briefcase slung over her shoulder.

His place of business stood in the midst of an older part of Monterrey, and like most banks unformed guards with guns were posted at the entrances. Lindy eyed them warily, but marched right up to the door. Then smiled broadly as they murmured, "Bueno Señora," and hurried to open the heavy massive doors for her. She found the information desk where a beautifully groomed Spanish woman sat.

"May I help you, Señora?" she asked in perfect English.

Lindy sat down. "Buenos Dïas! Señorita," she returned easily even though butterflies were dancing in her stomach. She read the nameplate on the desk. "Señorita Cruse," she went on, "I recently moved here and I need a safe place to keep all my important documents." She leaned closer to the lady, "and I'll need a large container, I have so many papers."

Señorita Cruse smiled at her and said, "It'll just take a few minutes to fill out the forms." Then busied herself collecting the necessary papers for Lindy to sign. Of course Lindy had her fictitious identification with her and produced her Lola Lang driver's license, and social security card. Fortunately, when she'd had these done in Dallas months ago, she had been blond then too and still wore the brown eye contacts when the occasion called for them.

After tapping information into her computer, the woman finally led Lindy back into the bowels of the bank and to the vault which contained walls of numbered drawers. She pulled out a large box and opened it for Lindy and said. "Here you are Señora, just ring the buzzer when you have completed your business." The woman closed the door and Lindy was left in complete silence. It was so quiet, it was spooky. She looked around warily and shuttered.

Just how safe was this bank? Did it have observation cameras? She looked around casually but couldn't see anything that might look like one, but then if they did she realized it would be well hidden.

Well hell, she pretended unconcern, fluffed her hair then opened her briefcase, leaned in close and quickly slid the bills in the drawer. Several minutes later she rang the buzzer for the attendant.

As they came out of the vault, Lindy asked, "Is Mr. Guiness in?"

"Do you have an appointment to see him?" the woman asked.

"Well no," Lindy murmured apologetically, she hoped "but could you tell him I stopped in." Lindy asked.

"I'll check for you Señora Lang." And she hurried out of sight.

Lindy had intentionally taken care of her business before letting him know she was there. Five minutes later, the man appeared with his hand outstretched.

"Lola, I am so honored to have you in my place of business. What can I do for you?"

Lindy clasped his hand in greeting. "Al," she gushed, "I'm taking advantage of your safe deposit box for now, but I'll want to get together with you and go over different strategies for my investments," then added, "I look forward to your expert advice, of course." She released his hand and felt like wiping her own on her dress after coming in contact with him.

"My dear Lola, I'll be more than happy to assist you." Al Guiness said. She felt his eyes rove up and down her body. Today the banker was dressed in assorted shades of blue. Suit, shirt, tie, shoes and socks accentuated his tanned complexion perfectly. His snow white hair and van dyke styled mustache was a startling contrast and added to his British air.

Pig, she murmured under her breath and suddenly his next thought flashed through her mind. YOU SILLY LITTLE BITCH, I'll get you this time, he'd been thinking just then. This hadn't happened to her for some time and when it did, it always startled her when she realized she had just read another person's thoughts. She immediately pasted a smile on her face.

"You're looking beautiful today." Al continued, "Are you free for lunch?" He ran a manicured hand through his mustache.

So you think I'm a silly bitch, well just wait and see! Lindy's thought burned to escape her lips.

Instead she calmly smiled at the man and replied, "I've got several errands to take care of Al, but I would love to join you."

She sensed danger, but she needed him!

-20-

"I'll see you all later," Reed said to his friends at the Woodsmen café after wolfing down a country breakfast. He was home and feeling good after a sound night of sleep in his own bed.

"Are you going to take the Formula out?" Stan asked. "I heard the walleyes were biting yesterday." He inhaled hard on his Camel cigarette.

"Hell, yes," Reed said and added, "I just might stay out on the boat for a few days. I haven't had a chance to really try her out, and SUDDENLY SUMMER is about over, with all this goddamned work interfering."

"Must be rough," one of the guys at the counter said good-naturedly.

"Yup," Reed grinned, "and someone has to do it!" He put his smoke out and laid some bills on the counter. "See you all later," he said again, saluted his buddies and left. On the way back to his house he stopped at the local grocery and stocked up on food, then the liquor store for an assortment of top shelf necessities.

Back home, he packed up supplies, collected his fishing gear and took off out to the dock. His boat was a thirty foot Formula cruiser that could sleep six. It had a queen size bunk, a bathroom with shower and a kitchen down stairs and a pull out bed topside if you wanted to sleep under the stars. Just enough room for him and God, how he loved it! The motor purred smoothly as he backed it away from the dock and headed towards open water. His dark glasses cut the glare from the morning sun. He lit a cigarette. Damn, this was heaven!

Birch Lake was deep, startling blue and full of walleye. If you squinted hard you could see the homes across the water. Some lived there full time and some were week-enders from large cities around the country. All of the houses, complete with private sandy beaches were priced in the millions, and where the residents selfishly guarded their paradise from marauders of every kind. No obscene loud motors were allowed, ever, to muck up the serenity.

Reed shook his head at the pretentiousness of some of his neighbors who had bought in over the years, but what the hell. Live and let live. After testing the boats performance, he dropped anchor out in the middle of the lake and settled in, and even though it was still before noon, he opened a beer and got his line ready to work on catching his dinner. By afternoon he took off his shirt, donned cut-offs and stretched his bare legs out. But the elusive walleye stayed away.

That's why they call it fishing, not catching, he mumbled as he laid down his rod and reel. Between the beer and the sun, he was just a little drunk, but loving the feeling as he made his way down stairs to his stocked refrigerator where he made a sandwich, then let the boat lull him into a nap on the bed.

When he came topside several hours later refreshed, he dropped his line again. There was no hurry, if nothing happened today, there was always tomorrow. He sat back on the leather seat and smiled inside, perfectly content even though the line in the water floated lazily. Giving up for the day a few hours later, he watched the sunset, then, the stars come out. He micro-waved dinner and settled in to enjoy a peaceful night on the water. When he looked toward the shoreline the lights from the homes twinkled now in the darkness. God, it was beautiful! He poured some brandy for a nightcap and tuned in soft music on a radio. As he sat out in his boat on the water a love song began to play reminding him of

Lindy. A sudden ache shot through his chest. He had to admit it had felt good to hold her again.

How would it have played out if he hadn't had to leave?

He took a big swallow of the brandy. Then he thought about Mona and her fight with cancer. Was she going to beat it or was she going to die? Goddamn, he was getting maudlin, and drunk!

Moonlight lit up the sky and had turned the lake into a shiny black basin of rolling waves. He drank and smoked as he reflected over his involvements. He wondered if Ginger, a cocktail waitress in town he'd had a liaison with now and then, would want to start up the relationship again. Maybe she'd shit-canned him for good this time!

Couldn't blame her, Reed muttered to the night. He listened for the weather report on the radio, and went downstairs.

Got to get up early and catch those buggers, he mumbled to himself as he settled in for the night. The air was just cool enough to pull the covers up on the bed and he slept like a baby lulled by the autumn breeze as it rocked the boat like a cradle.

As the sun broke out over the horizon the next morning, he awoke and jumped in the water to clear the cobwebs out of his head, ate a quick breakfast and filled his coffee cup. The sky promised another ideal overcast day, just perfect weather to catch that walleye for his dinner but after several hours, there was nothing happening. No fish, not even a nibble. Well hell, it was time for a beer anyway. Just one more cast and he would take a break. As he was reeling in the line, something caught. Jesus, this was great. A goddamn fish at last!

He began to slowly reel it in. By god, the fucker was heavy. He stood up in the boat as the rod began to bend over with the weight, praying the line wouldn't break. He forced himself to keep calm. Goddamn, the way it felt it must be trophy size. Man, he was pumped; just wait 'til his buddies in town saw this! After several minutes of intense resistance, Reed gave the line one fast tug and the catch burst to the surface.

He stared at it dumbfounded. His first thought was, it's a damn pile of rags! What the hell—he muttered, as he reeled it in closer. Then the waterlogged object abruptly spun over and a dead face stared up at him.

His top of the line rod and reel went flying overboard as he threw up his breakfast in the lake. The perfect day had turned hideous. When he finally got over the shakes, he got on his cell.

"Jesse," he said to the Sheriff in town, "I'm out here in the middle of the lake and I just caught a body!"

"Conners, what the hell are you talking about?" Jesse Monties was in his sixties, and had been the keeper of peace for decades. The only crimes that had happened in this small town had been an occasional domestic, someone getting rowdy after too many drinks at the Legion, or maybe a hormone driven youngster speeding in town. He didn't need something like this now, just when retirement and a pension was just months away.

"Jesus, are you putting me on?" Jessie wiped a hand over his sweaty face. He had just finished eating a pork chop dinner at the Woodsmen café in town and had thought about running home for a quick nap. He had to be alert and on the job when the tourists hit town and needed watching as they stopped in for the cocktail hour on their way through.

"Jesse, I'm serious," Reed said.

"God almighty, how could something like that happen here?" Jesse mumbled.

"How soon can you get out here?" Reed felt through his pockets for a cigarette even though his mouth tasted like road kill.

"Awright, awright, I'll have to get some help here," Jesse said as he tried to line up in his mind what was needed. "That no good deputy of mine will have to get the boat out. I've got to find the coroner, too."

"How long?" Reed asked.

"Don't know." Jesse grumped, "Soon's you see me I 'spose."

Reed put the cell in his pocket and glanced again at the gruesome sight. Was it a man or a woman? He couldn't tell and didn't have the stomach to study it further. Goddamn, he grumbled, what a way to end a good trip, and now I wonder what else is down there with the fish?

It was going on noon. He gathered up his fishing equipment then sat down to wait for Jesse, pissed at the turn of events. He poured himself a stiff shot of whiskey to ease the frustration.

After thirty minutes and still no sheriff, he took out his cell phone. Goddamn, he had to do something to take his mind off the gruesome remains he'd lassoed to the side of his boat.

Well hell, he muttered, I may as well make that call I've been putting off. And in seconds, the long distance wires connected the miles and the phone rang in Lindy's house in Monterrey, Mexico.

-21-

Lindy ran the last few steps in her haste to meet Al Guiness at the restaurant for lunch, not because he was a special man in her life, but because she had a plan that would tempt the socks off him. In her estimation he was a creep, but smart and dangerous, but one easily enticed by a woman's charm. And she needed him to exchange her US currency into pesos. She wasn't just talking about a few thousand dollars either. At last count, when she had sat on the floor and patiently counted her bills a few nights ago, it had come to one million, four hundred thousand and three hundred dollars. But Lordy, she had to quit spending so much. It had really gone down after buying the house, but real estate was one way of cleaning the dust of money.

Lindy knew she looked good this day in her Armani dress, and heads turned as she tottered on her high heeled Jimmy Choo shoes through the El Greco restaurant to Al's table. He stood up and when she extended her hand in greeting and he raised it to his lips, she almost cringed in aversion. Finally, they sat and Lindy tucked her hands in her lap under the table.

"It's so lovely to see you again, Lola. Have you been well?" Al asked in his clipped British voice as he looked her over.

Lindy smiled. "Why Al, how nice of you to ask, I've been just wonderful. I love your city!"

"I got to say it's agreeing with you, you look fabulous!" Al darted a quick look at her cleavage in the low neckline of her dress.

Lindy sat cool and calm as she felt his eyeballs burn through the material of her dress as he devoured the outline of her breasts. She leaned over further for the glass of iced water and pretended not to notice while she sipped daintily.

"I've met some very nice people at the country club, too." She went on not missing a beat.

"I heard you've met Rita, our famous artist?" As he spoke he motioned to a waiter who stood at attention nearby and who hurried over with a bottle of champagne nestled in a silver bucket of ice. "You may pour," Al said to him after swirling it around in his glass and tasting it, the young man busied himself filling their crystal goblets. Al nodded at him and turned to Lindy.

"Well my dear, Lola, I have missed you these last few weeks. I trust it's because your social life has kept you busy!" Al ran a manicured hand over his mustache and gray van-dyke whiskered chin.

Of course, Lindy didn't mention the fact that she had been home those times he had stood on her steps ringing the heck out of her doorbell. Right now something was creeping into her thoughts again. She took a slow breath to quiet her mind, while taking her time to answer him. "I have been so busy, and this past week I went to a bull fight."

"And what do you think of our national pastime?"

Lindy raised an eyebrow and shook her head. "Really, I don't think I can call it entertainment. Gristly is more like it!" She also didn't mention that she'd had to consume loads of Monica's tequila to keep from rushing away from the bloody scene as the animals were tortured in the arena. For God's sake, she was raised on a farm where cattle were valued and tended with care and had spent long summer days herding them on the prairie with only a bag lunch and a book.

I wonder what he would say if I told him that! More than likely he'd be appalled at being in the same room with a farm girl!

She watched as he took a drink of the wine and swished it around in his mouth before swallowing, then frowned at her and said, "No, no, my dear, it's an art! The Matadors have spent years learning how to skillfully lead the animal through the progression of control. I'll take you, Lola. I have a private box and I can assure you it's very comfortable."

Just then a picture flashed through her thoughts. Almost like a television screen flashing an action scene. She was in an enclosed room and was struggling as he forced her down. She blinked her eyes now as the scene disappeared.

Had he been trying to rape her or kill her? Her plan had been to keep the man hot and interested. Right now, he was practically drooling, but would she be able to keep him under control until she was finished with him?

While she sat demurely contemplating her options, Al motioned the waiter over and ordered their lunch in Spanish, and she almost giggled hearing the local language spoken with a British accent. She turned to Al as he said, "I hope you don't mind that I ordered for you. This is a five-star restaurant and I want you to experience some of their specialties!"

"I am starving," Lindy said and tucked her napkin over her knees under the table.

"I didn't have time for breakfast before I left the house this morning." And then she remembered the time she'd gone out to dinner with him and he'd ordered squid and didn't tell her what she was eating until after she had taken a few bites. "You didn't order something outlandish now, did you?" she asked.

"My dear, it is a surprise, but you'll enjoy it." Al raised his glass. "By the way, I want to congratulate you on your business. I heard your supporters are keeping you busy!"

Lindy dabbed her lips daintily with the napkin and took her time replacing it on her lap again, and wondered how he knew that!

"Oh, it's just a hobby." She shrugged her shoulders nonchalantly. Then thought, if he knew the amount of peso's her rich customers were thrusting at her for her prophecies, he might think up a reason to take a cut. From the first minute she'd made his acquaintance, she sensed his sly objectives, but that's what she needed him for.

The waiter bustled back with several covered dishes and began to spoon some small amounts on plates for them. The aroma was heavenly and Lindy's hunger pangs yelped in excitement at the sight of the beautifully presented foods.

"What is this?" she asked as she filled her fork with bright colored vegetables mixed with a browned meat. It tasted marvelous. A spicy dipping sauce accompanied the dish and Al spooned some on her food saying, "My dear, you must add this to really get the flavor of this delicacy."

"Really?" Lindy echoed, thinking it tasted great the way it was.

"This is a delicacy served only at several restaurants in this area. Only a few schooled chefs know how to properly prepare this." Al sat back and eyed Lindy's plate. "I can see you are enjoying it."

Lindy heaped the last morsel unto her fork and chewed. "It's wonderful." She said, and then asked, "It was chicken wasn't it?"

"No, my dear," Al said in his clipped British accent, "That was a dish using crotalo, rattlesnake, delicious wasn't it!"

Lindy was silent for a moment as the realization sank in. Then she abruptly stood, clutched her napkin to her mouth and ran. Ran like hell towards anything that might be a door into a restroom. Tears ran down her face as she tried to contain throwing up right there on the restaurant floor of this wonderful five-star place.

Damn that man and his stupid idea of what he thought constituted a delicacy.

What about shrimp or lobster, something decent most people would enjoy?

This all flew through her mind as she stumbled into a restroom and got sick. After several minutes, an attendant hurried to her with a wet towel and solicitously tsk, tsked as she wiped her face.

"Thank you, I don't have my purse with me, but I'll be back," she said to the lady and marched back to the table where Al was sitting calmly drinking his wine.

"Lola, my dear, I thought you would enjoy my surprise." He said and laughed.

"Al, you should be sorry. Please don't surprise me ever again!"

"I've ordered some tea, is that okay?" He asked as he stroked his mustache.

By now Lindy had, had it with the man and declared, "I'm not feeling up to par right now, so I'm leaving." She reached for her purse.

"Now?" Al stood up when he saw the angry look on her face. "I can accompany you and see that you get home safely!" he added.

Oh, for God's sake, Lindy thought, I've got to get away from this jerk. "No thank you!" She exclaimed and turned and left the five-star restaurant after stopping in the restroom to give the attendant a ten dollar bill for her help.

Bastard, she muttered on the ride home in a taxi. Only a tight ass limey would think that was funny!

The telephone rang as Lindy came into her house. She kicked off her sandals and picked it up, then sucked in her breath as she recognized the voice on the line.

"Reed," she murmured, too miserable to remember if she should be glad or mad at the man. "What's going on?" She asked then.

"Well, for one thing, Lindy, I wanted to tell you we found Ann Murphy! That place you told me about turned out to be where she was being held prisoner."

"Thank God, but did you get to her in time?" she asked.

-22-

Reed took another swallow of his whiskey as he sat waiting for the Sheriff and his men to get out to him on Birch Lake. The water logged body was secured to the side of his boat.

Goddamn, what a way to end the peace and quiet on the lake, he grumbled. Now, resigned to the situation and time on his hands he had remembered he'd meant to try calling Lindy again. It was early afternoon. The woman should be home now for Christ's sake, he mumbled. When her voice echoed over the wire a sudden jolt had rumbled through his belly.

It took a second as he tried to sort out that feeling, then failing said, "Lindy, uh -- I wanted to tell you that we found Ann Murphy. That building that you told me about turned out to be the place she was being held prisoner in!"

"Did you get to her in time?" She had held her breath as she waited, almost dreading his answer.

"Yes!" he said and she almost fainted with relief. Although, she had only met the Murphy's once, she knew that the family was Reed's dearest friends. That he, Murphy and the deceased Tanner Burke were like brothers.

"I didn't think you believed me when I told you that I saw Ann in that place," She exclaimed defensively.

He took a minute and lit a cigarette. "I didn't until I realized you were describing the exact place I was standing in front of." Lindy was silent as he went on. "I guess I forgot about the other times you have given me information that helped with a case.

"Imagine that," she answered.

Reed could hear the cynicism in her voice over the phone. Well, maybe she had something after all! He went on, "We got the asshole who took Annie." He didn't mention that he had shot the man.

"I remember that the Murphy's have three little girls. Thank God, they still have their mother," Lindy added.

"Yeah, that's one happy family!" Reed paused and took a swig of whiskey and a drag of the cigarette as he wondered how she would take his next piece of news. Apparently she had been sound asleep before, when they had lain together in bed and he'd told her she was not on the wanted list in the US anymore. Also that, his company had gotten its money back!

"Lindy," he began, "there's something else. I told you all this before--."

"What?" Lindy asked when he didn't go on. "Reed is something else wrong?"

"No." he said, but looked around curiously as his boat began to rock. "What the hell," he mumbled, and then saw a whole convoy of floating vessels cruising towards him at top speed. The Sheriff led the parade with his deputy and the coroner, followed by numerous other boats.

"Reed, what is it?" Lindy stood puzzled and waited for his reply.

"Lindy, I'm out on my lake, and I pulled up something that needs investigating." He didn't have time to go into an explanation now. "I'll call you back."

Lindy said something that got lost as static crackled over the line.

Goddamn these things, he said and dropped the cell phone in his shirt pocket.

"Slow down now, this is a crime scene!" Jesse Montes, the Sheriff yelled out to everyone.

"Jesse, who is it?" Someone hollered over. "Is it someone we know?"

"Hold your horses, I just got here!" Jesse grumped nervously.

Reed put out a warning hand as the Sheriff's boat edged closer. "Jesse, I've got it secured over here." He pointed to a bundle he had tied to the side of his boat.

"God almighty," Jesse said. And for the next hour the men were silent as they rescued the remains and uncovered the awful sight.

"Careful now," Jesse warned the men.

"Is it a man or a woman?" Joe, a fireman and owner of the well drilling company asked as he leaned in for a closer look.

"Can't tell Joe," Jesse said impatiently, "we got to wait until the coroner here has had time to do his examining."

Reed stood back as they loaded the body onto the Sheriff's boat and finally the commotion simmered down.

"Reed, I need you to come in and give me your statement," Jesse had said as his boat chugged off.

"I'll be there as soon as I can," he agreed. Then, muttered goddamn, as he cleaned up the mess left by all the commotion on his boat.

And once again Birch Lake was quiet. He blew out a cloud of cigarette smoke as he wondered who had had the misfortune of ending up in the water filled grave.

It all left a bad feeling in his stomach. How could something like this happen in his town? All the residents relished every minute of the small town atmosphere, just like he did. Over the years, he had met most of them and found them to be okay. He couldn't think of one single person who had seemed to warrant an investigation.

But, he had to admit times had changed. More people were moving in and more were stopping on their way through, and it would be easy to dump a body in the lake as the small town slumbered.

Goddamn, Reed swore, pulled up anchor and turned his sleek craft towards the shores of Birch Lake. And, forgot all about calling Lindy again as he had promised. He headed towards his place and as always looked over at his spot with pride. Now that he lived there full-time he allowed his thoughts to wander to more pleasant things, there were still things he planned on doing around there. He was going to build a guest house, extend the deck around the side of the house, and have landscapers come in and terrace the hill that sloped down to the water. And he saw he needed more white sand on his beach. All these things took up space in his mind and pushed the ugly scene from out there on the water away as he neared his property. He tied up the boat and spent the next hour cleaning and gathering up his things. After a shower he headed into town and to the Sheriff's office.

Jesse Montes had been born and raised in and around the lake area. He was a Mexican and had married a girl from a prominent Scandinavian family and had gained privileges and then position as he was let into the tight clan. After years now of being the keeper of peace, he was tired of kissing up; to the family, the townspeople and even his spoiled wife and kids. He was still a good looking man with dark Latin features; graying hair around his temple and sideburns and in his handlebar mustache, a little overweight, but still looked good in his pressed brown uniform.

In moments like this, he secretly had thoughts of kissing it all good-by and going to a far off island to do whatever he wanted. This panorama was flitting through his thoughts now as he sat at his desk, his office knee deep with townspeople.

"Hey Conners," he said standing up, "come on back!"

Reed nodded to the crowd and followed Jesse to a back room. "You got full house, I see. Got any news yet from the Coroner?"

"Nah," Jesse said and handed him a cup of coffee. "I'm not expecting anything for hours yet." He motioned Reed over to a table and they both sat.

"Okay Conners, tell me how you found the body. I need the time and the date for the record." Jesse took out a notepad and pen and began writing.

"Did you see anything or anybody out there that looked suspicious?" Jesse asked.

Reed shook his head. "Nothing at all, I spent the night out there. Looked to me like the body had been in the water for a long time!"

"Yup, that's my take." Jesse mumbled as they went back out to the front later. Now the place was empty except for his deputy who sat importantly at the desk. He jumped up as they came into the room.

"Let me know if I can do anything for you." Reed said then as he walked to the door. "I'll give you a ring in the morning."

The sun was sliding over the horizon as he left the Sheriff's office. By now his stomach demanded food, but not having shed the revulsion of the afternoon, he headed to the Legion club for some of the local medicine.

-23-

The phone lines crackled with static as Lindy strained to hear Reed's voice. She puzzled over his words, "'I'm out on the lake and pulled up something that needs investigating!'"

What had he meant? Then suddenly a picture of a young man's face flashed through her thoughts. And the name Sam!

She stood in her kitchen, still in the Armani dress and Jimmy Choo shoes she'd worn when she'd met Al Guiness, in shock now at the vision she'd just seen.

She rubbed a hand over her eyes. "Reed, are you there?" She whispered, "I think I know who it is!" But the line had gone dead.

She dropped the phone on the cupboard and put her head in her hands as a dull ache arched across her brow and then around to back of her head. As it circled it gained in momentum until she swayed in dizziness and grabbed unto the edge of the granite covered cabinet to keep from falling. After a moment and finally gaining some semblance of rightness, she managed to walk to the couch in the living room and lowered herself gingerly to the safety of the cushions. She whimpered and closed her eyes. She'd often have visions or bizarre thoughts lately but had never experienced such pain. What was happening to her? Should she call 911? Did they even have 911 in this country?

She put one of the accent couch pillows over her face and lay there and grappled for answers. She could call Monica. That's what she'd do as soon as she could sit up and move. Then, as fast as the headache had come on, it left!

She sat up and tentatively looked around, then stood. Finding things firmly back in place again she went to her bedroom, undressed and put on a comfortable robe. Coming back to her living room, she sat down in one of the stuffed red easy chairs and picked up a book she had been reading, all the while the persistent memory of that young man's face prominent in her mind.

Who was he? She didn't know anyone by the name of Sam! Did it have anything to do with Reed and whatever kind of fish he'd caught out on his lake?

She sucked in a breath and took two more, then stretched her feet out on the hassock. She brushed her hair off her face and groaned. She was so tired of all this: the visions and predictions that constantly interrupted her, unannounced at all times of the day or night. And lately, it had been happening more and more.

The sun was starting to sink toward the horizon in the Mexican sky and the rays streamed in through the open blinds. Jasmine scented the air from the bush that stood just outside the open front door. She listened and thought she heard the familiar scratch of cicadas. All of a sudden she was lonesome, and scared. For what or whom, she couldn't place at the moment, but suddenly all her bravado and zest seemed to have vanished.

She looked around at her gorgeously furnished house. Everything was perfect! She lived in a beautiful country, had loads of money and had carved out a social life.

So how come she felt this way?

She tugged her robe closer and stared off into space. Honestly, she had to admit that no matter how much money she could get her hands on and how beautiful her home, she still wasn't happy. Really happy! Not like she had been before her husband got sick, when they had finished renovating that old relic of a mansion and had settled into a cozy warm life. And dreamer that she was, had assumed the bliss would go on forever!

She swiped a lone tear that slid down her cheek. She wondered wherever he was, what would he think about her actions? Then cringed as she knew how mad he'd be that she'd had burned the place, after the work they had done sanding and refinishing all the woodwork and floors in the house. The back-breaking days and nights he'd put in making it into a showpiece. Although, now she preferred to think that the fire had been an accident!

Lordy, she whimpered and straightened up; she had to get away from all the depressing thoughts that had suddenly sabotaged her psyche. She picked up her phone.

When Monica answered she forced a cheery greeting and said, "Girlfriend, let's go somewhere and check out the nightlife!"

Monica's husky laugh echoed across the line. "I was just settling in to take it easy tonight!"

Lindy got up and paced around her living room, then the kitchen and went on, "Monica, could you please, I've got to get out of here tonight!"

"Why, what's up?"

Lindy blew out a long breath. "I'm so down in the dumps. I just need to get out for awhile." Actually she wanted to talk but would even her good friend understand her?

"Well, I guess I could go," Monica said, "but it's going to take me an hour to get ready. I've been out in my yard all day but I need food."

"Thanks," Lindy said. "Let's brave a taxi ride and I'll pick you up this time. You can leave that silver bullet you drive at home in the garage!"

Already Lindy was feeling better as she soaked in a perfumed bath and took her time getting ready. She put in her brown contacts, expertly applied her make-up, swirled and fluffed her blond tresses. Then stepped into one of her special outfits; this time a black fitted sleeveless low cut slip of a dress, and her new Prada sling backs. Adding her Mother's diamond earrings she was ready. As she checked herself in a floor length mirror on her way out to the waiting taxicab, she looked good, and things were okay again.

Dining in Monterrey is more than just eating out; it is another one of the most popular leisure activities in town. Every night the restaurants fill up and every night the adventurous diner can sample a different cuisine. The variety of styles matches the range of cuisine; from greasy spoons that serve regional specialties to rooftop gourmet restaurants with gorgeous views of the city and countryside.

"I'd like to show you one of my favorite places Lindy," Monica said as they clung to the sides of the taxi as it careened around corners, vying for space on the streets downtown.

A short time later, surviving the hair-raising cab ride, the two forty-something aged women arrived at The Bella Vista, one of the finest restaurants in the city. Lindy's blond hair gleamed like silver in the neon lights as Monica tossed her black mane of hair over her shoulder.

"Buenas noches! Pedro," Monica said as they stepped in the door. She slipped a fifty dollar bill in his hand.

"Señorita Monica, Gracias." Pedro tucked the money in his pocket and smiled showing perfect white teeth.

"This is my friend, Lola Lindy, from the US," Monica said as she returned his big smile.

Pedro turned his attention to Lindy, bowed and exclaimed, "Señorita!" His white tuxedo coat accentuated his dark features. Always loving the machismo of Latin men, Lindy felt better yet and blew him a kiss.

"Have you got a table outside," Monica asked?

Pedro smiled grandly and nodded. "For you my beauties, uno!" And the women followed him through the dining room and out to a covered veranda where the tables were covered in white linen. Small lamps glowed in the center with a low vase of fresh roses nestled next to it. Heads turned as they tripped daintily behind Pedro, and in appreciation Lindy couldn't help herself and winked at several of the onlookers. Yes, she was feeling good!

Pedro pulled out their chairs for them and waved to a waiter to immediately see to their every wish. And within minutes, the waiter came over carrying a silver bucket with a bottle of champagne nestled in crushed ice.

"Compliments of Pedro," he said and opened the bottle with flourish and poured the sparkling wine.

"Well, this is wonderful," Lindy gushed as she daintily sipped. Then found her long silver cigarette holder in her purse and lit up a smoke as she looked around the place. "My Lord, this is beautiful," she exclaimed.

"I thought you'd like it. When I first came to Monterrey, I worked here." Monica waved to a group of people who sat across the room.

"Really, bartending?" Lindy asked.

"No, I was a waitress. And I made a ton of money."

"Hmm--, I bet you did." Lindy said as she eyed the glamorously dressed people at the tables. An hour flew by as the two women talked, laughed and drank champagne then the waiter placed menus on the table before them.

"What do you suggest I order," Lindy asked Monica as they decided that they'd better put some food in their stomach.

"Well, for God's sake, don't order beef!" Monica said as she drained the last of her wine and busied herself refilling their glasses.

Lindy looked at her friend with a puzzled look on her face and asked, "Why not?"

Monica laughed heartily, "Because, you just might get horsemeat!"

"Really, horsemeat?" Lindy gasped and rolled her eyes. And then froze as she looked up into the face of the approaching waiter as he came back to their table.

Good Lord, he seemed familiar! Then she realized he looked just like the young man in that vision that had flashed through her thoughts when she had been talking to Reed earlier.

As her eyes strayed to his name tag she almost fainted when she read Sam!

-24-

The Legion club in Birch Lake was jammed with locals as Reed walked in and joined the afternoon crowd. He pulled out his cigarettes, lit up and blew smoke towards the ceiling to join the clouds of it already there.

The cocktail hour hadn't officially started, but today since the news had spread about the body found in the lake, everyone had hurried to the local gathering place to hear the latest. Reed had to park the Corvette over on the next block as the streets were filled with pick-ups and RV's; even old man Harrison had his big yellow Cadillac edged right up to the front door of the saloon.

Ginger, the bartender, reached up on a shelf for the bottle of Crown Royal and poured Reed a double shot on ice and slid it over to him.

"Heard the news," she said, "Anybody know who it is?"

Reed hefted the glass and savored the whiskey as it warmed its way down his throat. "Not yet," he replied, "hard to tell, it's been in the water so long."

"Jesus," the bartender said, shook her head and headed over to new customers that had just come in.

Jerome was at the bar, wearing his usual plaid flannel shirt, bib overalls and his feed cap pulled firmly over his bald pate. Stan, one of the firemen, cook and owner of the Woodsmen Café was there, and even Flo the waitress of fifty some years, had slipped a coat over her uniform and hurried over when she heard the news. Most businesses had closed their doors early. The well-drilling and sewer company, Herman's Hardware, even the bank president was there. The bar hummed with brisk business and in the event anyone needed to do business with any of these people, most customers knew where to look for them.

Sheriff Jesse Montes came in and was immediately the center of attention as he came over to where Reed stood at the bar.

"Christ, I need a beer but I'll settle for a soda," he groaned and his constituents nodded sympathetically toward him. "We're going back out and drag the bottom of the lake, soon as the crew from Minneapolis gets here," he said loud enough so most of the people heard him. "I want to see what's been holding the body down there so long."

"It's going to be interesting." Reed nodded.

"It should give us something to go on," Jesse said.

"Anyone been reported missing lately?" Reed asked.

Jesse took a long swallow of the soda. "Nothing's come in." He wiped his mustache on the bar napkin, then added, "But I sent out inquiries to the five state area!" He drained the last dregs in the glass and banged it down on the bar. "Well, that's it for me."

He looked around at his friends in the saloon and said, "Folks, if any of you here has seen anything going on in the last few months or even weeks out of the ordinary, I need to know." He pulled the visor of his cap down lower on his forehead as he turned to go and added, "You know where to find me!"

The door closed on Jesse and the locals closed in on Reed. Stan, who had been at the scene, leaned in. "What a gristly sight," he said, "I think the corpse looked like it might have been a male."

"What makes you think that? All we've got is some rags and a pile of bones." Reed asked curiously.

"Well," Stan scratched his head and looked thoughtful. "I've been thinking. I remember the Fourth of July week-end when the town was flooded with strangers, Christ there must have been fifty tents spread out over in the park. Mostly guys, but some women too.

"Booze and fights?" Reed blew smoke rings.

"I heard Jesse made a few trips over there. I had to throw them out of my place a couple a times. They had money to spend!"

"Do you know where they were from?"

"No, but from what Flo could make out it sounded like they had gone to college together. Drove swell cars!"

"That so," Reed answered thoughtfully. "Well, the reports should be back in a few hours." Taking a last swallow of the whiskey, Reed put some bills on the bar. "I'll see you all later," he said and nodded to his friends, then took off in the Corvette. He headed towards the peace and quiet of his home.

His place was about five minutes down the road from town and by now the sun was going down sending long shadows across his private road as he sped through the heavy woods. The wild assortment of overgrown trees leaned into each other above and formed a tunnel of colorful foliage, then opened up to a breath taking scene of emerald green pines and gleaming clumps of birch in his yard. He parked the Corvette in the garage, and then mumbled goddamn, as he stood for a minute and gazed longingly out at the lake.

He had been looking forward to taking it easy and since he wouldn't be going out in his boat for awhile, he had his books. Deciding that, he cooked a steak and settled in at the round oak table in the kitchen. The last vestiges of sunlight cast a purple glow over the lake as he sat next to the huge glassed in bay windows and ate his dinner.

Finishing that, he turned some music on low and relaxed in his recliner with one of his John MacDonald mysteries. He had the author's complete collection and now finally, could enjoy another adventure of super sleuth Travis McGee who lived on his boat the Busted Flush in the Florida Keys. The character was smart and intuitive and often times operated just outside the law. Darkness settled in over his haven on the peninsula of Birch Lake as MacDonald's character settled the havoc created by roustabouts. Putting the book aside several hours later, he got up and poured himself a brandy. And again the afternoon's scene burned its way back in his mind.

He just couldn't forget it! This had happened too close to home! He had seen death before but this one was bad. To see the remains of a person reduced to almost nothing was a chilling sight!

What was the story behind this bundle of water logged remains? No amount of whiskey silenced his thoughts as he sat in his recliner.

Goddamn, he muttered, his book collection was great, but reading hadn't blocked out what he'd brought up on his hook on his lake.

Well, the hell with it, he grumbled abruptly getting out of his recliner. He couldn't just sit here and do nothing. Even though, he had no official position in town, he drove back into Birch Lake. Jesse's office was dark, but his deputy pulled up in his Jeep just as he was leaving.

He rolled down the car window. "Did the divers get here from Minneapolis yet?" he asked the young guy.

"Yah, Jesse just took off with them in their boat. I need to get some things, then get out there!" The deputy unlocked the office and disappeared inside as Reed waited in the doorway. After a few minutes he had gathered the items and came back to where Reed stood.

"Care if I ride out there with you?" Reed asked. Actually, he had known the deputy since the young man had been a toddler, being the son of one of his buddies.

"No problem," the guy said and they drove their vehicles down to the dock where numerous cars were parked next to the water.

And as they neared the activity out on the lake in the boat, the Sheriff's voice carried across the water, and they heard more shocking news as he roared, "God almighty is that another one?"

-25-

Lindy gulped her champagne and tried to compose herself after glimpsing the resemblance between their waiter and the face of the young man that had flashed through her thoughts earlier. She'd been talking to Reed on the phone, when he said he'd caught something on his hook while fishing that needed investigating. And now this young man who was waiting to take their order in the restaurant was wearing a name tag that said Sam; the name that went with the face in that quick scene.

"Señoritas, what can I bring you?" He asked and stood ready and waiting.

Monica lifted her champagne flute. "Salad! Sammy, it's so good to see you again. How is your mama?"

He smiled broadly and said, "Gracias, she's happy to be at home."

She turned to Lindy and said. "Sam's family owns this place and his mother was my boss when I started working here."

Lindy listened and politely raised her glass.

Monica continued, "She started this place decades ago, then it was next to a tattoo parlor. Can you imagine?"

Lindy wondered, could you order a sandwich and go over there and have lunch while they burned and inked their artwork in your flesh? Shaking her head to clear the picture from the thought, she suddenly had to forcefully straighten her face to keep a silly giggle from escaping her lips.

"Really!" She murmured then in reply.

Monica added, "Everything that comes out of the kitchen is cooked by one of her personally trained family members."

"Wow," was all Lindy could say then thoroughly impressed as she scanned the menu again. "Everything sounds delicious, but I don't have the faintest idea what it is."

"Let's start with some appetizers," Monica pointed out several items to Sam who then rushed off to the kitchen.

"This is really a beautiful place," Lindy commented again looking around.

"There's talk about opening another!" Monica lit a cigarette and the smoke spiraled up into the star filled sky.

Minutes later, Sam returned with the beginning of their three hour feast. And, during the course of the evening they enjoyed Ceviche, a national dish of raw fish and shellfish, turtle steak which did taste like chicken, braised lamb and poached swordfish. All of it listed under exotic names and highly spiced, accompanied with fresh vegetables. Several hours later for dessert, Sam brought out a huge platter of fresh fruits of every color and description, nestled in ice and creamy dipping sauces.

"Delicious, isn't it," Monica said.

"Lordy, if I ate like this often I'd be big as a house," Lindy grinned as she looked at her friend.

"Eating out is what we do here." Monica said and tossed her head to keep her hair from falling in her face. "The basic menu is tortillas, beans and rice and the drink is tequila. Add something from the sea, various red meats, and that's our menu, all done up in creative variations according to your pocketbook. Then we have loads of fruits and vegetables available year around."

In Lindy's travels, she had dined out in five star restaurants and the cuisine here measured up equally with some of the best places she'd been in. She recognized the colorful presentation and knew it was considered as important as the content of an item.

"I'm impressed," she said. "Who owns this?"

"It's the Mercado's; there are three brothers who took over for their mother. Then there are their sons; Pedro, whom you met at the door and Sam and Paco who also work as hosts and waiters. Sam and Paco are twins, identical. Wives and kids work here too."

"Really." Lindy murmured.

"Oh yeah, this is a tightly run family business. They're rich and powerful and controlled by Mama Mercado. She comes in unannounced at times and raises holy hell if things aren't running according to her standards."

"Are they?" Lindy asked curiously. Having been in the restaurant business for years in her career, she was familiar with the operations.

Monica laughed. "They all know if they want to work for the "Big M," as their mother is called, they have to tow the mark!"

"How old is the mother?" Lindy lit a cigarette and inhaled the smoke.

"She's in her eighties now. There's a picture of her in the foyer."

"Oh, I remember seeing it when we came in the door," Lindy said and added, "looked like someone with a lot of authority."

"She did and still does," Monica said. "She has a lot of health problems now."

"Serious ones?" Lindy picked a strawberry off the plate of fruit.

"I don't know for sure, they're all pretty quiet about it. I spend the holidays with the family every year."

Lindy nodded. "I know it's an honor to be included in a family's festivity in this culture."

"That first year I was here I was terribly lonely and Mama Mercado took me home with her and showed me such love and caring," Monica said with a catch in her throat, "She saved me!"

Lindy ran a hand through her spiky blond hair. Checked each ear to make sure her mother's diamond earrings were still safely enclosed over each lobe. Then asked, "Monica, why didn't you ever let someone know where you were when you disappeared years ago?"

Monica hung her head. "I know I should have. After I broke up with who I thought was the love of my life, I was devastated and just needed to heal. Then I just worked like a demon and the years fell away."

"But Monica," Lindy huffed, "You could have let me know where you were!"

Monica leaned over and touched her wrist, "Lindy, you were busy fixing up that mausoleum of a house and you were happily married, you didn't need me to take you down."

"Lordy, years went by," Lindy scolded.

"Yeah, I know and I'm sorry." Monica raised her glass. "Hey, let's not get maudlin, Lindy. We're both here now in this sexy country so let's celebrate!" And, they began toasting each other and right away two well dressed good-looking men pounced on them drawn by their high-spirited antics.

"Señoritas," they echoed and bowed from the waist and reached out a hand.

"Si, gracias," Monica said and got up off her chair. Lindy followed suit and realized they were being asked to dance.

"Well, I don't know this dance but I'll try," she said to the smiling man and let him draw her over to a small intimate dance floor.

"Gracias," was all he said and clasped a muscled arm around her waist and swirled her in a circle of spins that left her in a dizzy fog as the room swam before her. She hung on for dear life with a silly smile pasted on her face as the man gyrated to the beat of the Spanish music. She caught a glimpse of Monica and saw she was dancing effortlessly to the music.

"Lord, that was hard," Lindy exclaimed as they came back to their table. "What the hell was that dance? She asked curiously.

"That is called the Paso do'ble," Monica answered and downed half of the champagne in her glass.

"That was what we were doing?" Lindy gulped hers, caught up in the beat of the mariachi music.

The rest of the evening the two women drank their champagne, smoked cigarettes and danced. At 2:00 AM the musicians packed their instruments up and disappeared and the crowded room began to empty.

"Sam, we need our bill," Monica motioned to the waiter with a look of disapproval on her face. He had taken off his white server's coat and was sitting at the next table whispering in the ear of a beautiful woman. She'd noticed his obvious flirtation all evening.

Brought back to the moment, he guiltily jumped up and came over. "Señoritas, no ticket!"

"No charge?" Monica asked.

"Sí, Pedro says no ticket!" He smiled and hurried back to the table where the woman was waiting.

"They do it all the time," Monica murmured and they both left a pile of bills on the table for a tip.

As they walked by the next table where the waiter was sitting, Monica playfully tapped him on the shoulder and said, "Paco, you better take time out of your busy love life and do your laundry and quite wearing your brother's things!"

"Sí, sí gracias," he said and smiled.

Making their way out of the restaurant Lindy looked at Monica curiously.

Monica laughed, "Sam and Paco are constantly playing jokes on everyone. Remember they are identical in appearances; the only difference is Paco is the womanizer of the two!"

"So this was Paco wearing Sam's uniform and nametag. Did you know?" Lindy asked curiously.

Monica shook her head as they sidestepped tables and people on their way out to the street. "Oh sure, I can always tell. But Sam is gay and the serious one, and wouldn't fool around here at work."

As Monica straightened out the true identities of the two men, the vision Lindy had glimpsed earlier while talking to Reed came back to haunt her. She paled as the picture of the ravaged body of the young man and the name Sam sprang to the surface of her thoughts again.

What should she do? She couldn't tell Monica that quite possibly one of the Mercado family members was dead! Was it even true?

"Come on, we need a taxi," Monica said and hurried Lindy out to the street. And, instead of giving the driver their home addresses when they settled in, she instructed the driver to take them to a place called the Hacienda.

"Where are we going?" Lindy asked curiously still in a quandary worrying about what to do.

"The night's still young," Monica said and took out her make-up and began to redo her lipstick. "Relax Lola Lindy. To properly close an evening out we dance until daylight!" She spritzed perfume over herself and flashed Lindy a smile.

And the taxi driver eyed them admiringly in the rear-view mirror all the while driving at break neck speed around the traffic circles of downtown Monterrey.

-26-

Jesse Montes's voice carried across the lake to Reed and the deputy as they neared the crime scene.

"Goddamn, it sounds like they found another body?" Reed yelled over the noise of the motorboat as they raced. The surface of the water was black and still like the night, but as they got close the area was filled with garish search lights and action. Now the water seemed to rise and fall with a mournful sigh.

The deputy slowed the departments craft and sidled in closer just as divers hoisted a body over the side of the craft. Reed recognized the men from Midwest Search and Rescue as they assisted Jesse and the Fire Chief as they laid the remains of what was left of another corpse on a blanket. An eerie silence spread over the men as they stood horrified by the unsightly ravaged body, again, only a pile of bones and rags. After a moment Jesse took command and spoke to the divers.

"Did you see anything else down there?" he asked.

Taking off their gear the two men shook their heads and heaved themselves over the side of the craft.

"Okay then, let's go in." Jesse adjusted his cap and grumbled; "Now I got two bodies. What the hell is going on?" And within minutes the boats headed back into town, their lights lending a carnival appearance to the parade.

The coroner/medical examiner, who also owned the funeral home stood waiting with the official van when they docked, and the undertaker whisked the body into the vehicle and took off with the siren blaring. By now, this was the wee hours of the night and the townspeople were usually safely tucked into their beds. But Birch Lake was a quiet village and finding bodies in their waters was very unsettling and soon, lights began coming on all over the town as people came awake and fumbled for robes and went to their windows.

As the men got in their cars and took off from the dock, Reed gunned the Corvette into action and followed Jesse back to his office.

"What can I do to help?" he asked the sheriff after the place quieted down.

Jesse held up a hand and picked up the phone. "Susan," he said into the receiver, "I'm going to be tied up here for the rest for the night. We got another one out of the lake." He replaced the receiver and said to Reed, "The wife nags about being home alone at night," he grumbled as he went over to an alcove and started a pot of coffee.

"Conners," he said, as he finished and went to his desk and swept a mess of papers over to one side. "I'll take all the help you got!" Sitting down he continued, "I should have some information soon from the coroner."

"Have you gotten any inquiries from the missing person's bureau lately?" Reed asked and took out his cigarettes after seeing an ashtray on the desk.

"Not anything," Jesse answered and sat back and opened a drawer in the desk and withdrew a slim cigar. He raised it to his nose and sniffed, then lit up.

"I should be hearing from them today," Jesse said.

Reed unzipped his light leather jacket and leaned back in his chair. "Stan said something interesting earlier. That maybe this could be connected to that gang of people who showed up here over the July Fourth holiday."

"Bunch of rude shits!" Jesse commented dryly as he blew smoke in the air. "They were here for three, four days. I had to go out several times to quiet them down. The park edges up against those new houses, you know."

Reed knew the area. A developer had come in and bought prime lakeshore and built large luxury homes which were soon bought up. The residents were referred to as the "swells" by the locals. "I remember," Reed nodded.

"The tenants called and bitched like hell about the loud music and the fireworks they were shooting off."

"Who were they?" Reed asked.

"Some class reunion if I remember."

"Did you get the name of the school?" Reed stood up and went in search of a cup for the coffee that had finished perking.

Jesse ran a hand over his face and mumbled, "Nah-- didn't think it was important at the time to find out."

"Did you get license plate numbers?" Reed asked.

"That I did, but it didn't tell me anything! All were rentals from Brainerd and Bemidji, probably some from Minneapolis, too!" Jesse exhaled a cloud of smoke that swirled over his head. "I was glad to see the last of them when they pulled out. Left trash all over the place!" He hunched over his desk.

"Stan wondered if these bodies might belong to someone who had been with that crowd," Reed opened doors in the little alcove that served as a cupboard.

"God almighty," Jesse said and just sat at his desk as Reed found a second empty cup and poured coffee for both of them. Reed studied his friend's face. Jesse looked tired, damned tired.

And Jesse was deep in thought, and could count on one hand the number of weeks he had left to serve as Sheriff and he just didn't know if he had the energy to get through this. The wife was bored and bitching about his long hours and the in-laws were coming to spend weeks again at the house. He closed his eyes for a minute and let his thinking ramble over a plan he'd been working on for several years now. Really a dream escape plan! And maybe that was all it was, just a pipe-dream. As Reed set the cup of coffee down on his desk Jesse forced his thoughts back to the present.

The small room at the Birch Lake Sheriff's Department was silent as both men drank their coffee and blew smoke towards the ceiling. Soon the sun would come up over the forest to the east and send its colorful rays over the lake and another day would begin.

By now the Woodsmen café was firing up its grills and plugging in the coffee urns getting ready to throw open it's doors promptly at five AM. Flo bustled in wearing her usual white nylon uniform and apron. A red, lacy edged hanky peeked out of a pocket on her left shoulder and matched her red perfectly-permed hair. The radio blared country music and soon the mouth-watering aromas of bacon and freshly brewed coffee wafted through the exhaust and swirled out to the block-long business district. By now most of the town was up and if they opened their doors or windows and got a whiff, they knew instantly what time it was.

"Want to get some eggs?" Reed asked as a whiff slipped in through the cracks around the window in the small office.

"Ahh—yup," Jesse said and stood up. He switched off the lights and they walked across the street to the café. Already several vehicles were lined up waiting for the place to open and just then Flo appeared and importantly unlocked the door. Soon she was flying around the room filling orders; thanking God she'd worn her old foam filled nurse's shoes that day.

Within minutes, Reed and Jesse had steaming plates of crisp bacon, eggs over easy and potato home fries with onions and green peppers. Butter dripped off the toasted cinnamon bread as Reed took his first bite. The men were silent as they wolfed down their cholesterol loaded breakfast, enjoying every minute of it.

"Well, that was good," Reed commented dryly after wiping the crumbs off his chin, "but it means I'll have to spend an extra hour doing sit-ups for the next week!"

"The wife won't even keep decent food in the house," Jesse grumbled as he used a piece of toast to mop up the last of the eggs from his plate.

"Tough," Reed agreed and raised his cup for a refill as Flo came around with the coffee pot.

"Top mine off too, will you darlin'?" Jesse lifted his cup and shook his head. "Another night with no sleep."

Reed was wide awake now, but knew he'd feel the effects of no sleep as the day wore on.

"Hey buddy," he said now, "why don't you take off and catch a nap for a few hours. I've got some ideas I want to run down and I can meet up with you later today."

"Nah--," Jesse shook his head. "But, what you got in mind?"

"Jesse, I've got to agree with Stan that these two people must have been here with that bunch of hell-raisers over the Fourth of July. For starters, I'll go and check the rental outfits in Brainerd and Bemidji," and added, "I can call down to Minneapolis. They would have had to produce identification to get the wheels."

"Right," Jesse said. "Then we've got to question the residents around the park area. Could be someone saw something interesting!"

"I could help with that." Reed put out the cigarette and stood.

"Appreciate it Conners! Okay, I'm on my way back to the office to start the damned paper work. Let's meet up here at five!"

-27-

As the taxi careened around corners, narrowly missing other vehicles, Lindy and Monica clutched the car seat for support. It was after 2:00 AM on a week-end night and downtown Monterrey was lit up like Christmas. The two women had left one night spot and were on the way to another.

"I can't believe all these people are still out?" Lindy commented stealing a peek out the window at a street corner.

"We're night people here." Monica laughed, "We don't really get moving until the cocktail hour!"

Lindy nodded, "I think I like it."

Monica bent over at the waist and scrubbed her hands through her hair and made it stand up in a cloud of wild curls.

"Wow that looks good!" Lindy commented eying her friend's long hair then checked her own in her compact mirror and did the same to her short spiky hair-do.

Within minutes the taxi came to a screeching halt in front of huge double doors in front of a hotel. El Cid was the name and another sign proclaimed the Hacienda cantina just inside the door.

The taxi driver jumped out, opened their door and held out his hand for his money.

"Gracias Señoritas," he said and unabashedly counted the number of bills they pressed in his palm.

Latin music rocked the lobby of the hotel as the two women teetered on their stiletto sandals to the door of the club. As Monica opened the door the throbbing music fell out on their ears and the flashing lights blinded them momentarily as they stood outlined in the glare.

Grabbing Lindy's arm, Monica pulled her into the room, through the gyrating mass of people on the dance floor and over to a bar that lined a long wall.

"Good lord," Lindy yelled over the music, "this is crazy!" The crowd looked to be a mixture of tourists and local jet setters. All of them dressed fashionably and dancing to a tango beat.

Lindy's sleek blonde appearance and Monica's wild dark look caused a slight stir among the customers as they perched on their stools. Monica waved to friends scattered around the room, then leaned over the bar towards the bartender and kissed the air.

The bartender beamed. His coal black hair gleamed in the lights as he stood before them.

"Señoritas," he said expectantly.

"Carlos, this is my friend Lola Lindy. We'll have some tequila," Monica said

"Sĩ Gracias," he bowed and expertly filled their orders. And again the women danced and were the center of attention.

Hours later, as dawn broke they bade their acquaintances goodnight and gathered up their purses. Caught up in the flurry of the departing crowd, Lindy glanced over to a corner booth where several Latin men were still seated. She suddenly stumbled and caught her breath.

Rio, the Mayor of Monterrey was there. The man, who had drugged and raped her just a few months ago. He had broken into her house and knew her real identity! When she dared steel another look, she almost fainted as she recognized the faces of the other men seated with him. On unsteady legs she almost ran out of the hotel.

"Monica, did you see Rio in there?" She gasped once they were outside, as they waited for a taxi.

"Sure, he gets around." Monica waved down a cab.

Lindy faltered and whispered, "Do you know those men that were with him?" Lindy's anguished eyes were huge in her pale face.

"Sure, I don't know them well, but I've seen them around town for years. The D'Agustino family, and the Mercado's who I worked for and Rio, the Mayor are all related!" Monica stated as a taxi rattled to a stop for them. "All three families are related, cousins I think," she added.

Lindy stood frozen to the spot. Horrors, this was her worst nightmare!

"Come on, what's wrong?" Monica asked as she looked back out the door of the car at Lindy when she didn't move.

Suddenly realizing the need to get away fast, Lindy jerked to attention, climbed in and slammed the door of the cab.

"Oh God, oh God," she moaned and took a shuttered breath. Her heart thudded in her chest.

How could this have happened? How could she have walked right into the country the D'Agustino brothers called home? The men the FBI had arrested for drugs and worse, Mario, the man she had had a romance with, and had been a witness as he murdered a man.

She clasped her bare arms around her chest as a chill crept over her body. She remembered the threat blazing in Mario's eyes as she had sat on the witness stand in South Carolina and pointed him out as the murderer to the court. That look in his eyes had been no mistake! He would make her pay!

"What on earth is wrong?" Monica asked seeing Lindy's pale face in the morning sun's rays. "Are you sick?"

Lindy sat motionless, too scared to move but her mind raced.

What the hell should she do now? Surely Mario and Rio had seen her dancing and whirling around the dance floor. Laughing and having fun while she sat at the bar. Seeing these men again jolted her back to a frightening reality, and seeing them together doubled her panic.

She opened her purse and fumbled for her cigarettes. Finally getting one lit, she tried to still her shaking hands as she held it to her lips and inhaled.

"For God's sake, what the hell is wrong?" Monica asked again.

Lindy finally managed to whisper. "Those men with Rio," she swallowed and her voice wavered, "They're the men I testified against!" By now, Monica had pretty much sobered too after seeing Lindy's fear.

"You testified against the D'Agustino family, for God's sake why?" Both women clutched the seat as they careened around a corner.

Lindy looked up to the driver to see if he might be listening to their conversation. Then, whispered again, "I saw Mario kill a man!"

"What are you talking about? You know them?" Monica asked, aghast at the revelation.

Lindy swallowed over her fright and leaned in closer and said, "It's a long story Monica. I met Mario and his brother in South Carolina last year. We dated for awhile and one time when we were out on the ocean in his boat, I saw him shoot a man. The FBI forced me into testifying against him for them in a trial. He and his brother had been arrested for bringing drugs into the US!" Lindy blew out a breath and added, "They got off!"

"This is bizarre. I can't believe the upstanding D'Agustino family would be involved in drugs! Are you sure, Lindy?"

Lindy took another drag of the cigarette. "Of course, I'm sure. I was there!" She huddled into a corner of the cab. "He will kill me," she whispered!

For once Monica was silent. After a minute she said, "Good God, I've heard an occasional rumor over the years, but in this country you don't poke around in other people's business."

"He will kill me," Lindy repeated and whispered, "I've got to do something fast!" Just then the cab came to an abrupt stop in front of her house. She had a handful of bills ready and flung them at the driver and scrambled out. "I'll call you later," she whispered to Monica and ran. She slammed and locked the door in her house and dropped down on the couch, totally scared stiff.

Lordy, what would she do now?

-28-

After bringing up the corpse on his hook while out fishing and then watching as another ravaged body surfaced, Reed had given up on getting any sleep that night. Both he and Sheriff Montes had agreed that the visitors who had camped in the city park over the Fourth of July week-end were suspect. During their stay, the sheriff had been called out numerous times to investigate the commotion residents had complained about, and he had noted all the cars parked over there were rentals. Figuring the people had flown into Brainerd, Bemidji or even the twin cities, rented a car and drove the remaining miles to Birch Lake, Reed took off for the hour drive to Brainerd first. He'd start the most obvious and get the names of the people who had rented those vehicles. It was still early and he should be getting close when they opened for business.

He was tired. He had just started his long awaited break after weeks of hustling in the investigative business, and on his second day out on his lake, enjoying the goddamn peace and quiet, he had the misfortune of catching a body on his fishing line. Which was bad enough, but then several hours later another body had shown up! He shook his head and groaned as he drove; that sure as hell put an end to my paradise!

He slipped George Strait's latest CD in the player and settled into the drive. The northern countryside rolled by showing off the last of its vibrant fall colors. In the hills around the resort town of Nisswa, a mist hung in the valley forcing him to shift gears in the Corvette and slow to almost crawling. Further down the highway, just as the sun was coming up, a deer sprang out of the ditch and ran across the road. He cussed, he knew better than to speed through this part of the country especially at this time of the day. He drove on, slower now, but the image of the two pathetic corpses continued to haunt him. Also possible scenarios of how they could have ended up in the lake.

Then while in the debts of these deep contemplations, Reed suddenly remembered he'd completely forgotten to call Lindy. Regret flashed through his thoughts. He hadn't meant to ignore her, but things had just gotten in the way again. Well, he had time now. He dialed her number and heard the phone ring in the distance. He thought over what he would say to her. Well hell, he frowned, the important thing right now is that she know that she is a free woman! Over the miles the ringing echoed on and on, and again, there was no answer.

And he had to admit he was relieved. This misunderstanding between them had gone on too long already, but he was not anxious to open that door of communication now. Not in the middle of this apparent murder investigation he'd volunteered to help with. He cleared his throat and pushed away a small sliver of guilt that she was walking around thinking she was still a wanted woman, owing his company a million dollars! But how the hell could he let her know how she stood with the law if she couldn't be found? And he had tried time and again to straighten it out with her.

Not getting to bed the night before with all the commotion going on, Reed Conners was in a foul mood as he approached downtown Brainerd. Even in this small town at this early hour the streets were jammed with traffic. The upcoming week-end, plus a promised sunny fall day brought out countless cars and vans loaded with families and pets to swell over the resort area and muck up the country-side.   He leaned on his horn as a RV slowly lumbered through a stop light.

Finally locating the address he needed, Reed parked the Corvette. Rudy's Rentals it was called and the nametag on the shirt the man behind the counter wore said Rudy.

"You need some wheels," he asked as Reed stepped in. Rudy was overweight, bald and his face was round and flushed.

As Reed approached the desk he reached out a hand. "Name is Reed Conners," he said and after shaking hands showed Rudy his ID. He went on, "I'm from over in Birch Lake. I'm giving the Sheriff a hand," he said waiting a minute as Rudy studied his identification.

"Yah, I know Jesse," Rudy said looking concerned. "What can I do?"

Not wasting time Reed said, "Over the Fourth of July week-end we had a slew of people in town camping in the park. We're thinking they flew here to Brainerd and then rented cars to drive to Birch." He wiped an impatient hand through his sandy hair as it fell over his forehead.

"Over that week-end you say," Rudy said thoughtfully. "Yeah, I remember, that whole week was crazy. Why, something happen?"

"Well, something did, and that's what we're trying to piece together." Reed didn't want to say too much, talk spread like wild fire around the area.

Rudy looked at Reed expectantly and then volunteered, "For Christ's sake, I had to borrow cars from all over the country to fill the demand! I raised the prices and they didn't care!"

"I'm wondering if I could get a list of the people who rented from you that whole week," Reed asked, hopeful the guy wouldn't ask too many questions.

"Well," Rudy mumbled and stood back, "What's going on?"

Reed hesitated, not wanting to divulge too much. But if he didn't clue Rudy in, Rudy could refuse to give out the information he needed and that could mean it might take days to get a judge to issue a warrant for the release of the names.

Reed made a quick decision. "Rudy," he said, "I need your help but you need to keep this quiet."

"Trust me, I'm a business man," Rudy pledged.

"Okay, here's what has happened, Rudy. We fished up two bodies from our lake yesterday and from the looks of them we figured they had been in the water for a few months!"

"Jesus," Rudy said and his ruddy face paled. "You think that someone who rented a car from me did it? It's possible but of course we don't know yet. That's why I need to start checking out these people!" Rudy shook his head. "Okay," he mumbled a worried frown on his face. "Give me a few minutes." He turned to his computer.

As Reed waited impatiently another thought came to mind. "Hey Rudy, did you happen to catch what the occasion was that brought all these people here?"

"I didn't, but you know," Rudy stopped punching keys on the computer and scratched his head, "my clerk will be in soon and she probably heard. She likes to kibitz with customers."

Reed took up a magazine and paged through the colorful pages, but still the awful scene of the ravaged bodies haunted him. He tried again to force the thoughts aside. As soon as he got home he'd get on his phone and see what he could dig up about these people.

Thankfully, within minutes the silence was broken as Rudy's printer began to spew out pages containing names, addresses and telephone numbers of his customers who had rented vehicles during the Fourth of July holiday week.

"That should do it," Rudy said as he handed Reed the copies. "I own the place across town too so this is from both places."

"Appreciate it," Reed said. Handing Rudy his card, he added, "Can you give me a ring if your clerk remembers anything?"

Checking his watch, Rudy said, "It won't be long."

Reed left Brainerd and headed back towards Birch Lake anxious to get started tracking down these people. The list totaled thirty four names, with addresses from all around the US.

What the hell had brought these people to his part of the country? As he grumbled over this the same scenery flew by as he cruised just a bit over the speed limit. But now the country gleamed brilliantly as the morning sun climbed higher in the sky. He opened the window and a whiff of burning leaves fanned into the car. Fifteen minutes into the trip, his cell phone rang and Rudy's voice came on the line.

"Conners," he said, "My clerk just got here and she says they were all in the restaurant business!"

"That's interesting," Reed answered.

Rudy added, "She thinks it might have something to do with a school they all went to."

"Yeah that helps, anything else," Reed asked?

"That seems to be it Conners. I'll get in touch if something else comes to mind!"

Reed closed the cell phone and concentrated on driving. He figured when he got back to Birch, he'd stop by Jesse's office first to see if anything had come in from the medical examiner, then head home, make a pot of coffee and get started on the list.

The Sheriff was at his desk busily filling out reports when Reed got there. "Any luck," he asked?

Reed nodded. "I got a list of everyone who rented cars from both places. Anything new come in here?"

Jesse looked up from his paperwork. "Preliminary examinations show they were both male."

Reed nodded his head in the direction of the local funeral home in the next block. "Does he have room over there for these two? Doesn't he have full house after the flu hit the rest home?"

"Yeah, he's got them stacked up. His hands are full being the medical examiner, the coroner and the undertaker." Jesse shuffled the papers looking for some notes.

"What else you got going?" Reed asked.

"I've got the deputies out checking the park, course if there had been anything of importance over there it would more than likely be gone by now." Jesse shrugged his shoulders. "They'll start door to door this afternoon."

Reed turned to go. "I'll get on these names and give you a call if I come across something interesting."

At home, Reed settled in at the oak kitchen table with his coffee and the list. The view of the lake through the large windows was breathtaking in the noon sunshine. A family of loons swam by with a baby riding on the back of one of the parents. Even through the closed panes of glass, Reed heard the protective squawking they voiced as they guided their precious cargo over the waves.

Reed's first call was to a man in New Jersey. No answer there, but he left a message asking the person to please return the call, collect of course. The second one was a wrong number, the third a no answer. As he went down the list, if he got lucky and connected with someone, they either hung up or refused to answer any of his questions. One told him to "go fuck himself!"

He took a break and lit a cigarette. His gut told him he was on the right track and sooner or later he would get lucky!

And then his next call was a pleasant surprise when a woman answered and said she was visiting, her son was out, but she could take a message.

After identifying himself Reed took a chance and asked, "By any chance do you know if your son went on a trip up to northern Minnesota over the Fourth of July week-end?"

Expecting a curt reply, he was surprised when she said, "Maybe, I'm sure that was the time he was there!"

Hitting pay dirt Reed took a swallow of his potent coffee and wagered another inquiry. "May I ask what the occasion was?"

"Well let's see," the women said and after a minute went on. "Yes, yes, that was their annual get-together. You see they all went to chef's school together."

Reed asked conversationally, "Do you get to visit your son often?"

"No," she hesitated, "only once in a while when he has time. He's so busy!"

The woman sounded frail.

"What business is your son in?' Reed asked then but feeling guilty for pumping the lady for information. He ventured further and asked, "Where is your son's business located?"

Now her voice wavered, and then sprang out garbled. "Oh, you see he owns those places with the chickens on the roofs!"

For a minute Reed was stumped, chickens on the roofs? What was she talking about? "Do you mean McDaniel's?" he asked.

"They're just small places!" She sounded apologetic. Reed thought.

Did the woman's son own one of the biggest take out fast food chains scattered across the map? Or did she mean those two Golden Chicken diners in Minneapolis. He studied the area code on the number he'd dialed and realized it was from around the Minneapolis area.

"They get together once in a while," she added then, now very articulate.

"When do you think I could talk to your son?" Reed asked.

"Well, I don't know," she said sounding vague. "He promised to take me out to breakfast today and he still hasn't come to get me!" Then she clunked the telephone down and the line went dead. Apparently she was done talking!

Feeling guilty about pushing her for information, and then not getting a chance to properly thank her for talking to him, Reed shook his head in sympathy. The poor woman sounded as if she might be suffering from Alzheimer's or the after effects of a stroke.

Should he call back? Well, maybe later. For now, he knew the group was a gathering of individuals affiliated with the food business. So now all he had to figure out was; what the hell might have happened that would have caused two of these culinary folks to get tossed into the lake in his town?

-29-

Getting home at dawn after partying with Monica, Lindy huddled in shock on the couch in her living room in her dress and high-heels.

How could this have happened? She had traveled thousands of miles to escape the repercussions of testifying against the D'Agustino brothers, and now she had unknowingly walked right into their world. Mexico was their home! They had been just across the room at a table with the Mayor of Monterrey in that dark cantina. Surely they had seen her and Monica there!

Had they followed her home? Was someone outside her house right now?

She clasped her arms around her chest as she peered at the windows. Had she checked the locks lately, especially the one on the back door? She couldn't remember! With a sinking feeling she realized then, no lock would stop them when they came for her. Fear prickled at her heels.

The people she feared the most lived right here in her adopted city! She hadn't dared look back at them when they had left the cantina, but she was sure, right now, there were plans in motion for her.

She had to get away fast. Now, tonight! But where could she go? If she did manage to escape, how long would it be before they would find her again? She was up against dangerous men, and now she would have the brothers, plus Rio after her!

Suddenly all the fire went out of her as she realized she had run out of options, in the end they would find her! Alone and helpless, she cried out. She was going to die! Tears ran down her face, streaking her mascara.

But I'm not ready, she protested. I want my life! She took a sobbing breath and for a moment wondered how it would feel to have to give it up. She covered her eyes to shut that out and, in anguish cried out Reed's name. After a minute, she took another breath, this time a steadying one. Reed, yes he could help her! He always knew what to do.

She had to leave, get away from this house right now before Mario found her. But she had things to do before she could leave the city. In her bedroom she changed into a shirt and slacks, hastily packed and grabbed her make-up, a big purse, and her important papers, then, called for a taxi. Chills ran down her back as she dashed outside and ran to the cab minutes later, fearful any second someone would grab her.

The sun was heating up the Monterrey morning and she swallowed over a lump of sadness that caught in her throat at having to leave her beautiful home.

"Take me to the Posada Hotel," she informed the driver, deciding on a busy tourist attraction on the opposite side of town. As usual he took off at a hair-raising speed, but now Lindy didn't mind. And keeping close watch out the back window of the cab, no one seemed to be interested in her actions. Yet!

Wearing large sun glasses and a scarf over her blond tresses when she arrived at the hotel, instead of signing in as Lola Lane as she was known in Monterrey or her real name, she used one of her favorites and wrote Lana Loyalton with a flourish.

"And how long will you be staying with us Señorita Lana?" a desk clerk asked.

"Several days," Lindy said and added, "I'll pay cash for it now."

"Sí Señorita," the young man put a hand over a stifled yawn.

Grabbing the key, she ran to her room and locked the door. Lordy, she needed coffee and after pacing around endlessly, room service finally delivered her order. Now she needed to make a plan! She guessed by now her picture would be plastered on wanted sheets at all the borders, so she had to work out a way to get back into the US without getting arrested! She had to get back home.

When she'd crossed the border months ago, she'd dressed as a pregnant woman and worn a wig. Of course, the bulge that protruded out of her midsection was a pillow stuffed with money. Her heart lurched in her chest as she relived that stressful trip, but she had no choice now, she'd have to chance it again to get back to the US.

First of all though, she needed to collect all her money which she had hidden in safe deposit boxes around town. She hurriedly began to make the rounds of the banks to collect her million plus dollars. And luckily she hadn't invested it yet. Each stop produced a fatter purse, but fashion had declared it chic to carry large bags this season, so she smiled at the guards at each establishment as she glibly went about her task. On the second day, at Al Guiness's bank, she ran smack into the man as she came out of the vault. Lordy, she had hoped she could slip in and out without seeing him.

"My dear Lola," he said in his clipped British voice, "It's a pleasure to see you."

He reached for her hand and brought it to his lips. She cringed inwardly as his cold hard lips touched her skin.

"Why it's nice to see you too, Al," she lied. Monica had told her he was dangerous, and one of the clan as she had begun to think of the men that were forcing her to run. She swallowed hard as she realized, more than likely he knew who she was, too!

"Have you come to discuss investments, I'm free this morning for you, Lola." Always groomed elegantly, today he was attired in black cashmere suit with a gleaming white shirt and tie. His gray hair and van-dyke beard clipped to perfection.

For just a second, Lindy's edgy thoughts tricked her and she had to stifle a sudden nervous giggle as she wondered if he ever allowed sex to muss his perfect appearance.

She faked a smile. "Al, I can't today, I just stopped in to put some things away for safe keeping, but next week I'll have more time."

"Promise me Lola, in the meantime, the markets are up. I can make you rich and famous!" He ran a hand over her arm as he stood close.

"That's for me!" Lindy declared. "I'll call and we'll get together." She blew him a kiss and hurried out of the bank, but she could feel his probing eyes drilling into her back as she fled. Creep, she thought, too bad you won't get a chance to play with my money.

She had one more stop to make and then she would be ready to make that trip back home to safety.

But would Reed Conners help her or would he toss her to the wolves?

-30-

Reed took another swallow of his coffee as he sat at the oak table in the kitchen and pensively studied the lake, and wondered who the hell had used it for a grave for its victims? Never before, had anything like this happened so close to home!

He lit a cigarette, and then forced his thoughts back to what he'd been working on. Before him lay the list of people who had rented cars in Brainerd that week of the Fourth of July. But again as he continued down the list, he was met with voice mail, hang-ups and rudeness. Finally giving up, he stood up and shuffled the papers into a pile. By now the sun was going down sending long shadows over the sandy beach and the dock where his boat gently rocked.

Goddamn, this was a great time to launch, but now, all accesses were closed until further notice.

He swiped his hair off his forehead with an impatient hand. He was pissed and hungry. After spending the whole day on the phone, he had gotten nowhere, except for that woman in Minneapolis who might or might not have something to add.

Did she know something that held the key to this homicide? Or was she a lonely woman suffering from an illness. He'd try contacting her again first thing tomorrow, he muttered to the walls.

Standing in his shower a short time later and letting the hot water sluice over his tense shoulders, he tried out a few tunes. Anything, to take his mind off the events of the last days and after trying out several country hits he settled on an old church song, he learned as a kid when his folks would take him to Sunday school. His voice resonated throughout the log house as he scrubbed.

Minutes later, dressed in freshly pressed jeans, another favorite Italian knit sweater and a pair of his highly polished Western boots, Reed wheeled the Corvette through the now darkened woods, unto Highway #371 and headed towards the night life of Birch Lake.

When he first had thoughts of retiring his law business and selling his ranch in northwestern Minnesota and settling in the small town, he did wonder if the small town lifestyle would bore him to death.

He'd renovated the cabin and made it into a showpiece, landscaped the yard and built a huge garage for his toys and settled in. When he had gotten too restless a few years back, since he had previous investigative experience, he had taken on a job with an insurance company that a friend owned. Only part-time he had demanded, and now after finishing a case last week and being away from his place it had looked and felt really good to be home again.

Goddamn, he needed to get to the bottom of this hideous anonymity going on in his town and his lake and get his life back.

He recognized most of the vehicles in town as he drove through the three blocks of Birch and pulled up at the Legion Club. Tonight a sign on the door proclaimed it was spaghetti night, entertainment by the Traveling Troupidors, and a meat raffle at intermission. A fun filled Friday night was planned for the residents ready to dance, drink, and most importantly, catch up on any new gossip in their town.

Reed opened the door to a smoke filled, polka rocking filled room and made his way to the bar. Ginger glanced up at him as she expertly mixed drinks for the harried cocktail waitress. A smile lit her face as she topped a glass with beer foam as he slid on to a stool.

"Hey cowboy, the usual?" she voiced over the loud music.

Reed shrugged his shoulders. Being a true-blue lover of jazz and good country, he just couldn't get into the mind-set of polka hell-raisers, but generously gave the locals credit for doing what they loved. Taking a relieved breath after the noise died down, he nodded an affirmative to her question and watched as she reached to the top shelf for the most expensive whiskey for miles around.

"Good seeing you, Ginger, how are things?" Reed asked and put a cigarette to his lips.

"How are things?" she repeated and grinned as she worked, "Well, let me tell you, my ex lost his job so now I'm behind on my mortgage, the kids need clothes for school and I'm late with my period!" All this was said as she put his drink down on the bar, took his money and made change.

"How did things go so wrong? You were on cloud nine about that new romance this summer," he said then.

"Well, that was months ago, then he just disappeared." Ginger turned away to take care of some new customers as the band of merry makers went into another tune, this time the "Tennessee Waltz." Reed took a big swallow of the drink then grimaced, Goddamn, that song! Every time he heard it, it brought back memories. Memories he would just as soon forget! As the locals swayed to the grinding notes of the song a cloud of memories spread through his thoughts as he remembered. That song had been popular way back, decades ago, when he and Lindy had first met. And it had continued to haunt him after all these years every time he heard it. Goddamn it!

Momentarily lost in thought about her again, Reed turned to see Jerome, the town's oldest known resident sitting next to him on the bar stool. His feed-cap topped his bald pate firmly and Old Spice after-shave filled the immediate space.

"How are you?" Reed greeted him.

"Oh, I've been better." Jerome spoke slowly and nodded his head. This evening he was wearing the usual faded bib overalls, plaid flannel shirt, but had on a bright new looking tie. "Do you know yet," he asked then not wasting any more time on other pleasantries, "who those are you found out there in the water?"

Reed took a drag of his cigarette and blew the smoke towards the ceiling fan that circled above the heads of the locals as the majority puffed away. "Nope, we don't know as yet, but we don't think it's anyone from around here."

"Heard you're checking out those city rough-necks who raised such hell here over the fourth," Jerome said and took a hefty drink of his whiskey sour.

There was no such thing as keeping the investigation quiet in this town he knew, so he acknowledged Jerome's curiosity by nodding his head. Letting a few minutes go by and hoping he would go on to something else, Reed was jerked to sudden attention as the old man said, "Took some pictures with that new fangled camera the kids gave me when I was at the park one time this summer, got that bunch of bums on some!"

"You've got pictures of them?" Reed asked.

"Yup, didn't mean to waste the batteries." Jerome wiped his sagging mustache on his wrist.

Reeds interest peaked. "Jerome, would you consider turning them over to the Sheriff's Department to be held as evidence?" He asked then.

"Hell," Jerome said and adjusted his cap, "They ain't any use to me!"

"If I gave you a ride home and brought you right back here, could I get them from you tonight?" Reed asked.

Jerome looked askew for a moment as he thought it over. Then a grin broadened his lined face. "Well, I guess that's okay," he said importantly. "But, I'll lose my spot," he added nodding at his stool and place at the bar.

"Ginger," Reed called out, "Can you keep Jerome's stool for a few minutes? We'll be right back."

Outside, Jerome looked doubtfully at the low slung car and Reed hurried over to help fold him into the Corvette and they sped off to Jerome's house a few blocks away.

"Come in, come in," he said as they stopped a few minutes later and Reed helped him out of the car again.

Reed looked around as memories abounded. "Jerome, I haven't been to your place since the folks would bring me along over for card parties," Reed said then.

The white, salt box styled house stood on a corner lot but now, decades later, the yard was bare of any of the flower beds and shrubs that were there when Jerome's wife was alive. A one car garage stood off to the side, and he knew it held a vintage turquoise Edsel that was spit polished weekly by Jerome. And then, it only emerged when a neighbor would drive it around the block to rotate the tires for him.

Jerome flicked on a light in the kitchen when they came in the door and immediately went and opened a drawer and began rummaging in it.

"Yup, here they are," he said and handed the pictures to Reed.

Reed quickly flipped through them and slipped them in his pocket. "Thanks Jerome," he said and then added, "Your drinks are on me for the night."

"Appreciate it," Jerome said and adjusted his feed cap more securely. Back at the Legion Club, his stool was waiting for him. The band had cranked up the volume and now rocked the place with their rendition of "The Blue Skirt Waltz."

"Take care of Jerome," Reed said to Ginger and laid some bills on the bar, then escaped the noise.

Goddamn, the night air felt good as he headed to the Woodsman. Although he usually supported the Legion's efforts, tonight the spaghetti supper they were serving didn't appeal to him. He wanted a steak; loaded with garlic. Then he wanted to study those pictures. Something about them had triggered a recollection!

And for some reason, it had something to do with Mexico!

-31-

Lindy had a plan. Actually, it was the same one she had used to protect her fortune earlier by coming to live in Mexico. And now that these murdering thieves were forcing her to leave, she wasn't about to leave a single cent behind in their country.

She called the Monterrey airport and made reservations to as far as she could go, which was Tijuana, then headed to a department store. She needed a dark wig, a maternity dress and some sensible low shoes since it wouldn't look very convincing if she tottered around in her spike heels. Her plan was to impersonate a pregnant woman again who had visited her husband's family in his native country and was going back home to the US to wait for the arrival of their first child. Her passport would show she had been there for several months. Certainly they wouldn't remember her face or name after all this time, and the picture wouldn't show she had been big as a house then too, stuffed up with her money filled pillow.

Having bought the black wig and a hideously big dress, she hurried back to her hotel room, all the while keeping an eye out for anyone who might be following her. Sure, Mario and Rio, or both would be catching up with her any minute.

She tossed her clothes on a chair and got into bed. By now it was getting dark and Lordy, how she needed sleep. But her worries wouldn't let her rest. She had to get away, out of the country now! But she had hours before she could start her journey.

She picked up the phone and called Monica. "Hey girlfriend," she greeted her.

"I know it's the middle of the night, but did I wake you?"

"Are you kidding, it's my weekend off and I don't waste time in bed. What's up?"

Lindy sucked in a breath. "Monica, I need your help. I've got to get out of here and back to the US before Mario catches up with me. I told you he will kill me!"

"You really think so?" Monica exclaimed.

"Absolutely! I've got to go back home and beg Reed to help me!" Lindy's voice shook as she talked.

"Lindy, I don't believe this. You're leaving Mexico?"

"Soon," Lindy said and realized the less Monica knew about her actions the safer she would be.

"But, we just got together!" Monica protested.

"Lordy, I know. I might come back, you just never know. But I need a favor."

"Okay, what? Damn, wait, I need to grab my smokes," and Monica dropped the receiver on a noisy tabletop. A minute later she came back on the line, puffing hard as she lit up. "Okay," she said again.

"Do you know any real estate people?" Lindy asked.

"Sure, I have a good friend who owns her own company."

"Can I get her name and number?"

"Sure, but why Lindy?"

"In case I might need to unload that house of mine!" Lindy said with a catch in her throat.

"Well, I guess-," and Monica gave Lindy the name and phone number of the woman. "Now Lindy, let me know what you decide to do," Monica implored and they hung up. A minute later Lindy left a message on the realtor's voice mail with instructions to follow later.

Finally after a restless night in the hotel room, Lindy dressed in the maternity dress, adjusted the wig on her head, stuffed her belly pillow with her million dollars and waddled, effectively she hoped, out to a taxi and then into the airport. She carried a straw bag which held her make-up and cheap cardboard suitcases with her clothes. The place was jammed with natives and tourists and the noise ear-splitting. She paid for her ticket in cash and boarded the plane, then finally was able to put her head back against the seat, relieved after getting this far away. Then her thoughts plummeted. She'd left behind another home, Monica and all her new acquaintances and especially the business she'd started.

She wondered if the images and messages she got from the universe had stopped. She hadn't seen or heard anything for days, not since Reed had called her and then been side-tracked and had swiftly hung up on her.

She shuddered as she remembered the picture that had flashed through her thoughts then of a dead man and the name Sam! Should she have called Reed back and told him what she had seen? Actually she hadn't known what to do, but now, she would see him soon and she could explain it then.

The trip lasted hours it seemed and they finally landed in Tijuana, the border town just outside San Diego. Here Lindy followed as everyone disembarked and walked across a bridge and entered the custom department, and there if you passed muster, a few more steps would put you on US soil. Lordy, she was nervous but forced her concentration on lugging her money stuffed cumbersome body over the uneven pavement leading up to the fearsome barricaded enclosure. The temperature hung in the nineties as the sun blasted down on her, and she could feel sweat soaking her underarms. She wiped a hand over her face as a trickle ran down her forehead from under the heavy black wig. By now, the pillow dug into her belly, and she thought she heard the bills crackle as she moved.

"Next!" The guard's voices echoed as two dozen lines of people waited for their turn to be allowed through the gates. Tourists hugged bags of purchases they'd made in the flea markets. Wheelchairs holding sick loved ones were pushed through by families who had sought out help from some of the many clinics offering alternate medicine. Dozens of vehicles of every description lined up awaiting admittance back to the states. The noise and the nauseous exhaust fumes co-mingled with the heat and raised the level of tension to a nerve racking high at the border crossing.

Lindy stepped up to the gate. The guard was huge and peered at her with hard black eyes from under the visor of his hat. His uniform fit snugly over his muscled body and she blanched when she saw the gun holstered on his hip

"Your passport," he barked at her.

She swallowed and handed it over. She'd had on a black wig when she had the picture taken.

Now the guard looked her up and down and studied her face a second time, then said, "Lola Lane, I remember you, you still haven't had the niña?" He pointed at her belly.

Her heart lurched in her chest and she put a protective hand over her stomach. She gawked at him. How could that be? Why would he remember her?

Her voice squeaked as she managed to say, "Excuse me?"

The guard studied her passport again. "I checked you in when you came across months ago!" It seemed the noise in the terminal hushed as his voice carried over the crowd. She felt her face pale and thought she'd pass out right then and there from fright. Now they would grab her and throw her in one of those dank dark prisons and no one would miss her or care. The thought scared her so much, she started to cry. Big drops of tears slid down her cheeks as she stood forlornly clutching her cheap belongings, looking like she was ready to give birth right there.

"It's twins," she whispered desperately at last. "Pretty soon now," she added as the guard continued to examine her passport. With a smirk on his face he started to say something, and as she stood petrified waiting for the ax to fall she looked down at herself in horror as a puddle of water began to collect around her shoes.

The guard stepped back and gaped. "The nina! Señora, you need to get to a hospital," he exclaimed alarmed and nervously shoved the passport back into her hand. "Wait over there!" He indicated a chair and yelled into his cell-phone as she waddled towards it, her heart in her throat.

Lordy, she'd been so nervous she'd wet her pants! And he'd thought her water had broken and was about to give birth! What the hell would she do now?

His eyes were on her as she sat down in her wet clothes, embarrassed and totally at a loss as to how she could get out of this fiasco. As she waited doomed for sure, a bus roared up and as soon as the doors opened to let a noisy group of people out, right off their boisterous antics caused such a chaos that they momentarily disrupted the operation of the border crossing. This was exactly the diversion Lindy needed and she quickly disappeared into the mass of people and slipped through the border blockade, and was back on US soil!

She flagged down a taxi. At her first stop in a convenience store restroom she changed clothes and threw her dress and wig in the garbage can. Then transferred her money into the suitcase, slipped a baseball cap over her blonde hair, hailed another cab and was on her way to the airport in San Diego. By evening, she stretched luxuriously in her first class seat on the plane headed north and let her thoughts ramble as she sampled the champagne. She had gotten her million dollars safely out of Mexico, escaped Mario and Rio's expected threatened revenge and would be home soon. Reed would keep her safe!

Then suddenly her lovely thoughts were interrupted as a picture flashed before her eyes and a chill crept up her spine!

-32-

As Reed drove back home after spending the evening in Birch, he had that same niggling feeling he'd had earlier when he had glanced through those pictures he'd gotten from Jerome. Pictures, Jerome had taken months ago as he had tried out his new fangled camera, as he called it, he'd gotten from his kids. He had gone to the town's park and focused on the picturesque setting for practice and had gotten a group camping in the background at the time in some of his shots. He'd been disgusted to have wasted some of his batteries on those city slickers, but it had sent Reed's blood racing when he had found out about them as they had sat in the Legion Club. Now he had the pictures in his pocket.

Unlocking his door and switching on the lights as he went through the house and into his office, Reed sat down at his desk and laid the pictures out. They were in color and after studying them he counted thirteen people.

Goddamn, now he was getting somewhere! All he had to do now was put those faces next to the names he had on his list. After getting the coffee pot going he went back into his office and got busy on the phone.

"Hey buddy," he said to his friend Bernard, the computer genius who lived in Minneapolis, "I need your help. If I fax some pictures and a list of names would you match them up?"

"Sure," the man said and Reed could hear the whine of his wheelchair through the telephone lines. "You in town, Conners," he asked?

"Nope, I'm home up here at the lake." Reed walked out to the kitchen and poured a cup of coffee as he talked. "Just got here a few days ago, and we've got two possible homicides."

"No shit. Nothing ever happens up there!"

Reed was back in his office and sat down at his desk. "Yeah," he grumbled. "You got time?"

"Man, nothing but-- send it through!"

And after several hours Reed's phone rang with the news that ten of the names had a face to go with them leaving three.

"Three of them apparently don't have or never have had a driver's license in the US. Of course," the man said, "it could mean many things, one of which they don't even live in the US!"

By now the moon was full and Reed stood and stretched his back. His mouth tasted like swamp water after the whiskey he drank at the Legion and then the coffee he'd downed while he sat going over the case at his desk. He needed sleep and called it a night.

When he got up in the morning, his body felt like he'd been hit by a tank. He had noticed lately that the waistbands on his jeans were getting a little tight.

Nah, he grumbled, then resigned to the inevitable, went to a closet and found his old running sweats he'd hung away a while back. Goddamn, this really was a pain in the ass, but no way was he going to allow himself to turn into a fat old man!

Years ago, when he'd had his law business he used to burn up the miles running to ease the tension especially before a hard case came to trial, then when he'd moved and became semi-retired he figured he didn't need it any more.

Well, get real, he mumbled now as he yanked the brim of a cap down over his eyes, laced up his running shoes and took off out the door down the road in a slow trot to warm up. Minutes later puffing away, he made it out of his hilly half mile wooded drive and out to the highway. He figured he'd jog into town and back and that would make it an even four miles. A good run! And a few of those and he'd be back in great shape in no time. No sweat!

Later on shaking legs, he collapsed on the grass back in his yard. Goddamn, he mumbled again, what a bitch!   But now he was sure he could feel fresh blood cursing through his veins.

Later in the day, he stopped in to see Jesse at the sheriff's department and caught him up to date on the ID's of the ten men who had been in the park. Together they studied the pictures.

"Most of them live around the area so I figure I'll have to make a trip down to Minneapolis and track down these guys," Reed said now.

"Hold on, we don't know that they are even involved!" Jesse absentmindedly played with his mustache.

"Jesse, there's something about that week-end my friend, that spells trouble!" Reed stood up.

"Yeah, could be," Jesse replied. "But hold on, I've got my deputies going door to door so we'll wait and see if someone will come forward."

Reed turned to go. He was restless and impatient and the slow pace of his town began to bug him. He was used to being in charge, but of course, Jesse was the boss here.

There were two meeting places in Birch, one being the Woodsmen Café and the other the Legion Club. And leaving the sheriff's office, Reed saw the

Legion was swamped again this early afternoon with familiar vehicles from around the community.

Business was brisk but just as many customers sat with coffee cups as cocktail glasses before them on the bar. But as the sun climbed higher in the sky and then started to descend the cups would be replaced and the tinkle of ice cubes would intermingle with twang of the jukebox.

With time on his hands, Reed went in and joined the throng of early merrymakers. It was a Saturday and the place was already lively. Normally he wouldn't be spending a clear fall day in a bar, but until these mysterious deaths were cleared up, even if the lake was open to the public, he wouldn't have enjoyed being out there on the water after what had happened.

Ginger was back behind the bar. "Good to see you Reed," she said, "Your usual?"

"Too early, got any more of that coffee?" He reached for his pack of cigarettes and lit up.

"I feel like I'm working in a coffee shop," Ginger joked as she placed a mug of it down on the bar.

"Joints jumping," Reed said as he looked around. He recognized most of the patrons and nodded greetings as he glanced around the room. It wouldn't be long before they ambled over and pumped him for information.

His mind was still occupied with those pictures he'd gotten from Jerome and the people in them. That woman he talked to earlier on the phone in Minneapolis, the mother of one of the men had said they had all gone to school together years ago and occasionally got together.

Of the list of twenty three people who had rented cars that week in Brainerd, how many had camped at the park and how many were in the area for other reasons?

Who were those three unidentified men in the pictures?

Would the two bodies they'd fished out of Birch Lake match any of the twenty three faces in Jerome's practice film?

As Reed sat at the bar in the Legion Club in Birch Lake and tried to find answers, Johnny Cash mourned a lost love.

-33-

As Lindy lounged in her first class seat on the plane another picture suddenly flashed through her thoughts. She sucked in a shaky breath and clutched her carry-on bag more securely in her lap. Then sank further in her seat and tucked the brim of her cap down lower on her forehead.

Lordy, she'd just seen another dead body under water! And it too seemed like it was in Reed's lake.

It had been several days since she'd had any kind of vision and then had seen that first one, and heard or somehow felt the name Sam. And just now for God's sake, a picture of another corpse, a man it seemed, had slid across her thoughts. His hands had been tied and a large object had been attached to his feet that pulled him down.

And for just a fleeting second, she had glimpsed the anguish in his eyes as he had sunk helplessly down in the water. She sensed these images could only mean one thing. No wonder Reed had cut her off when she'd called him earlier. When he said he had caught something strange on his hook while out fishing on his lake, it had been a body!

She clasped her arms around her chest and sat motionless. Maybe if she sat perfectly still and didn't move a muscle nothing else could sneak up on her. She stared off into the beyond as the plane droned on somewhere over the central states. It would be several more hours before they landed in Minneapolis. She forced her thoughts onward.

Her lovely silver Lexus was gone, long ago, and she would have to rent a car and drive the last several hours of her journey. She should be in Birch Lake around dark.

A shiver went through her body as she thought about that. Reed would be surprised to see her; and maybe even ticked off! But he would know what to do to keep her safe from the D'Agustino's revenge! She was sure of it!

Maybe she should call him as soon as they landed and tell him what she'd seen. But would he believe her?

She hesitated. Over time she had learned that
sometimes the things that flew through her thoughts
was just a bunch of junk that made so sense. He
probably wouldn't believe her anyway, she decided.
He had sounded pretty grouchy when they last talked
and she sure didn't want to irritate him now.

The monotonous drone of the plane finally lulled
her into a nap and the last couple of hours flew by and
she awakened as the flight attendant announced their
approach into the Minneapolis airport. As the plane
dropped the last few feet onto the tarmac and the
landscape rushed by in a terrifying flash, she closed
her eyes and held onto the precious bag in her lap for
dear life. She loved flying except for this. Always
worried whether the brakes would hold or the big
metal tube they were encased in would hurtle into
endless space and they would be lost forever. She
clutched the bag tighter, if anything happened now;
she would lose the fortune she held. But finally she
felt a decrease in speed and sneaked a peek, then blew
out a breath as the scenery slowed and she saw the
terminal ahead. She forced herself to relax.

Then finally it was time to disembark and now
later, she was on the road out of Minneapolis and
headed north. Here the freeway and suburbs were
familiar as she cruised along in her rented red SUV. It
was late afternoon on a clear fall day. The sumac
bordering the road had turned a blazing orange and
the tuberous flowers a deep maroon. The stately pines

stood green and proud surrounded by the maples as they showed off their spicy colors of autumn. How she had missed her home state!

Several hours later as she turned off Highway #371 just out of Birch Lake, and unto the gravel road that led through the wooded area to Reed's homestead, the trees leaned into each other overhead and formed a tunnel of brilliant colors. Then suddenly she was there. Right in front of his house!

She turned off the car. Lordy, now that she was there, it didn't seem like such a good idea after all. She sucked in a breath. Maybe she could turn the car around and leave quietly. Maybe he wasn't even home! But he was, and he did see her and his muttered "goddamn it," echoed through the house and outside, and through the open window in the car to her as he strode down the steps toward her car.

"What the hell?" he growled as he stood there beside the SUV. "What are you doing here?"

Lindy tried to smile, but her face froze, so she busied herself opening the car door and slid out from behind the wheel.

Well, he had the nerve after all she'd been through! She took off her sun glasses and cap, and then fluffed her blond tresses. She'd worn comfy black shorts and a black tube top and now bent over to reach her wedgies from the floor in the car.

A flash of heat rushed over Reed. Goddamn, that's all he needed right now. He had two deaths to contend with. He'd planned to telephone her later when things quieted down! His thoughts sputtered defensively.

"Reed Conners," Lindy said as she straightened up, "don't you dare talk to me like that!" She put her hands on her hips and stared at him.

Reed gaped at her. "Well, I mean," He said, "this is a surprise. Why didn't you let me know you were coming?"

Lindy's defiance crumbled as she thought she saw just a bit of concern cross his face. "Some things happened," she said, "and I didn't have time!" The setting sun dazzled the water on the lake in the background.

"Like what?" Reed managed to ask as he stood uncertainly.

First he was pissed at her abrupt appearance, now he was worried about what had happened to make her leave so suddenly. She blinked back a threatening tear. Lordy, she was ready to crumble to the ground in a pile of bones if he didn't let up. "Reed, I am so tired. Can I come in?"

He reached out a hand. "Sorry, goddamn Lindy, you just took me by surprise that's all. Here let me get those," he said then and reached in and took her bags out of the car, unaware he was holding her million dollars in one of them!

"You're traveling light," he said then as he motioned her to follow him into the house.

Should she tell him why? But she just nodded.

-34-

As Reed led the way into his house, he suddenly stopped in the foyer and looked around uncertainly. He eyed the guest room down the hallway and his bedroom, and then just set Lindy's bags down in the tiled entry.

She was a wreck. Her nerves totally unraveled as she waited for him to move on in to the living room. She peeked around him and saw the fire burning in the huge stone fireplace that covered one whole wall, and housed his collection of books on the side shelves. She recognized the chandelier of deer antlers over an oak table that hugged two fat caramel covered leather arm chairs in front of it.

Still standing just inside the door, Reed turned to her and asked, "Would you like some coffee or something?"

She had just traveled hundreds of miles to get away from those men in Mexico and managed to get her fortune safely back across the border, she surely wasn't in the mood for coffee.

Hiding a plaintive note she said, "What I would like is a good strong drink, a dozen cigarettes, and a long soak in your Jacuzzi!" She adjusted her tube top, kicked off her wedgies and stepped around him into the room, then dropped onto the plaid couch. She looked back at Reed, who hadn't moved.

Well hell, he walked over to the bar in a corner of the room, and poured Crown Royal from a decanter into a glass and handed it to her.

"Thanks," she said and sat back and crossed her legs. "Apparently I interrupted something?" she said looking towards the light in a room down a hallway that she knew was his office.

Reed sat down across from her on the matching sofa. He swept his tousled hair off his forehead and mumbled, "I'm helping the sheriff with a new case."

Lindy sipped the whiskey and felt the warm liquor sizzle her insides. Reed put his arm over the top of the couch and leaned back.

The knots in her stomach had begun to loosen up and she said, "Reed, something happened and I didn't know what else to do!"

What now? He was in the middle of an investigation! He frowned and then resigned, decided he might as well let her ramble on and get it over with. "What's up," he asked?

Lindy sucked in her breath, "Reed, the reason I had to leave Mexico so fast was because I ran smack into Mario D'Agustino!" She put the glass of liquor down and raised her hands in the air. "And listen to this, he lives there in Monterrey. His whole family does!"

Reed lit a cigarette as he digested this piece of news.

Lindy shivered. "Reed, he recognized me!"

"Are you sure it was him?"

"Yes, I'm sure!" Lindy exclaimed and reached for the glass of whiskey on the table again. After downing the last of the amber liquor, she whispered, "I'd recognize him anywhere!"

Reed blew smoke towards the ceiling as he listened to her talk.

"Reed," Lindy said and wiped her eyes, "I got away just in time. But he will find me and kill me like he said!"

"Nah, he won't find you here." Reed said shaking his head.

"How do you know?"

They were sitting across from each other on the matching plaid sofas and now Reed got up and moved to sit by her. He put a hand on her arm. "Lindy, this is a small town, and I'd know the minute he set foot in it!"

"How can you be so sure," she asked.

"Trust me, I've got ways!" Reed sat back and blew a smoke ring and nodded his head, already at work on a plan to get even with the asshole.

All along, Lindy had had this feeling, but she couldn't dwell on it at the time because she had other things to worry about, like getting out of Mexico. And, she felt more strongly than ever, after seeing the second image while on the plane of another drowned man, that there was a definite connection between them and Reed's lake. Especially, after seeing the headlines in the local paper at the station when she'd stopped for gas in Brainerd.

Now she said, "Reed, listen to this," and went on. "Right after we talked on the phone last week, after you told me that you had pulled up something strange while you were out on your lake fishing, I had a vision of that scene and in it I saw a man who had drowned, and his name was Sam!" She shook her head slowly. "Don't ask me how I know his name, I just know!"

She sucked in her breath as she went on. "You remember my friend Monica don't you? Well, she lives in Monterrey now. We went out to a restaurant for dinner a few nights ago and she introduced me to the owners, the Mercado family. Also, I met one of a pair of identical twins, Paco Mercado.

She drained the glass of whiskey and asked, "Could I have another?"

"Might as well join you," Reed said and went back to the bar. Ice cubes crackled in the glass.

"There's more Reed, then Monica told me one of the twins was missing. His name was Sam, Sam Mercado. And that same night we ran into Mario.

As Lindy took another drink of the whiskey and felt its burn slide down her throat, she suddenly felt faint and dropped her head back against the couch.

The sun had slid below the horizon and the glow from the fireplace sent long shadows through Reed's living room. As he reached over and switched on a lamp on a table next to the couch, as the light reflected off Lindy's face, he asked, "Are you okay?"

Her stomach rumbled an answer just then.

"Come on," Reed said and stood up, he took her hand and started towards the kitchen.

As they came into the room, he switched on the lights. "Here take a seat and I'll scramble you up some eggs and toast. How's that sound?"

Lindy settled on one of the cushioned chairs at the oak table. She was starving as the only food she'd had since the night before was that measly bag of pretzels on the plane from San Diego.

Now she watched him hustle around the room, beating eggs and slicing bread. He was wearing sneakers, faded jeans and an old sweat shirt that had U of M printed in big letters on the front. Dressed so differently from his usual attire of shined boots and pressed jeans.

As the eggs cooked and the toast browned, his thoughts were on what she had told him.

Was she unto something? Could there be a connection between what she thought she saw in those scenes that floated through her mind and the drowned men found in his lake?

"Here, eat," he said minutes later and set the plate of food down for her and took a chair opposite her at the table.

"Wow, this looks wonderful," Lindy murmured and began to eat. This was what she had been hurrying back to. He was already taking care of her.

It was getting on to nine o'clock in the evening as Reed and Lindy sat at his table in the kitchen. Moonlight shimmered over Birch Lake and classic country floated softly though-out the house from a state of the art sound system.

She finished eating. "Thanks Reed," she said and sighed, "That was so good!"

"You were looking pretty fagged out. Are you feeling better now?" Reed sat with his elbows on the table a few feet away.

"Much better than I have for days." Lindy remarked.

"You're looking pretty good, too," he said and winked at her.

Too rattled to let go of her worries so easily, Lindy missed his innuendo and said tearfully, "Reed, you do believe what I saw, don't you?"

"Well, but what does all that have to do with what's going on here?" Reed asked evasively, all the while weighing all this in his mind.

Lordy, couldn't he see what it all meant? Patiently, Lindy went on. "I'm just telling you, as farfetched as this sounds, I know all this is connected; my visions of the drowned men, Sam Mercado's disappearance, and the bodies found in your lake!"

"It's a long shot," Reed said shaking his head. All though, he had to admit she might be on to something, it had happened before!

Well, if he didn't think her information was worthwhile, to heck with him! For now, she was totally wiped out. Lindy stood up and rubbed her eyes, and then said, "I need to sleep for about two days, do you mind if I stay overnight?"

-35-

Lindy declared that she needed to sleep for two days and looked at Reed expectantly for an invitation to stay at his house. When he hesitated she took it for a negative response and replied defensively, "I'm going into town to the Dew Drop Inn and get a room." She picked up her plate and glass and set them in the sink, then started out of the kitchen and toward the front door.

Reed followed, suddenly at a loss for words. "Lindy, stop, wait," he managed finally and hurried after her. "You don't have to do that!"

Lindy whirled around to face him. "I wouldn't want to impose, Reed!"

"I'm sorry I don't mean to be rude. It's just this dilemma we have going on here in town!" He brushed at his hair impatiently and jammed his hands in his pants pockets.

"Well, okay then," Lindy said and went to pick up her bags, then added, "I'll use the guest room if that's okay with you?" Then she headed down the hallway.

Feeling somewhat foolish Reed said, "Help yourself to all the hot water you want and there's plenty of towels in the closet. The timer on the coffee pot turns it on at eight o'clock in the morning, should I bring you some in bed?"

Not in the mood for any dilly-dallying right now Lindy said, "Reed I just need to sleep!" then added, "Thanks, but I'll let you know when I wake up."

He had to admit he was just a little bit relieved and went back to his office and sat down at his computer. Now that Lindy was tucked in for the rest of the night, he had time to go back to his own work.

The minute she had told him the D'Agustino's lived in Monterrey and then mentioned the Mercado name he'd been deep in thought. He knew Mario was from somewhere across the southern border, but had thought South America. Well, the sucker was closer then he thought! Reed turned on his computer and went to his phone list and dialed a number on his cell phone.

When the call was answered with "Dallas Police Department," he asked, "Could you connect me with Detective Emanuel please?" As the lines clicked and connected, Reed lit a cigarette and blew a smoke ring.

When the man answered, he said, "Hey Manny, how you doing buddy?"

And recognizing Reed's voice right off, he replied, "Conners, where the hell are you?"

"In paradise, my part of the country," Reed said. "How are you?"

"Great and working my ass off as usual. You coming down?"

"Nope. Why don't you come up here and go elk hunting with me this fall? Get a look at this part of the world?" Reed arranged papers on his desk as he talked.

"Well maybe. But Jesus I hate the cold!" Manny joked. "Conners, I often think back to when we worked the John Thomas case and the time we staked out the Red Dog bar here in Dallas waiting for him."

"Yeah, already over a year. That asshole is tucked away in the slammers over in Wisconsin."

"Glad to hear it. What's up, Conners?" Manny asked then.

Reed put the cigarette out and leaned back in his chair. "Tell me all you know about the D'Agustino and the Mercado families in Monterrey, Mexico. Also, the Mayor of the town whose first name is Rio, I don't know his last."

"Jesus, you're nosing around in dangerous territory my friend!" Manny said. "We don't mess with them, but they come and go across the border all the time."

"I've already had a run in with D'Agustino for drug trafficking."

"And you're still alive? Conners, I'm telling you stay away from them! They're all from one family. The Mama's are all sisters, all three. The Mercado's own all those Tex-Mex joints, you know," Manny added.

"Yeah?" Reed said.

"Yep, they're money and power."

Reed lit another cigarette as he listened, then blew a string of smoke rings and watched them drift slowly towards the fan in the ceiling and then disappear.

"What do you know about Sam and Paco Mercǎdo," he asked Manny then.

Manny cleared his throat. "Well, they're both players. Rich, smart and good looking and get this, they are identical twins. They travel around a lot setting up those taco places. They're big in the US; there must be some near you up there!"

"In Minneapolis but not this far north," Reed said. "Hey, Manny, you going to be in your office for while?"

"Yep, I guess."

"I'm going to fax you some pictures, there's guys I need to ID, take a look and see if you recognize them will you?" Reed was already standing at the machine.

"Okay, shoot them down here. I'll get back to you." And they both clicked off their cell phones, hundreds of miles apart.

After sending off the fax to Manny in Dallas, Reed studied the pictures again which of course were copies. The original being property of the Birch Sheriff's Department now. Of the thirty-four people who had rented cars that week-end of the Fourth of July from Rudy's Rental in Brainerd, there were still several that couldn't be identified. And after Lindy told him of her visions and mentioned the name Sam, right away he'd thought of his friend Manny who lived in Texas, and who would be well acquainted with the underworld just across the border.

Thirty minutes went by and Reed went out to the bar in the living room and poured another shot of Crown Royal and settled back at his desk. He'd thought of knocking on the door to the guest room to see if Lindy was still awake, but then decided not to. She'd been a little huffy earlier so maybe she just needed some sleep like she'd said. She had traveled a long way that day after all.

His cell rang just then.

"Hey," Manny said, "Sorry, I got another call I had to take care of. Okay pal, those two faces you circled on the pictures are two of our finest: Sam Mercado, beloved son of Mama Mercado. Billionaires. Queer as a three dollar bill. The one he's holding close is Miguel D'Agustino, burnt out youngest of the brothers! Story goes; he's strung out most of the time testing their products, which is grown in their homeland. Old families, old money and they run the country! What the hell brought them way up your way?"

Reed sat back and studied the ceiling. "Damned if I know. But I sure as hell am going to find out! We fished two bodies out of our lake, and it could be those guys!"

"Oh Jesus, get ready for an explosion of notoriety!"

"Yeah, goddamn it!" Reed knew that the minute word got out what it would be like. "I've got to go see the sheriff and let him know. Thanks buddy, I'll keep in touch!"

He hung up and left the house. By now it was going on eleven o'clock, but he knew Jesse would be still in his office as he was a known to stay out until the last car had left his streets for the night.

As Reed cruised into town, it was still full of cars as the younger crowd stayed out until the last call for booze could be gotten at the Legion. He pulled up in the lot outside the sheriff's office and walked in. Jesse was at his desk and puffing on a cigar, copies of the pictures spread out before him.

"Conners," he said through a cloud of smoke, "Thought you went home?"

"I did," Reed said pulling a chair around backwards and resting his arms over the top. His voice was low as he said, "Jesse, we got trouble! Big trouble!"

Jesse's face reddened. "What the fuck are you talking about man? How can it be worse?"

"Listen to this," Reed said and went on to tell him about the pictures he'd sent to Manny, and his identifying them. And even about Lindy's arrival and her story.

"Jesus Christ," Jesse said, "I can't believe this is happening in my town. Now of all times! I've only got a few more weeks in office and then I get my retirement." He wiped a hand over his face and swore again. "This will bring in those assholes from the FBI, you know!"

"Yeah, you're right. What do you think? Maybe the best thing to do is-- you get in touch with them right away. They like that. Then they can contact the Mexican government. We need to compare DNA samples, but first we need to find out if these two have come up missing!" Reed shook his head. "We could be way off base."

Jesse played with his mustache as he pondered Reed's suggestion. "You know, I've got a distant relative down there, I'm going to give him a call, he would know if something is going on!"

"Yeah, good idea, and maybe you should call Carl, over at the funeral home and have him get some DNA samples ready." Reed looked towards the alcove for the pot of coffee that always simmered on the burner, but saw the top of the stove was bare. Then, noticed the bottle of Jim Beam, almost hidden amongst the books and papers on top of the filing cabinet.

"You want some scotch?" Jesse asked following Reed's glance around the room.

"Nah thanks," Reed shook his head and stood up. "Think I'll catch some sleep, but I'll meet up with you tomorrow."

The minute he walked into his house he knew something was up. He'd expected Lindy to be sound asleep and the place peaceful, but instead the place was ablaze with all the lights on. He hurried in not knowing what to expect and found her wearing his favorite blue terry robe and a pair of his wooly socks pulled up to her knees.

"Where did you go?" She wailed and swiped at her eyes.

"Why, what's wrong?" Reed asked at a loss for more words.

"Why do you have pictures of these men? I went looking for you and found them on your desk!" Her eyes were huge as she held out the pictures as they stood in the living room.

"Why?" Reed asked curiously, "Do you know any of these people?" He had intended to ask her first thing in the morning.

She tightened the robe around herself and pointed, "Reed," she whispered, "I think this one is Sam

Mercado and the other one looks like he could be one of Mario's brothers." She took a shaky breath as she looked at the pictures again, "Oh God, I'm almost sure of it!"

-36-

Lindy stood in the middle of the living room with the pictures in her hand as Reed had rushed into his house. Her voice shook in the quiet night as she whispered, "Reed, this is bad!"

"Lindy come on, sit down." He took her arm and led her over to the couch.

She pulled her arm out of his hold and yelled, "Reed don't you understand now they will come here for sure!" She stared at him with terror in her eyes.

"Slow down, Lindy, we don't know anything for sure yet," he said trying to calm her.

She finally sat down and dropped the pictures on the coffee table. "Lordy, I knew when I had those visions." Her hand shook as she wiped her eyes.

Reed picked the pictures up and pointed, "Lindy, these men have been identified but we don't know yet if the bodies we found in the lake belong to any of them! We need DNA tests!"

She tightened the belt on the robe. "Well, what are you waiting for?"

He pulled his boots off and went on patiently, "The sheriff is checking the missing person reports from all around the country first. We'll see what that turns up."

"Reed, how can you be so--," Lindy turned to him, and then shook her head as she searched for the words. "Don't you understand I'm a sitting duck here? Don't you see?" She stood up, "Let me use your phone!" She had an idea that would speed the snail pace in this town.

"It's pretty late at night," Reed said but handed her his cell.

She ignored his comment and dialed a number in Mexico. When the call was picked up, she said, "Hey girlfriend, don't ask where I am, but I need to ask a question. Is Sam Mercǎdo still missing?"

Silence followed as she listened, and then said, "Thanks." She flipped the lid closed on the cell and handed it back to Reed, her face as white as a sheet.

"Sam Mercǎdo and his boy pal D'Agustino have not been seen or heard from for weeks. The families are out for blood!" Her voice quavered as she repeated what Monica had said.

Reed listened intently.

"She said that no one got too worried about them at first because they were known to go off and go canoeing or white water rafting. And get this; they have friends around this part of the US!"

"What caused the alarm?" Reed asked.

"She said the families began to get phone calls from friends, inquiring about their whereabouts and began to check on them."

Reed thought for a minute. "Well, like I said we don't know anything for sure yet until tests are completed."

"How can you be so calm?" She glared at him. Was the man intentionally dawdling?

By now it was going on two in the morning, and the moon's glow danced off the gentle waves on the lake. In the distance a loon called softly for its mate. Now that Reed was back home she felt safer, and like he said, as yet there was no proof that the bodies found in the lake belonged to those men. But Lordy, if it turns out that one is Mario's brother--, she shivered in horror at the thought.

Reed hid a yawn. "Lindy," he said, "I've got to catch up on some sleep, and you better get some too." He stood up, and then glanced back at her as he took off towards his bedroom. "Are you going to be okay?"

She blew out a breath. "Of course," she said as he went in his room and closed the door. She looked around at his house. He had a lot of windows and she didn't see one shade or drape in sight. The kitchen and great room took up one whole side of the house with huge windows to the east, north and south, with the bedrooms, office and baths to the west. The floors were satiny wood with scattered colorful rugs. The color scheme was cream, beige and taupe.

She had been in his home several times since he'd moved here and been impressed with his taste. Now as she looked around, she wished that he had seen her house too. It had been lovely, until those giant carpenter ants started devouring it!

She sat now on his couch in the middle of the night at loose ends. She did have the house in Monterrey, but she couldn't live there now. Not after finding out Mario lived in that city. She'd have to give it all up. Not only her home, but her new friends and also the lucrative business she had just started.

She wiped at her eyes again and then instantly brightened, but she still had her million and it was safely tucked under the bed right here in Reed's house!

Maybe she'd stay around and buy her own place in this nice little town. She stared off into space and thought about that for a while. Then she had another thought, maybe she'd go back to Newport, Rhode Island. She'd loved the area but with a start, remembered working those tours in the Ashton mansion and having experienced that first vision, and how frightened she had been.

It seemed like so long ago since her life had been so rudely interrupted by her husband's death and then that fire! It seemed like a lifetime ago.

She sagged down on the couch and reached for a pillow and as mourning doves began to hum in the distance, she finally fell asleep.

***

One thing Reed really welcomed about his semi-retirement was, not having to get up at the crack of dawn and rush off to his office to contend with the problems of clients. Now in his forty-ninth year he was enjoying life and only worked when he felt like it, or when Ed, his boss at the insurance company heckled him enough to get down to Minneapolis to work a big money case. His daily routine usually began waking up to the aroma of freshly brewed coffee and spending a leisurely morning with the newspaper out on his deck in the sun or by the fireplace and his books.

But not today or any time soon, he grumbled since he'd made that decision to get in shape. And he would unless it killed him! He donned sweats and running shoes and as he went through the living room on his way outside, found Lindy curled up sound asleep on the couch.

Should he wake her and tell her to go back into the guest bedroom? Guess not, she'd been pretty pissed and he couldn't blame her. The slow pace of small town investigations tried his patience too. He got a wooly blanket and covered her.

The brilliant sunshine lit up the autumn colors of the birch trees and bushes as he took off in a slow warm-up trot down the road. Birds chirped merrily in the branches and lacy butterflies floated in the cool morning. He sucked in deep gulps of air as his tight muscles complained and hurt like hell. Worse than the day before he mumbled, but he forced one foot in front of the other and tried to work out a limp.

Finally making it back home, after finishing the four mile run, he slumped to the ground in a heap of sweat and fatigue, and groaned "Goddamn!"

-37-

Lindy was still asleep on the couch with the blanket Reed had covered her with pulled up to her chin. While she thought she gave the world the impression of being an independent socialite, to him she still looked like a kid lying there curled up in a ball.

In the past, when she would appear out of the blue and they would spend time together, after a few days they'd both go on their own merry way and that was okay. But now she'd been messing with him for months, ever since he had picked up that goddamn fraud case his company had reopened against her.

He grumbled as he stopped in the kitchen and downed a glass of water. His whole life was suddenly screwed up. Since the sheriff had closed the lake he couldn't take his boat out on the water and go fishing to get away from the hullabaloo either. And now goddamn it, murdering drug lords would likely appear to wreak havoc, not only to avenge Lindy for squealing to the Feds about them, but to get even with the town because two of their own had just happened to stop in and had been tossed in the lake! He ran a hand through his tousled hair.

Had they figured out yet that Lindy was here in the same town that the drowning took place?

It wouldn't take long for them to make the connection and figure out that she would run back here for his help. And when they traced the campers to Birch Lake too, the Mercădos and D'Agustino people would be overly enthusiastic at finding they could take care of two vendettas at once.

As he stopped in his bedroom and stripped, then stepped into the shower in his bathroom, his thoughts were totally immersed in the dilemma going on. He didn't hear the door open, wasn't aware until he felt a warm body snuggle against his back and arms clasp around him.

"What the---," he managed to say and turned to see Lindy standing stark naked in the shower stall.

"Do you have any shampoo?" She asked nonchalantly and stuck her blond head under the water.

Reed fumbled for the bottle, and finally managed to say, "I thought you were sound asleep!"

She remarked dryly, "I was until you woke me up with your grumbling!" She poured shampoo on her head and began washing her hair, then peeked at him through the foam and added, "I don't remember you being such a bear in the mornings!"

"Yeah?" Reed answered at a loss for words.

As Lindy stood unabashed in all her glory she asked, "Now that you woke me up, what are you going to do about it?"

The water sluiced over his shoulders as he thought about that. Then he reached over and began to play with the bubbles. When she poured out more soap in her hand then began gently massaging his chest with the warm fragrance, after a few minutes of her attention, he just muttered "Goddamn."

This time when they made love, after the first wild thrill of each other's lust, they dried each other and settled down in his bed to a slow expression of their feelings. Something they had felt previously from time to time, but not something either one dared to explore further, or wanted to for that matter. As they lay in his king-sized bed, their legs entangled, lulled in the afterglow of their lovemaking their thoughts rambled down the same path. Time had suddenly crept up on them, Reed was just about to turn fifty and Lindy had traveled far and wide, and just maybe, now they should think seriously about a future together. But soon, all their possible scenarios were forgotten as the lovers fell into an exhausted sleep.

***

Lindy awoke and turned to see Reed sprawled next to her. Here she was in his bed again! She remembered tossing and turning fitfully on the couch trying to sleep and feeling so lonely. She chewed on her lower lip as she thought about their love-making. Lordy, she had to admit again, no matter who was in her life, Reed held the strings to her heart.

She slid out of the bed, showered and dressed, and went outside and down to the water's edge. As she watched gentle waves roll over the surface of the lake and splash against the dock, she remembered the terror she had felt when John Thomas had trapped her out on it. Her stomach rumbled a reminder as she sat down on the sand.

Just then Reed's voice startled her out of the fear filled thoughts as he strolled across the beach clad in pressed jeans and a blue sweater.

"Hey," she greeted him. "Are you feeling better today?"

"Yeah much," he grinned as he sat down on the sand next to her.

"Did you get some sleep?" she asked.

Reed skipped a small rock across the water and squinted in the glare of the bright morning sunshine, then turned to her. "I slept like a baby!"

"That's good," Lindy said and searched his face and wondered if he was still pissed at her? No, she didn't think so.

He reached in the pocket of his shirt for his cigarettes. "Are you still smoking?" he asked.

"When the occasion calls for it," she smiled relieved at his apparent ease.

And minutes later, as the smoke curled around them in the late morning sunshine, she asked curiously "Reed, you still have my suitcases I left here, don't you?" Then as an afterthought frowned, "You didn't give my stuff away, I hope!"

Reed stood. "Come on," he said, "I've got something to show you."

Lindy scrambled to her feet, and trailed after him through the sand on his man-made beach and toward his garage; where he threw open the door.

"This look familiar?" He asked as he switched on a light that gleamed on a silver Lexus?

"Lordy, it's my car! But how did you---," Lindy gasped thunderstruck.

"The Minneapolis Police Department impounded it you know." Reed stood with a hand stuffed in a jean pocket.

She whispered, "I thought it was gone for good!" She wiped tears from her eyes. How she loved that car, even better then the black BMW she'd had at first.

"Well, it cost a little, but goddamn I didn't feel the state should get it!" Reed took a drag of the cigarette he still carried and the smoke curled towards the ceiling in the garage as they stood just inside the door.

Curious, Lindy went over and opened the door of the car and peered inside. And there he was, Rex, her protector. The life sized stuffed, black Labrador dog she had bought still sat on the front seat. She ran her hand over the fur.

"I wondered about that," Reed said and shook his head at her.

"Well, I had a few scary moments on the road." She added, "He looks real doesn't he?"

Reed grinned, "Yeah had me going for a minute. Come on, I've got those other things of yours." They headed into the house and over to a hall closet where he pulled out two suitcases. Her eyes widened happily as she recognized them. They held all those beautiful clothes she had bought in Hilton Head and Newport.

"This is unbelievable," she chattered and hugged him, then bent down and threw them open.

"Reed, thank you so much," she said again as she pulled colorful outfits out of the suitcases and studied them. "Wow, I remember this," she would exclaim.

Reed started to walk away then turned and said, "Lindy, I'm going into town and see what the sheriff has come up with." And then added, "And you can reach me on my cell."

Well, now that will keep her busy, he assumed as he cruised down the road. Several times, he had had thoughts of finally getting rid of her things, but then would put it off. And now luckily, that could soften the blow when he would have to come clean and tell her she wasn't a wanted person any longer. Christ, why hadn't he just told her that too, while she had been in such a good mood?

Then he wondered briefly, could it be that he felt he had power over her and didn't want to let go? He shook his head. Well hell, he'd have to think about it later when he had more time!

As he pulled up to Jesse's office in town, the parking lot around the sheriff's office was jammed with cars.

Goddamn, maybe they were getting somewhere, finally!

-38-

Reed nodded to the crowd that had gathered in the sheriff's office as he made his way to Jesse's desk. The air was heavy, not only caused by the late summer temperature, but also from the number of locals jammed into the small office wanting to get a close look at real FBI agents.

"Conners, you're here," Jesse said looking relieved. He wiped his brow and nodding toward the side of the room said, "I called them like you suggested and they were here bright and early."

Reed glanced over at three men standing in a huddle, all clad in blue suits and wearing sun glasses. "Figures, I knew as soon as you mentioned the D'Agustino name, you'd get their attention."

"Well, as much as I hate working with these assholes, they did get the DNA from our medical examiner and it's on the way to the crime lab in St. Paul," Jesse said. And then added, "The lab has this new fangled machine that can identify DNA right away, they say. So, as soon as the DNA gets there from the Mercădo and D'Agustino families we can get the show on the road. If there's a match, we will know tonight!"

Reed grinned. "They're good for something then!" Just as the men came over to him.

"I understand you found the first body," one said. "What can you tell us about that?"

Even though he had to give the Bureau the credibility it deserved, every time Reed got close to the arrogant bastards his temper went up. Swallowing his ire now, he reached out a hand and said, "Reed Conners." But a little irritation still echoed in his voice as he asked politely, "And you are?"

"We're from the Federal Bureau," the second man said.

Reed lowered his hand when none of the three offered theirs. "Well, I hope you are prepared," he said shortly.

"And why is that," the third one piped up.

"Obviously, you haven't had the pleasure of dealing with our neighbors from across the border before!" Reed shook his head in disgust. Christ, leave it to the bureau to send them three rookies fresh out of training school.

The agent who appeared to be the leader of the group said, "You need to bring us up to date, Mr.—."

"Conners," Reed remarked dryly. "And the sheriff has my signed statement!"

The three agents looked appalled for a moment at his audacity, then went back to their corner and began whispering amongst themselves.

Reed turned to Jesse then and noticed his hands shake as he shuffled papers on his desk and asked, "Hey buddy, are you okay?"

Jesse shook his head, "Nah, only got a coupla hours of sleep." He put a hand on his stomach and added, "Didn't even have time to feed my ulcer, they got here before the sun came up."

"Well, to hell with that, come on. We'll be over at the cafe," Reed announced and stood aside for Jesse to follow.

"Transfer my calls to my cell," Jesse said to his deputy as he and Reed walked out of his office. They didn't look in the direction of the agents, and after a few minutes when the locals didn't see anything more, they followed.

"I figure by dark we'll hear something from down south," Reed said as they crossed Main Street. "We better be ready!"

"Yeah? Jesus." The Sheriff wiped his forehead with the sleeve of his tan shirt and pulled his cap down firmer on his head as they stepped into the café. "I'm calling in all the guys," he said then and punched in a number on his cell. "Joe," he said, "I need volunteers, can you gather the men? Come to my office in one hour and I'll bring you up to date then," he said into his cell.

The noon hour had passed at the Woodsmen Café as Reed and Jesse sat down at the counter. It was Tuesday and the daily special was roast pork with baked apples, and mashed potatoes and gravy. The comfort food brought in regulars from far and wide and the mouth-watering aroma still hung in the air, although now it was mixed with the smoke of cigarettes.

"Afternoon, good looking," Reed greeted the waitress as she stood refilling salt and pepper shakers. Flo looked over and a smile spread over her lined face.

"My two favorite guys," she replied and came over with plastic glasses filled with ice water. Her crepe soled shoes swished over the tiled floor in her haste.

Next to Jerome, Flo was another of the town's oldest residents. Some said she could be getting close to eight-five or possibly ninety years old, but no one dared ask for sure. She had been a waitress in the same place when Reed had come up to the lake for vacations with his folks when he was a kid. She showed up for work every day and kept the other wait people on their toes, and if they didn't measure up there was hell to pay. She still made her daily stop in the Legion for a whiskey sour or two after her shift, but mainly just to keep up with things, she claimed. Now as she stood before Reed and Jesse, the fluffy lace hanky that always peeked out of her uniform pocket over her left shoulder drooped, and her permed French twist listed to the left after the rush. She was a little pooped, she had to admit, but she had to straighten out the mess those knot-head waitresses had left undone before she could leave.

"Stan cooked an extra roast today, so we've got some left." She said as she placed silverware down on the counter, and then stood with pencil poised ready for their order.

Jesse nodded and joked, "Sweetheart, marry me will you?" Then picked up the glass and drank most of his water.

"Ah, go on, I'm too much woman for you to handle," Flo replied without missing a beat. She grinned at them and wrote something on the ticket, then swished off to the kitchen.

Reed lit a cigarette and sent smoke rings spiraling across the room and asked, "Did we order?"

"Yup," Jesse grinned, and then wiped his forehead again. "Okay, Conners, now what do you think we should plan for?"

"We're going to have to plan carefully," Reed said as Flo bustled over with heaping bowls of a luscious looking salad. "There now boys, when you clean your plates, I'll give you some dessert," she chirped.

Both men took her advice seriously and began to eat. Reed remembered his earlier determination to slim down, but decided he'd get serious tomorrow.

"Well, I guess we better get back and see what those guys are up to now," Jesse said later and slid his empty plate off to the side after feasting on the day's menu.

Reed agreed and put some bills on the counter. "My treat," he added.

"Thanks, next time it's on me!" Jesse said.

"Jesse," Reed said as they stood up, "I've been thinking, what about setting up road blocks?" Reed asked diplomatically. "That way we'd know who shows up?"

"Jesus, that's what we gotta do!" And after a minute of thought Jesse dialed a number on his cell again as they walked out of the café.

"Now, here's what I want you and the boys to do," Jesse said to his star deputy. "I want road blocks set up at all the entrances into town. I want each and every vehicle stopped and every ID checked before it is allowed to enter into this area. Got that?"

"Good thinking!" Reed said as they walked into the sheriff's office. Then added, "Oh yeah, you better let them know that we're especially looking for those foreigners from across the border when you get the men together. And have them carry cell phones!"

As Reed and Jesse came into the office, Reed wasn't surprised to see the FBI men had taken over Jesse's space. The most serious looking of the three sat at his desk with files in hand. Jesse exhaled and muttered under his breath, "Oh Christ," then walked over and said, "Excuse me!"

"Oh, sorry." The blue suited young man stood up and put the file down, then nodded toward the others and all three walked to the door and went outside. Reed watched them go to their black town car and settle inside.

Jesse sat down at his desk and straightened his papers, then checked his watch. "Jesus, I hate the waiting. What do you think another couple of hours?" He looked at Reed.

Without hesitation, Reed said, "The Federals will notify the family's right away, today, if the DNA matches!"

He lit another cigarette and blew smoke toward the ceiling. "If they are looking for revenge, and I'm sure they are, they are warming up their jets as we speak. But I don't think it'll be before the close of the day," And hearing the tremor in Jesse's voice tried to reassure him. "Hey buddy, who knows, maybe it'll turn out to be those bones belonged to some idiots from Timbuktu, and we'll have gotten heated up about nothing!"

"Yeah?" But Jesse wasn't buying it and got up and opened a locked gun case that stood hidden in a closet. Calling his deputy over he said, "I want each man to be armed when they take up their posts. Call them in, will you please?" And the deputy went back out front to his desk and to gather the town's posse.

Not expecting anything to happen yet, Reed said to Jesse, "I've got to take off for awhile, you got my cell number and call me if anything comes in before I get back!"

It had dawned on him, if and when the D'Agustino's came to town, it wouldn't take long for them to find his place and get their revenge on Lindy for turning Mario in for murder. If the DNA proved it was the young brother that had died in the lake, they wouldn't hesitate to even the score. A life for a life! Goddamn, he had to get Lindy to a safer place, right now. The Corvette roared through town and out to his island.

The first thing he saw as he swung into his yard was that the red SUV rental she had driven was still there, and then when he checked the garage her silver Lexus was there too! But for some reason, dread began to chill his thoughts. He reached inside his jacket for the .38.

He opened the door into the foyer and saw her suitcases were still in the same place, but now all her colorful clothes were scattered around the floor. In pieces, he realized as he looked closer. Goddamn,

everything had been slashed! Her dresses, shirts and
pants and sundresses, she'd excitedly held up for him
to see lay there now in shreds.

The hair on the back of his neck bristled. He stood
still and listened. Then took cover behind a stuffed
chair and waited. Not a thing moved and then the
only sound he heard was his own heart pounding
furiously in his chest. Then he realized he was too
late. Someone had already gotten her!

-39-

Lindy had waved to Reed as he got in the Corvette and left for town.

"Call me if you need me," he had said, "I'll be back in a couple of hours." It was close to ten o'clock in the morning. The late fall day promised to be beautiful as the sun burned the dew off the trees and bushes in his yard. As she sat on his sandy beach, a gentle breeze rippled the water on Birch Lake and sprinkled the scent of burning leaves in the air.

Most of her fears had diminished since being back in her own country and now, after their night of making love, she began to daydream. She imagined herself living in Reed's house, and becoming a part of his life. And maybe even marriage!

Well, she had to admit she liked being free and single now, but there were those times in between that could become pretty bleak. As she sat in the sand she thought long and hard about her future. And finally after making a decision, she went back into Reed's house to hang all those clothes of hers in his closet.

***

The first thought Lindy had, was why couldn't she open her eyes? Then she fell back down into the darkness of oblivion and lay motionless. After some time, maybe minutes or even hours a small trickle of self-preservation awakened her instincts again and she began to struggle for her life. As if gripping onto the edge of a cliff, she pulled herself up and out of the fog.

However, to her bewilderment when she tried to move, she found her hands were tied behind her back and her ankles were bound together. When she realized she was blindfolded she knew this was not a dream or a nightmare.

This was real! As a hysterical sob began deep in her throat, it was stopped by a gag stuffed in her mouth! She struggled to breathe. Fighting back hysteria, she forced herself to think.

She could hear the hum of tires over pavement and realized to her horror then the hot cramped place she was in must be the trunk of a car. She fought to focus. The last thing she could remember was that she and Reed had made love and she had decided to stay in his town.

But when was that?

She had gone back into his house to hang up her clothes that were still in the suitcases in the hallway. She had been kneeling on the floor, folding some lacy under-things when someone had grabbed her from behind and held something over her face. She remembered then for just an instant, the immediate feeling of falling down some dark filled abyss.

My God, that was it. This was what she had been terrified off. Mario had found her and now he would make good his threat to kill her. Her heart thumped crazily against her ribs.

She felt the car slow and turn, and then suddenly she was flung back and forth against the close confines of the trunk, helpless to brace herself against the assault of pot-holes in a road they had taken.

Finally coming to an abrupt stop, she heard a key slid into the lock and then the trunk was flung open. Blessed air cooled her sweaty body, but she forced herself to stay still and lifeless. Then someone grabbed her, roughly pulled her out of the trunk and dropped her to the ground. She lay momentarily stunned. Then felt the dampness of the ground, smelled the heady scent of pine trees and realized they must be in a wooded area.

She heard voices in the background and listened intently, and then to her dismay realized neither one belonged to Mario! But only slightly relived, she realized that only meant he'd sent someone else to do his dirty work. When she heard one of them apparently talking on a cell-phone say, "Bueno, Sĩ Señor Mario, we got her, the Señora," a tremor shook through her. Then the man's voice became muffled and she couldn't hear him describe the area where she was hidden. Or know that Mario had replied, "I'm on the way up there now."

But she did hear the soft swooshing sound of rubber soles crush the moist soil of the forest floor as someone came toward her and she was dragged over the rugged ground and that's when she began to fight. Fight for her life. She raised her bound legs and tried kicking with all her might. She struggled but to no avail. She was tied up and couldn't move, and with the gag in her mouth she couldn't scream. She was totally helpless!

"Sorry, Señora, we got our orders," a man said gruffly.

She was going to die now!

Then to her astonishment he pulled her upright and slammed her against what felt like a tree. His sweat and foul breath assaulting her as he hastily tied her firmly to its trunk. She felt him step away, heard car doors slam and then the vehicle accelerated and started off away from her. She sat motionless for long minutes, the hum of insects the only sound in the woods around her.

My god, she couldn't believe it, she was still alive. They hadn't killed her! Then when she realized they might change their mind and come back she really panicked. She strained to listen. If she could just get the damn rag out of her mouth or the blindfold off.

She began to frantically move her head back and forth against the rough trunk of the tree, winching in pain as her hair caught in the bark. The blindfold loosened slightly, but soon her strength began to ebb. She felt a chill in the air and realized the sun must have begun its descent in the west, and would soon darken the forest around her.

Helpless, she sat alone in the vast wilderness. She had escaped sure death from her two-legged captors so far, but soon the four-legged night prowlers would start their silent trek to capture their evening meal.

Could she survive?

***

As the men drove out of the woods in the north, one made a call. "Bueno, Señor Mario, its all set!"

"Gracias," the man answered, "Now get lost!"

-40-

Reed stood in his living room with his .38 pointed, ready to blow the bastards to hell. He sucked in a shaky breath and listened. Nothing moved. The house was silent! Stepping over the slashed remains of Lindy's clothing lying scattered on the hallway floor, he went into the kitchen, and then searched the rest of the house. He opened closets, and even got down on his knees and searched under the beds. There was no one there. He came back to the hallway and looked again at her clothes. And now as he stared down at the mess he saw a switchblade embedded in the middle of the pile.

Sweat broke out on his face as the reality of the situation dawned. While he had been dawdling around in town with Jesse those ass-holes from Mexico had silently crept into town right under their noses. And now they had Lindy! He lowered the gun.

All along something had been nagging at the back of his mind about those photos he'd gotten from Jerome. One face had looked somewhat familiar. Now he knew it. It was because it resembled the D'Agustino brothers. And when Lindy's friend Monica who lived in Monterrey, had said D'Agustino's younger brother Miguel and Sam Mercado; sons from the two richest and prominent families were missing, he made the connection. He slipped the gun back in the holster under his arm, locked his doors and hurried out to the Corvette.

"Jesse, he exclaimed to the sheriff in town, "They're already here. Those assholes grabbed Lindy Lewis!"

"Ahh- shit." Jesse slid his chair away from his desk and started toward the door.

"I've got all the roads covered leading into town; how the hell did they get in?"

"Apparently we were too late," Reed said. "But now we can use the feds sitting out there in their car twiddling their thumbs."

"Yup, you're right," Jesse said and opened the door and waved the three FBI men to come back inside. And after bringing them up to date about Mario's threat and the kidnapping, they finally got busy and called out search and rescue, and put out a five state alert for her.

But Reed had some doubts about the D'Agustino mob killing Lindy. Would they want to chance the national notoriety they would get if they were caught? After all, most of their drug business was done right here in the good old US.

"Goddamn, I've got to do something," he said to Jesse just as the sheriff's phone rang. Then saw the man's face pale and turn beet red as he listened to the caller and then put the phone down.

"That's it," Jesse said then, "That was the crime lab and they confirmed the DNA matched." He shook his head and groaned, "Christ, we got the D'Agustino and Mercădo boys right here!"

"Yeah, I knew it," Reed said and headed for the door. He sucked in a breath to steady his nerves. For the first time he was worried, really worried about Lindy.

Why the hell hadn't he made her go into hiding when she had turned up at his door? Now it could be too late! Goddamn, he couldn't forget that good feeling he had had in his gut when he'd left her sitting on the beach earlier at his house.

As he drove through town his cell phone rang, and to his surprise Detective Emanuel, his friend Manny from Dallas was on the other end.

"Buddy, what's up?" Reed asked.

"Hey, after we talked I figured it wouldn't hurt to check out your part of the country." Manny's raspy voice echoed in the phone.

"Yeah? Are you planning on a trip up this way?" Reed asked as he headed out on the main highway.

"Conners, I figured those bastards you're tangling with have been getting their own way too long."

"Goddamn right." Reed remarked and heard angry voices in the background. "Where the hell are you, Manny?" he asked curiously.

"I'm trying to get into your town, but some cowboys are pointing shotguns at me!"

"You're here?" Reed shifted into second and cornered a curve.

"Yup, figured I'd check out your town." And then added in his Texan drawl, "Be around in case you might need help!"

"Come on aboard, we just got confirmation on the DNA. We've got them alright."

"Holy shit!" Manny remarked.

"Manny, I'll be right there, I'm just down the road from you." Reed gunned the Corvette then slowed as he approached the roadblocks at the city limits sign ahead. Two pickups faced each other across the highway blocking traffic and two townsmen were standing guard, their feed caps pulled down firmly over their foreheads.

"This here gentleman says he knows you," one volunteer fireman pushed into municipal service said, holding Manny at gunpoint as Reed pulled up. Sweat streaked the man's face as this was the first time he'd been called out to wear a badge and carry a firearm.

"Hey, he's okay," Reed said after hurriedly getting out of the car. "He's a friend of mine," he added and the locals put their guns down with relief. "Good to see you, Manny," he said and they shook hands. "Follow me into town and I'll bring you up to date." They parked Manny's car in town and Reed motioned for him to get in the Corvette. Manny whistled as he opened the door and got in Reed's car. "Nice," he said and checked out the Corvette.

"Thanks, buddy. Now here's what we got," Reed said, "The boys from across the border got here earlier today, right under our noses. Remember Lindy Lewis? They grabbed her!"

Manny stuck a slim brown cigarette in his mouth, fumbled for the lighter in his shirt pocket and took his time lighting it.

He raised an eyebrow. "You banging that chick again pal?" he asked.

When they had worked together on the John Thomas case, they had formed an easy friendship. Sometimes during their stake-out in Dallas, they had discussed some personal topics and Reed had told Manny about his occasional trysts with Lindy.

Reed nodded his head slowly, "Can't seem to let it go. It's a long story." He continued, "Listen to this, she had an affair with Mario, one of the D'Agustino brothers and was a witness to a murder. When she was forced to testify for the FBI, Mario threatened to kill her. She showed up here yesterday and now sometime today, they grabbed her."

"And you figure its payback?" Manny asked.

Reed shook his head. "Goddamn right! That's how they operate. Listen to this Manny, we had a bunch of people here in town a while back. We think the two that ended up in the lake were with that gang."

It was late afternoon, and as they came into Birch Lake Manny remarked, "So this is your town?" He looked down the next block where the buildings ended. "This is it, I see vehicles but where is everyone?"

Reed checked his watch. "Well, at this time of the day, I'd say the Legion club!"

"Any chance you could take a few minutes so I could grab a burger over there and you can let me know how I can help?"

"Sure thing, and I need to check in with the sheriff." Reed swung into a vacant parking spot next to the well-drilling company.

Heads turned curiously as the two men walked into the Legion club. Some stools were open at the bar and Ginger came over.

"Hey, cowboy," she greeted Reed and went on, "Who is your good looking partner?" She checked out

Manny's graying ponytail, droopy mustache and faded jeans.

"A friend from Texas," Reed said. "Manny meet Ginger, the hottest bartender around these parts."

"Oh yeah, I can see it." Manny took her hand and kissed the inside of her palm.

Reed forced himself to calm down while Manny ordered a quick burger. He took out his cell and connected with Jesse.

"Nothing yet," The sheriff said, "but we've got search parties covering a fifty mile radius. We'll get those ass-holes! I heard that a detective friend of yours from Dallas is here in town."

News traveled fast in the north country. "Yeah, he's a good man," Reed said. "We're across the street here while he grabs something to eat and then we're ready to take off and help you!" His mind worked furiously. Goddamn, they had to find Lindy fast! The longer it took the less chance of finding her alive!

As Manny ate his hamburger, Reed went over the case with him and then laid the photos out on the bar for him to see. Ginger leaned over and glanced at the pictures curiously.

She looked closer. "Oh God, let me see those!" She leaned over the bar and then pointed to the face that belonged to Sam Mercado. "This is him," she exclaimed, "this is the guy I was going out with and then he just disappeared!"

Reed recalled her saying months ago she had met a new guy, complained that her ex old man was behind on child support payments, the kids needed school clothes and she was late getting her period.

He pointed to Sam's face in the photo now. "This is the guy you were going out with?"

"That's him," Ginger whispered and peered curiously at him. Then her face paled and she gasped, "Why, what's going on?"

"Ginger, bad news. The bodies we fished out of the lake belong to a Sam Mercado and Miguel D'Agustino."

Ginger sucked in her breath and murmured, "Oh no, not Sammy, now I have a real problem!"

-41-

"I've got a phone number I need to check," Reed said to Manny as they stopped in the Legion so Manny could grab a quick burger. When he had contacted the people who had rented cars over that week-end in July, when they thought the drowning had occurred, he had talked to a woman in Minneapolis who was visiting her son. She had been one of the few people he had called who had been at all helpful. She had thought her son had been with a group of people on a camp-out in the north in July. On a hunch Reed dialed the phone number and to his surprise a man answered.

After identifying himself and then the reason for calling he asked, "How well did you know the deceased?"

The man paused then answered defensively, "I didn't know them. They were friends of friends. Christ, I don't have time for this!"

"Well my friend," Reed said, "you better make time."

"Are you threatening me?"

Reed laughed into the phone. "Nah, but we know where to find you. You could be arrested for obstructing justice in a murder investigation!"

"Ah shit, man," he muttered and Reed could hear him bang something against a hard surface. "I was sorry I ever agreed to join that bunch of weirdoes and I left!" Then he added, "Things started getting pretty rough."

"Like how?" Reed asked.

"Hey, I'm a business man now and I can't afford to get mixed up with people like that."

"Yeah?" Reed lit a cigarette. "I'll make a deal with you, tell me what went on and I'll do all I can to keep you out of the papers."

The man huffed his frustration. "Do I need an attorney?"

"Nah, it's just between you and me." Reed blew a smoke ring over the bar in the Legion as he talked.

"What the hell, okay. The whole gang was into drugs, and then a fight broke out between these two gay guys. One had picked up a woman!"

"Do you have names?" Reed asked.

"Miguel and Sammy! That's all I know, I didn't get the last names. Some greasers from south of the border I heard," he added then.

"They were a couple?" Reed asked

"Yeah, looked like they were lovers and Miguel went crazy, man. When this drug crazed greaser threatened to kill Sam for cheating on him, that's when I said adïos and got the hell out of there!"

Reed thanked him and hung up. Manny had been listening to the conversation and when Reed told him what he had learned Manny replied. "I've heard this D'Agustino is nuts. That he's burned his brain up sampling their merchandise. Sam Mercado is his cousin, you know, and they've been hanging around each other for years."

"Yeah, I heard the families were related." Reed finished his beer and stood up. "We're going to search the area for Lindy," he said to Manny. He moved over to a group and told them to pass the word around that a local search crew would form at the sheriff's office in thirty minutes to begin to check the residential area around Birch Lake. By now word had leaked that a woman, a friend of Reed's, had been kidnapped and that it could be connected to the drowning!

It was late afternoon as a crew of about twenty Birch Lake residents stood together outside Jesse's office. The Legion had closed early since everyone was ready to do their part in catching the marauding person or persons who dared put any of their people or their friends in danger.

"Now hear this, you all heard that Reed's friend Lindy Lewis disappeared sometime early today." Jesse stood on the steps leading into his office as he spoke to the crowd and went on, "We decided not to wait the usual forty-eight hours so she has already been declared missing and an APB is out in the surrounding states. We suspect she may have been kidnapped by some foreigners from Mexico." Reed and Manny were off to the side.

"Here's her description," he continued, "Miss Lewis is forty four years old, has blonde hair and blue eyes. She's five feet, five inches tall and weighs around 120 pounds. She was last seen wearing a white shirt and black jeans. Now, first I want every building in this town searched; that is every house, garage, every structure and even old vehicles. Then let's meet back here in say, two hours. If you come across something that looks fishy, call me."

It was going on nine o'clock at night when the group of townspeople gathered back at the sheriff's office. Jesse, Reed and Manny stood together as the last group reported in. Nothing suspicious had been uncovered and now everyone waited.

"Jesse, we need to help search the woods," Reed had said solemnly.

"You're right," Jesse agreed, "But Jesus, Itasca Park is big; there are deep ravines, cliffs and swamps. I don't want to lose someone else!" Jesse took out a red bandana and wiped his face.

As the volunteers had moved through the town, the group had almost doubled. Jesse turned back to the people and went on, "Folks, I want to thank all of you, but now we need to help the feds search the woods!"

Reed lit a cigarette. He was apprehensive and edgy; this was taking too damn long. By now, Lindy could be lying out there somewhere, helpless and bleeding. Maybe even dead!

Goddamn, he felt like taking off and looking through the woods on his own for her, and he paced back and forth impatiently, and blew clouds of smoke into the damp night air as Jesse instructed everyone who could continue the search, to meet at the park entrance.

By the time the group assembled, Reed and Jesse had mapped the park off in grids. "Everyone form a line and stay an arms length from each other," Jesse said to them, "and do not lose sight of your neighbors!" And the somber group began its silent walk through the forest.

Reed and Manny were next to each other in the line. Flashlights had been passed out and each clump of weeds and every pile of brush was inspected, dead tree trunks were rolled over and the grass covered ground was thoroughly searched for clues as they moved into the forest.

Hour after hour they walked in the night and as the sun began to rise in the east, Jesse passed the word down the line that anyone who needed to stop and go home to get some rest should now. A good number of the people were of retirement age and looked towards Reed apologetically. He nodded his head in agreement as many of his good friends trudged back out of the wooded area to go back to their homes and sleep.

Reed was bone tired himself and his nerves were shot. Mosquitoes swarmed around his head and gnats chewed on his face. He looked at Manny.

"Jesus, don't these goddamned bugs piss you off?"

"Hell no," Manny said, "They don't bother me. These are nothing compared to the size of those we have in Texas!" And when Reed looked closely at him, there wasn't a single one chewing on him.

"I'm going on ahead," Reed said to Jesse as the group stood together a few minutes later. "I want to check out some spots up ahead here," he added needing to get loose from the rest of the searchers. He nodded towards Manny to follow and they took off into the dark woods. They moved quietly and only used their flashlights when they came upon a questionable patch of darkness. Time passed and by now the sun was just beginning to rise over the tree tops of the heavily wooded area casting weird shadow shaped images on the ground. Suddenly Reed stopped walking and raised his hand signaling Manny to do the same.

"Did you hear that?" he whispered to Manny who listened intently. Manny nodded. Someone or something was close by. They didn't move but reached under their shirts for their guns. The only sound in the forest was the twitter of birds awakening to a new day. Nothing stirred as Reed and Manny stood frozen, their gaze darting cautiously amongst shadows. Then a soft rustling could be heard again, but as they strained to listen it seemed to be moving away from them.

Reed motioned for Manny to follow. They moved cautiously staying behind stands of pines and brush. And finally in between the trunks of the trees, Reed got a glimpse of what and who they were following. It was Mario D'Agustino!

"It's him," Reed whispered to Manny. His first thought was to shoot the bastard on sight, but he forced himself to slow down when he realized Mario must be looking for Lindy too. He nodded to Manny and they moved along silently.

The forest was heavily overgrown with low brush that hid the movement and muffled the sound of their foot steps over the moss covered ground. The sun was still rising slowly and cast tall shadows over the area.

They watched as Mario impatiently slapped at tree branches and cussed at the bugs, but apparently knew exactly where he was going. Then coming to a small clearing he stopped suddenly and in a chilling voice they heard him say, "Buenas noches! Señora Lindy, this is for singing to the feds!"

He had found her and had a gun pointed right at her.

Lightening quick, Reed sprang out of hiding and within seconds knocked Mario to the ground using the butt of his gun. Manny vaulted over brush and shoved his sawed-off shotgun up against his head.

As Mario laid on the ground, his expensive clothes and gold jewelry covered in dirt and leaves, he grappled to raise the gun he still clung to. Spanish cussing spewed from his lips and asshole was one word Reed understood. Then in a split second's time Mario raised the gun, pointed it at Lindy and fired. But at that very same instant the bullet from Reed's .38 exploded into Mario's chest and his body fell silent as he lay on the floor of the forest.

Then finally Reed got a good look at Lindy!

-42-

Lindy had spent the hours bound to the tree fighting terror. Blindfolded and gagged, she was unable to see or scream for help. She was totally helpless. The deep forest was alive with scrambling night sounds, and then eerily quiet at times except for the howl of what she thought had to be timber wolves. Mosquitoes swarmed in clouds around her and attacked every area of her exposed skin. She could feel their bite through her clothes and under her hair on her head. Unable to do anything, within a short time her body had been on fire with the pain.

My God, this was the worst hell she could ever imagine! She tried to tune out the torture, but her scattered thoughts persisted.

Had Mario already killed her and she was in purgatory?

She had heard the kidnappers talking and knew he was on his way. Had he been here? She wasn't sure about anything.

One thing in particular agonized and saddened her; now time had run out for her and Reed! A silent sob wracked her body as she felt the great loss.

But, if she was already dead and might soon come face to face with her maker, she had to make amends fast! And Lordy, she needed to send Reed a message before it was too late. She had to tell him she had most of his company's million dollars; that it was in a suitcase right under the bed in his spare room. That he should return it to his company right away!

Using the last of her energy to fiercely concentrate and send the message through the universe to Reed, she sagged then and managed to turn off any and all fleeting feelings. Her life was over and done with. This was it! Time flew by or maybe it stood still in the hellish nightmare she was in, but suddenly she was jerked into consciousness when a familiar voice roared close by.

"Buenos noches! Senõra, this is for you for singing to the Feds!"

It was Mario. Now she was going to die! Right now! Then to her astonishment strange grunts and scuffling sounds arose next to her. Two shots rang out. One on top of the other and immediately something struck the side of her head. The last thought she had was, had Reed gotten her message?

Mario's bullet had found its mark and Lindy Lewis had been shot!

-43-

Reed and Manny stood in the Brainerd hospital unsure of just what was going on, they had just been told to wait for the doctor!

"What the hell does that mean," Reed growled. By this time his nerves were shot after no sleep the night before tramping through the woods and then the shooting. "Goddamn," he swiped his hair off his forehead, "Do they mean she didn't make it?" He shoved his hands in his back jean pockets.

"Nah, I think it's too soon to tell, they just got her here." Manny put a hand on Reed's shoulder.

Reed straightened his six foot frame. "Yeah, maybe you're right." He looked around and nodded towards a sitting area with couches and chairs.

"Christ, did you see a coffee machine around here anywhere?"

"I'll find one," Manny stated and took off down a hallway.

Reed sat down and picked up a magazine, but tossed it back on the end table. He took out his cellphone to call Jesse but changed his mind. There wasn't anything to report yet.

As he put the cell back in his shirt pocket Lindy's face suddenly flashed before him. She asked, "Hurry Reed, will you please do this?"

In that brief moment he had seen alarm in her eyes and heard distress in her voice. He blinked and shook his head. What the hell! He bent over and put his elbows on his knees and frowned. Even though she was unconscious, could she still use those psychic powers of hers he mumbled, confounded? Had she been trying to tell him something all along? But what? Jesus, could this mean that she had died? He swiped a hand through his hair again.

Manny came back carrying two paper cups of steaming coffee. "I hope you can drink it black, couldn't find anything that resembled cream." He set the cups down on a table. His gray ponytail swung around his shoulders as he settled across from Reed on a matching couch.

They drank their coffee and paged through old newspapers and magazines as they waited for some news. Reed was still puzzled about what Lindy had been trying to ask him to do. Finally in frustration, just as he was ready to yell at someone, a tired looking doctor in green scrubs came out of an elevator.

"I was told Reed Conners was waiting for information on a patient?" He said looking questionably at Reed and Manny who had jumped up from their seats.

"I'm Conners," Reed said.

"I'm Doctor Metz, Miss Lewis is my patient."

"How is she," Reed asked anxiously, "will she be okay?"

The doctor cleared his throat. "She was lucky it was a clean shot and the bullet just grazed the side of her head, but she's not out of the woods yet, we have to watch for infection." He blew out a breath and covered a yawn. "We've given her medication to counteract the poison from the insect bites, and that can take some time."

"All those bites, is that dangerous?" Reed asked.

The doctor nodded his head. "Very much so! You've heard of the West Nile disease, haven't you?"

"Sure," Reed said nodding, and then asked, "Can I see her?"

"Not a good idea," the doctor said then. "She's heavily sedated and I want her kept absolutely quiet. Sorry, maybe tomorrow." He turned and walked away.

Relieved, Reed said to Manny, "We may as well go back to Birch." But as they walked out of the hospital Reed was still perplexed about her plea to do something now! But what, he still couldn't figure out!

Jesse's office was swamped with people when they got back to Birch Lake. Tension was high. The men from the bureau were back in their corner with phones attached to their ears.

Jesse hung up his cell when he saw Reed and Manny come in. "Jesus, I'm glad you're back. How is Lewis?"

"She was lucky the bullet just grazed her. But the poison from bug bites are another concern now." Reed looked around, "what's happening here?"

"I just got a call from the Mexican authorities that a representative is on the way here." Jesse shook his weary head. By now, it was early afternoon. "I need to take your statements," he said then. And Reed and Manny took chairs at his desk as he turned on a tape recorder.

"Start when you two took off on your own until I found you in the clearing. And don't leave out one minute of the time!" He nodded towards the FBI men. "They will want to hear this!" So Reed and Manny very patiently explained the course of events again for Jesse and then the FBI. How they had come upon Mario just as he took aim at Lindy. How they were able to deflect his bullet, and finally how he got one instead.

"I'll take you to my place so you can settle in," Reed said to Manny after they had finally satisfied everyone. They were just getting ready to have a cold beer that evening when Reed's cell rang and Jesse's voice boomed in his ear, "The boys just told me three men just landed their plane in Brainerd and are on their way here!"

"Who are they?" Reed asked.

"Don't know." Jesse's voice cracked.

"We're coming in," and Reed and Manny jumped in the Corvette.

The sheriff's office was all abuzz when they got back to town. Jesse had gotten a chance to shower, shave and change into a fresh uniform but the FBI looked the same in their blue suits, white shirts and paisley ties.

Not more than twenty minutes had gone by when the door burst open and the strangers burst in. The FBI reached under their jackets for their holstered firearms. Jesse stood up from his desk.

"Hold it!" he growled. "Jesse Montes, I'm the Sheriff here!"

Reed and Manny stood off to the side and Manny hissed in Reed's ear. "Get this, the big one in front is Rio Prada, the mayor of Monterrey. The one carrying the briefcase is the biggest, meanest attorney in Mexico. The giant in the shades I would expect is their bodyguard!"

Reed leaned against a file cabinet and sized the group up.

"Oh yeah," Manny went on, "Prada is related to all three bodies. Mucho bucks and political friends."

"Oh shit," Reed said.

"I'm the Mayor of Monterrey, México," the one Manny pointed out as Rio Prada said to Jesse. "This is my attorney Anthony Ortega," he added. "Where are my cousins?" Mayor Rio Prada asked impatiently.

"The ME has them over at his funeral home. They haven't brought Mario's body in yet" Jesse answered, his face red and blotchy with stress.

"Who is the murdering son of a bitch who killed him?" Prada snarled then at Jesse.

Hearing this Reed stepped up and snarled back, "I shot the bastard! The sheriff has my statement." He glared at Rio Prada.

The federal men rushed over with raised guns. Attorney Ortega pushed his black rimmed glasses up the bridge of his nose, then reached over to ward off a blow Prada had aimed at Reed.

"To hell with his statement, I want that asshole to pay!" Rio Prada waved his arms as he shouted.

Reed was pissed and tired. Goddamn, he'd had it with all the commotion. He nodded for Manny to follow and they walked out the door of the sheriff's office.

He was going home!

-44-

Lindy's skin was on fire and the pain excruciating. And, oh my God, how she itched! If she could just scratch, but her hands felt like mittens covered them. In her drugged state she didn't realize bandages enveloped the cuts and blisters on them. When she tried to open her eyes, she couldn't lift her eyelids. Of course, she didn't know they were swollen shut from the insect bites.

Falling again into the oblivion of sleep, in a dream or was it a nightmare, she saw two young men quarreling; two men of Latin descent. She sensed a connection between them. Yes, they were lovers. It was as if she was watching a movie. She heard their names: Sam and Miguel. The same as in the visions she'd had earlier, and now the names had faces. She saw Miguel's rage as he accused Sam of cheating on their relationship with a woman!

She moaned in the quiet room again from the pain of the poison in her system, and a nurse hurried in and adjusted her IV and another jolt of medication hit her bloodstream. And like magic the pictures resumed. She saw Miguel stab Sam with a skinny knife blade, and then saw the horror in his eyes when he realized what he had done. She felt his anguish as he looked at his dead lover. Things grew fuzzy for a time, and then the final chapter to this sad story took place. A boat was out on a lake and she saw Miguel slide Sam's body in the water and then watched as he attached weights to his own feet and go over the edge. That was all. No struggling, no frantic call for help as the water accepted the two bodies and settled quietly in the night.

She moaned, and finally exhaustion overshadowed any more gruesome visions and she fell into a medicated slumber.

The next morning as she was slowly awakening from the drug induced night, she remembered hearing Reed's voice sometime earlier saying, "'Mario can't hurt you anymore! You're safe now.'"

What was going on? She couldn't remember. She opened her eyes. But she couldn't see a thing! She tried blinking and still couldn't see anything. She was blind!

Then she screamed. She screamed bloody murder!

-45-

Lindy sagged with relief after Reed and Manny left her room at the hospital. She had been fearful it was too late!

When she thought she was going to die at the mercy of Mario's hands out there in the woods, she had panicked thinking she was soon to meet her maker. And she had to atone for her sins, fast!

She had worried if Reed had gotten those messages she'd tried to send him. For him to hurry and return the money to his company, that it was under the bed in the guest room at his house. That she was sorry!

And then miraculously she survived! But even in her unconscious state lying so still in the hospital, anxiety had somehow tapped into her slumber.

What if her fortune was gone! But now, Reed admitted he hadn't understood any of the messages she'd tried so desperately to send to him. She still had her million, and now that she was going to live she needed it! And the best part was, Mario was dead! She didn't have to worry anymore; she was finally free of living with the fear of him finding her. The medicine had calmed her and the cooling cloth over her eyes had taken the swelling down somewhat from all those horrible bug bites. She shivered in remembrance. And the fire on her skin had cooled and most of the itching had subsided thanks to the drugs. Although, her head still ached from the wound, she was safe and on the mend after the terrifying situation she'd been in.

Feeling at peace, she finally fell into a deep, restful slumber and slept the day away. Footsteps awakened her toward evening and she lifted the cloth off her face as Reed, Manny and another man came in her room.

"You're looking better sweetheart!" Reed said and came over and kissed her on the cheek.

Lindy saw fatigue etched in the tired lines on his face and felt guilty. She guessed she must have caused it, all of it, by coming back expecting his help. Maybe she had made a mistake after all! She'd have to think about that later. She also recognized the man with him and Manny and tried to smile. "Mr. McGreger, what are you doing here?"

"Lindy Lewis, you're a sight for sore eyes." McGreger walked over to her bedside. "I heard about your encounter with the elements and then D'Agustino's attempt on your life."

"Oh Lordy," she sighed, "It's been awful!"

"I can well imagine. How are you feeling this evening?" McGreger put on a pair of horn-rimmed glasses and looked at her closely.

Lindy swallowed over a lump in her throat. Every one was being so nice. First, Reed and his friend Manny, and now McGreger. She hadn't had anyone who really cared about her for a long time. Middle-aged, a little overweight and a little rumpled, McGreger's brown eyes were magnified behind his glasses as he scrutinized her.

"I'm better," she murmured.

"I need to apologize to you. My dear girl, I fear you got the wrong impression when we talked before, on that other case," McGreger said. "But Lindy, I want you to know, I'm on your side. Now, I hear you've got this case already solved for us." He winked at her.

Lindy sucked in her breath. "They told you then. I saw it all!"

"Good job, my dear. I heard the tape. Now I just need to hear the story again straight from your lips. And I may have some questions for you."

Lindy settled back against the pillows, relieved she didn't have to defend herself to him. He was a believer.

"It all began when," she said relating again the horror of waking up in the trunk of a car. She told him of her helplessness and fear at being left to die in the woods. Then about hearing Mario's threat to kill her and waking up in the hospital.

"I'd had many visions," she went on with a tremor in her voice. "First, I only saw a drowned man with the name Sam and it wasn't until later that I saw the whole scene. Sam Mercado and Miguel D'Agustino were their names. I saw their life together; Sam straying from their gay relationship, with Ginger and then Miguel's revenge. And finally, the murder and suicide. Lindy lay back on her pillows and closed her eyes. They all thought she may have fallen asleep, exhausted from her efforts and stood uncertainly for a few moments. Then without opening her eyes Lindy said, "There is a letter! Written to Ginger from Miguel D'Agustino. It's lying unopened, under a pile of junk mail on her desk!"

MacGreger nodded his head and clapped his hands. "My girl, you are a genius!" Lindy sat up at his exclamation and he hugged her.

Reed looked on astonished. Then jumping into action said, "Come on, let's check this out. This could be just what we need!"

MacGreger had a smile on his face as they left Lindy's bedside.

As they got in the Corvette and minutes later on the road back to Birch Lake, Reed pulled out his cell-phone and called Ginger's house. After several rings a youngster answered and said his mom was in the shower.

"Can you remember to tell her to call me? My name is Reed."

"Yup, you've got that swell car!" The voice belonged to an eight-year old that Reed remembered seeing around town with his mother.

"Tell her it's very important. Can you do that?" He asked again.

"Sure," the boy said and then clunked down the receiver. Not more than five minutes went by and Ginger called back.

"What's up Reed, you haven't called me for a long time," she remarked dryly.

"Ginger, this might sound strange, but I need you to do something. This is very important and I'll explain later, I need you to look through your junk mail on your desk. Look for a letter addressed to you that you haven't opened."

"What the hell--," she muttered but he could hear her footsteps as she walked through her house. "How do you know this?" she asked curiously.

"Ginger, this is crucial. If you find it, don't touch it or open it! I'll explain everything later." The line was quiet as he heard her shuffling papers and swearing about the mess the kids had made again.

"Well, what the hell," she exclaimed finally, then, "hang on." Moments went by and then she said, "I'll be damned, here's a letter. For Christ's sake Reed, you better get over here fast and tell me what the hell this is about!"

"I'll be there in twenty minutes. And Ginger, I repeat, don't touch it!" He dropped the cell in his jacket pocket and shifted into fourth gear.

When they got to Ginger's house, her face was pale and her voice shook when she opened the door. "It's on the desk," she said leading Reed, Manny and McGreger into the living room and to the desk set in a corner.

The letter was addressed to her and Reed picked it up by a corner and opened it. A hand-written note read; Dear Ginger; Sam has got to pay for his sinful ways with you. Now I can't live without him. It was signed Miguel.

Ginger, Reed, Manny and McGreger stood momentarily stunned, and then reread the confession and suicide note. They looked at each other realizing what this meant.

"Have you got a plastic bag to put this in?" Reed asked Ginger who stood frozen at the turn of events.

"My God," she exclaimed tearfully, "I can't believe Sam is dead!" She wiped her eyes and sat down on a couch. "We were together just a few times, and then I thought he just wasn't interested." She sighed, and then got up and left the room to get a plastic bag.

"We've got to get to the Sheriff's office with this Ginger," Reed exclaimed then.

Jesse's office was a beehive of activity as Reed, Manny and McGreger rushed in. They were just in time to hear Rio Prada yell above the din, "It was that witch who put a curse on my family. That Lewis woman is the reason three of my family is dead!"

-46-

That morning as Reed neared Lindy's room in the Brainerd hospital, the hair on the back of his neck stood up as a scream echoed through the corridor. Manny was beside him and both men stopped dead in their tracks.

"Jesus, that sounded like it was coming from her room," Reed said and they took off in a run. The security guard stopped them at her door as another blood-curdling shriek cut through the air. Reed hurried in. "Lindy, its okay," he said and put his arms around her. But she fought him like a tiger.

"I can't see, I'm blind," she gasped and twisted out of his arms. She struggled to get out of bed, and wailed, "Mario, I don't want to die!" A nurse was in the room and between them got her settled back in bed.

"I'll get the doctor," she whispered and hurried out.

Reed stood by the side of Lindy's bed as she continued to whimper, "Help me!"

"Lindy, it's me Reed," he whispered, "listen to me, your eyes are swollen from all those bug bites and Mario is dead!" He was going to rub her arm as he reassured her but saw it was a mass of red swollen bumps. Within a few minutes the doctor came in the room carrying her chart.

"Glad to hear you're awake Miss Lewis," he said, "I'm your doctor." He reached out and touched her hand. "I've got a shot for you, it'll take away the discomfort, and the nurse will bring you some cooling pads to put over your eyes that will take the swelling down." He nodded at Reed and Manny and said, "Now gentlemen if you don't mind waiting outside, I need to examine Miss Lewis."

As they went out door Reed exclaimed, "Jesus," I've never seen her this way.

"Looks pretty bad and it'll take time." Manny answered as he followed Reed back to a sitting area.

"Yeah, we could have been dealing with an entirely different scenario. We all got lucky." Throughout the night Reed had awakened numerous times in a cold sweat, reliving the events of how the shooting had gone down. That Lindy could have died sent a sharp pain through his chest area. He had sat on the edge of his bed in the dark confounded; damn was he still in love with her?

He and Manny had driven to Brainerd early to check on Lindy, and then planned on getting back to Jesse's office shortly after. Reed said now, "I wonder what happened after we left last night?

"More shouting I'd guess," Manny remarked.

"Knowing Jesse, he'll stand his ground and won't let any of those arrogant assholes get to him. He's a stickler for procedures." Reed took out his cell-phone. "I'll give him a ring and let him know we'll be there shortly."

Manny shook his head in agreement. "Got any ideas as to who killed those other two guys that were fished out of the lake?"

"Not a clue," Reed said. When a deputy answered his call Reed asked, "Is Jesse in?"

"Nope, he'll be here shortly Reed, I'll tell him you called." Just as Reed put the phone away the doctor came out of Lindy's room, he nodded at them and disappeared down the hallway.

Now as Reed and Manny entered her room, she lay quietly tucked in under the covers. A white cloth lay over her eyes.

"It's me Lindy, Reed," he said and gently touched her shoulder. "I can see you're feeling better now."

"Reed," she murmured, "I remember what happened, that Mario is dead!"

"He is and can't hurt you now," he said, his hand still touching her shoulder. "And Lindy, Manny a good friend of mine from Texas is here."

"Manny I remember you helped arrest J.T. a long time ago." Lindy attempted to reach out a bandaged hand in greeting.

"Yeah, that's me kiddo," Manny grinned. "I came up to check on my buddy." The room was silent for a minute as Reed and Manny's thoughts went back to that time, then they were both jerked back to the present as Lindy said, "I know how Geno and Sam died1"

Reed frowned at her then asked curiously, "you do, how?"

Lindy calmly replied, "You see they had been lovers for years. Sam cheated on Geno by going out with a woman called Ginger who is a bartender in Birch. In a jealous rage Geno killed him and dropped him in the lake. Then in remorse, Geno took his own life by drowning himself."

Reed and Manny stood at her bedside, both of them momentarily flabbergasted.

Reed asked, "How do you know this Lindy?" Then he guessed. "Don't tell me it was another one of those pictures you see, was it?" He didn't know whether to laugh or swear.

Lindy heard the skepticism in his voice and replied defensively, "I saw it all Reed, it happened right out on your lake."

Reed cleared his throat and thought about it.

Manny chimed in. "Makes sense to me. Its well known Geno, Mario's youngest brother burned out his brains with all the drugs he stuck up his nose. He and Sam Mercado were cousins you know and always hung around together."

Reed remembered that Ginger the bartender at the Legion identified Sam from the pictures as the man she had dated and then had suddenly disappeared.

"You've got to believe me Reed," Lindy said urgently, "Geno killed Sam and then killed himself! Mario came here for two reasons: he found out I was here, and he wanted to get even with whoever had killed his brother and his cousin!"

"Yeah?" but Reed still looked doubtful. He always did when Lindy would tell him she'd seen some of those pictures.

She turned her head in his direction. A bandage covered one side of her head, her hands were bundled in gauze and her arms were covered in angry red welts. The outline of her small lower fame was almost lost under the covers, and he wondered for the umpteenth time why this slip of a woman could continually get under his skin with her stories.

Manny came to Lindy's defense and said, "It sounds like a perfectly good reason to me." Manny's mother was Latino, which made him half Mexican and he was brought up believing in the credibility of clairvoyance.

Reed thought about it and had to admit maybe it did make sense. But how could they solve these international murders on the evidence from a physic? Hell, he'd be laughed out of town! But so far it was all they had. He'd taken a tape recorder along thinking he might tape Rio Prada next time he began to rant and reached in a pocket. He asked, "Lindy, could you repeat what you just told us, and I'll tape it for the Sheriff?"

A tiny smile lit a corner of Lindy's cracked lips. "You mean you finally believe me?"

"Well, it might help," was all he would admit to. And Lindy told her story again as Reed held the recorder.

"Rest now," he said after she finished. He leaned over and touched his lips to her forehead. "I'll be back this evening to check on you, okay?" He turned to go.

"Reed wait," Lindy said with an apprehensive note in her voice. "Did you get my message?"

He remembered his frustration over some garbled thoughts that had been crowding into his head. He looked at Lindy curiously, "Something weird was going on that I thought was coming from you. What the hell was that about?"

She was silent for a few seconds then remarked, "It's just fine Reed," she said then and added, "It wasn't that important anyway!

He shook his head still confused but didn't have time to get into it further. "Sorry Lindy, we have to get back but I'll check on you later."

Back in Birch Lake, Jesse's office was a hive of activity. Prada's party hugged one corner of the room and today his demeanor seemed to have simmered down. Jesse and his deputy were shuffling papers at his desk as they walked in.

"Jesse," Reed said, "You've got to hear this," and handed him the tape recording he made of Lindy describing the vision she'd had.

Jesse put the recorder close to his ear and listened.

"Jesus," he said under his breath with a thoughtful look on his face. "Give me a minute to copy this, Conners. I need to keep the original." And after a few minutes he handed the tape-recorder back to Reed.

As Reed stood by Jesse's desk, he looked over to the corner where the FBI men stood and saw a fourth man had joined the party. After a second look he recognized the newcomer, walked over and stuck out his hand.

"Hey McGreger, good to see you again?" Reed grinned at him.

"Conners, didn't think I'd see you so soon! I heard what was going on here and thought I'd drop in."

"Yeah? You know then that two of the D'Agustino brothers are dead, also, the cousin?" As they talked, the two men walked out of earshot from the others.

"Christ, this is big! And a familiar name came up Conners," MacGreger said then, "Lindy Lewis! I'd wondered when Mario would try to get revenge for her testimony at his trial."

Reed went on, "She's been running ever since he was found innocent at his trial. She turned up here a few days ago."

"What happened," the FBI man asked? "I remember Miss Lewis well and how she helped us solve that case we were together on."

Reed shook his head. "I should have taken her more seriously and sent her into hiding, somewhere safe. She had been living in Mexico and ran smack into the brothers and found out the D'Agustinos lived right there too!"

"So she was living in Monterrey too. What a coincidence. How is she today?" MacGreger asked.

"She's going to be okay, but will have to stay in the hospital for a few days, I guess." Reed lowered voice, "I put guards at her door, just in case."

"Good idea." MacGreger nodded.

"I've got something I want you to hear," Reed said then, "Join me outside for a smoke, will you?" .

Outside the Sheriffs office the two men lit up. To Reeds way of thinking, MacGreger was the one and only Federal man he had ever run across that was worth a damn. The majority were arrogant and unfriendly. This man had been in the bureau for decades, seasoned and in charge, and Reed saw he dressed any way he god-damn pleased. Reed remembered him saying that more cases had been solved using clairvoyance then the public knew off.

"What's up," he asked Reed now as they stood outside. It was nearing noon and the aroma of roasting beef and garlic laced the air from the Woodsmen Café across the street. Locals were hurrying in to get a spot in the place before the outsiders ambled over.

Reed took the tape recorder out of his pocket. "You need to hear this. I just came from seeing Lindy over in the hospital." He turned the recorder on, then handed it to MacGreger who put it to his ear.

Reed saw the man nod his head. Saw his grin as he rewound the tape and listened again. Then as he said, "Conners, I've got to see that girl! I believe every word she said!"

-47-

Rio Prada suddenly shut his mouth when the attorney standing next to him clutching his Gucci briefcase barked, "Quiet!"

"We need to talk to you," Reed said nodding at Jesse, "and in private!"

Jesse stood up and led the way to a small room in back where he kicked the door shut and swore. "The whole place is nuts! Okay, what have you got?"

"We've got something you need to see!" Reed held up the plastic bag. "Read this. Geno D'Agustino wrote it and mailed it to Ginger, the bartender over at the Legion. Remember she had been going out with Sam Mercado and then he disappeared!"

Jesse took the plastic covered letter and read, and then exclaimed, "Jesus, we got a confession of murder and a suicide!"

McGreger stepped closer. "It sure as hell explains the mystery, Jesse!"

"I knew it would be something twisted like this." Jesse took out a red bandana and wiped his face with his free hand. "I've got to send this to the crime lab in Brainerd and have it dusted for prints. If we get a match we can close the case!"

Jesse called for his deputy to come into the back room. He handed the man the package containing the plastic covered letter. "Use your lights and don't let this out of your sight!" he exclaimed. He called the state office where the drowned men's DNA was held. "It's on the way," he said and closed the cell. "We should have confirmation in a couple of hours."

The sun was sliding over the horizon as the men stood in the back room of the sheriff's office.

"You got a back door out of here?" Reed asked.

When Jesse nodded toward one almost hidden by a file cabinet all four men stepped out the side of the building and headed to the Woodsmen café.

"My treat," McGreger grinned as they sat down in a booth off to the side. Flo bustled over with glasses of ice water.

"My goodness," she said somewhat flustered at the sight of such important men right there in her section. Her cheeks were rosy and her pencil poised.

As they waited for their order, McGreger said, "Jesse, when your deputy brings back the confirmation we need, I suggest you make an official announcement to the town and the newspaper!"

Jesse nodded his head. "I was thinking the same thing. I'll need you all to back me up."

"No problem," Reed said. "I'm waiting to see the look on that asshole Prada's face when he finds out one of his own was the killer and then did himself in. He's pissed off already after reading our statements about how Mario got himself shot."

McGreger drank half of his glass of water. "Man, there's nothing like the fresh water here." He wiped his mustache on the back of his hand. "I've met that attorney a few times over the years. He's smart and he's good."

Reed lit a cigarette. "And, it sounds like this Rio Prada met Lindy somewhere in Monterrey. Almost like he knows her!" He blew smoke toward the ceiling and looked thoughtful.

"He's the mayor, remember," Manny remarked. "It's a big city, but I'm sure he has a network of spies to keep him up with everything that goes on in his town. With Mario and the boys gone now, he's the only surviving male left in the D'Agustino, Mercado, Prada dynasty."

Reed just shook his head.

McGreger added, "And I've heard he's not an honorable man!"

Their dinner came then and the men were silent as they attacked their food with gusto. The special being corned beef and cabbage. They checked the time as they relaxed for a few minutes later with coffee, and a cloud of smoke hung over their corner as they each enjoyed their smokes.

"Lindy was right again," McGreger said then.

"That woman sure gets around," Jesse said just as his cell rang, and after a short conversation he closed the phone and said, "That was the lab, and it's a match. They're faxing over the confirmation!"

"Okay," he said standing up, "I need to make some calls and get ready to talk to the people."

McGreger took care of the bill leaving a hefty tip for Flo, and they crossed the street and walked in the door of Jesse's office.

The room was still packed with people; three FBI men, Rio and his attorney and bodyguard, and now, even more of the locals had come in to see what was going on. And all eyes were on the four men as they came in.

Jesse went to his desk and said to the crowd, "I will be making a statement shortly, until then I'd appreciate if everyone would clear out." He looked at his watch and added, "Thirty minutes!"

Rio's attorney stepped up to his desk and with a pissed off look on his face said, "I demand to know what's going on!"

Jesse glared back at him. "You'll find out as soon as everyone else. Now, excuse me, I've got work to do."

McGreger went over and joined his men and brought them up to date, then apparently told them to wait outside. The locals followed and then Rio and his entourage grudgingly moved.

Jesse was busy putting the facts together on paper while Reed, Manny and McGreger waited.

"Okay, let's take it outside," Jesse said as they walked to the door.

By now, the news had spread around town that the sheriff had solved the case and was going to make a speech. Good Lord, this was the most electrifying news in the history of Birch Lake and phones rang all over town. The editor of the local newspaper was there, front and center. Businesses closed their doors except for the Legion club, where Jerome still sat on his favorite stool and was told to watch the place, while everyone else hurried to the parking lot in front of the sheriff's office.

A hush fell over the crowd as Jesse, Reed, MacGreger and Manny came out of the sheriff's office and stood on the steps.

"Good evening folks," Jesse said right off after clearing his throat. "We have confirmation that the two men found drowned in Birch Lake were Sam Mercado and Miguel D'Agustino. Both of the men were from Mexico and here over the Fourth of July holiday. We have a signed confession from Miguel D'Agustino for the murder of Sam Mercado, and also a suicide confession from Miguel D'Agustino of his intention to end his own life!" Of course, nothing was mentioned about Lindy's involvement solving the case.

As the folks stood absorbing this news, Rio Prada roared, "That's bullshit. Sam and Miguel were friends!" He glared at his attorney and yelled again, "Do something!"

The attorney held up a hand to silence him and said to Jesse, "I'll need to see all this proof."

Jesse nodded, but calmly went on to answer questions and then introduced FBI Agent McGreger to the crowd, who went over more of the facts. All in all, the event took about an hour and finally with just a few of the locals standing rehashing the news, the town quieted down.

Back inside the sheriff's office, the air was thick with tension as McGreger stood by Jesse's desk while Rio's attorney studied the evidence.

"It's all a lie," Rio yelled, still not believing the facts. "That Lewis woman is behind this!"

"Quiet Rio," the attorney hissed under his breath, giving him a stern look. "Why do you hire me if you won't let me do my job?"

"Well, you haven't done anything yet! Someone has got to pay!" Rio Prada sputtered.

"The evidence clearly states the facts. Miguel killed Sam and then took his own life. I'm sorry." The attorney patiently explained to him and handed the papers back to Jesse.

Jesse stood up and very calmly declared, "I'm closing the case. This evidence is the proof we needed!"

"That's no proof. Anyone could have written that letter," Rio said with a sneer. "I'll have your job!"

"Now, hold on Prada," McGreger said stepping into the conversation. "I've gone over all the evidence and agree with the Sheriff. We are closing the case."

Finally after all his patience had diminished, Jesse jabbed a finger in Rio Prada's direction and said in a deadly voice, "Now asshole, I suggest you go see the coroner over at the funeral home, and find out when he will release the three bodies, then take your family and get the hell out of my town!"

-48-

After Reed, Manny and McGreger had left Lindy's room at the Brainerd hospital, a nurse brought in the next batch of drugs for the pain from her head wound and the insect bites. She'd felt the jitters coming on after giving the Federal Agent her statement about her visions of Sam and Miguel, but now, after the medication, hopefully she could get some relief. She checked to make sure the guard was still at her door and settled into the pillows. But her stress was not over.

It took a long time for her to relax and it was close to dawn when she finally fell into a restful slumber. But suddenly too soon, something awakened her. Her swollen eyelids flew open; still, she was only able to make out blurred shadows. She felt a presence! Someone was in her room. Standing close! She sensed a slight movement, but didn't move a muscle of her own as she forced her chest to rise and fall slowly. She strained to see through the gloomy shadows, then gasped as she felt the invader's eyes pierce the short distance between them. Every nerve in her body shrieked the alarm.

A late, fall storm was going on outside the hospital, and suddenly lightening streaked across the rain darkened sky and lit up her room. A man was standing there, right by her bed. She opened her mouth to scream, to yell, but just then a hand clamped over her lips. He bent down and whispered in her ear, "Lindy Lewis, you killed my family, now I'm going to kill you!" He put his other hand around her neck and tightened his hold. Lindy fought with all she had, but quickly felt herself falling, falling down into darkness.

For a split second, the room was silent as she laid immobilized, suddenly overcome with sorrow. Her life was over. Mario had tried to kill her when he'd kidnapped her. And now, someone else was after her.

No, not yet, she cried inside and seizing onto the last vestige of energy she had, she raised her knees and kicked with all her might. The assailant doubled over and instantly lost his hold. She let out a hair-raising scream and grabbed the remote and flipped on the light switch. As the bright light blazoned in her room she was astonished to see Rio, the Mayor of Monterrey, Mexico. Another member of that infamous family who had given her nothing but trouble! The man who had raped her!

Oh Lordy, she was so tired of all the dilemmas she had been through lately; forcing her to leave her new home in Monterrey and run for her life, again. All of it because of Mario!

And then the good Lord sent her a bolt of enormous energy and she hurled the heavy remote at him and just like in the movies, Rio's forehead caught it.

Chaos followed as the guard dashed into her room clutching a towel to his bloody nose, followed by security men. Lindy huddled in her covers and watched, scared out of her wits as they fumbled for power. In the commotion, Rio was finally handcuffed and hustled away still shouting, "She did it! She killed my family!"

No one noticed later as she tiptoed out of the room clutching her gown to cover her bare backside. She'd had it! She was tired of everything! No one saw her slip into a storage closet and change into a set of scrubs and head for an exit. Outside and careful not to attract attention, she hid in the shadows of the trees until a taxi came by and dropped off a customer. She scooted over.

"Thanks, just in time," she exclaimed and climbed in.

"Where to?" the driver asked.

She had to think. Where would she go? "Can you just drive for a few minutes?" she asked.

The driver looked at her in the rear view mirror, seeing the bandage on her head and her swollen eyes. "Lady, you don't look so good. Are you sure you should leave this place?"

"I'm fine," she fibbed, "I just fell down some steps and hit my head." While she talked she pulled the sleeves of the shirt further down to cover the welts on her arms. The driver set the car in motion.

It was after one o'clock in the morning on a Monday and the streets in Brainerd were quiet for now, but later in the week the Labor Day holiday would began. Hundreds of people would flock to the area to close their lake cabins and second homes for the coming winter. She remembered Reed saying to his buddy, "'Manny, as soon as we close this case, we'll take my cruiser out on the water and I'll show you how to really enjoy life!'"

She took a breath as all this went through her saddened thoughts. She wanted to belong too, and not always be on the outside looking in. And then, she recognized the familiar pattern that had crept up on her. That SUDDENLY SUMMER was over and autumn had arrived. A time again, when her confidence would dwindle and she'd feel vulnerable and exposed, afraid and lonely.

She had thought money would take away all those feelings when she had set out to collect the million dollars. But here were these same emotions again. The same sorrowful feelings that had haunted her ever since her husband had died, only more painful this time.

But she had to decide now, where was she going? The driver was waiting for an answer.

Was there something else out there waiting for her just around the corner? Or, should she go back to Birch Lake and settle into the comfort and safety of Reed's arms?

She had to make a decision. Now! And finally, she knew it was time! No more running. Her heart reeled for just a minute, and then she said to the taxi driver, "Would you take me to Birch Lake?"

The End

Lyn Miller LaCoursiere

Lyn Miller LaCoursiere loves to travel. She has a large loving family and joyfully hops on a plane when an invitation arrives to visit. She lives in Minneapolis, but spends as much time as possible by the ocean in the south. Lyn has published numerous articles in the Minneapolis Star Tribune and Minnesota Women's Press. This is her fourth novel in a series featuring Lindy Lewis and Reed Conners set in the Midwest.

Watch for
True Confessions: The Early Years

coming soon----

TO ORDER COPIES OF THIS BOOK

Please feel free to contact me through
my e-mail at
lindylewis1@msn.com,
or my web-site at
Mystery Novels-Lyn Miller Lacoursiere.com.
You can also find my books on **amazon.com** and
www.NightWritersBooks.com